THE SANDCASTLE MYSTERIES:

CATCHMEIFYOUCAN

AMEA LAKE

This is a work of fiction. Any names, characters, businesses, places, events or incidents are either fabricated products of the author's imagination or used in a purely fictitious manner. Any resemblance to actual persons, living or dead, or any actual events is purely co-incidental. Any views or opinions presented are solely those of the authors and do not represent any establishment or company.

We know that in real life people may use stronger language than is used by the characters in our book. However, we have chosen to stay within the parameters of a cozy mystery, which dictate that we as authors use only limited profanity, if any.

THE SANDCASTLE MYSTERIES:
Catchmeifyoucan

AMEA LAKE

Copyright © 2013 AMEA LAKE
All rights reserved including the right to reproduce this book or portions thereof in any form whatsoever.

ISBN-978-0-983-78001-4
Library of Congress Control Number: 2013948580

Printed in the United States of America

Cover design © by Gisela Bly
Book design by Donald Kerns
Graphics Editor-Matthew Kerns
Graphics Editor-Jonathan Kerns

Published by
Eight Women Writers
Jackson, NJ
www.EightWomenWriters.com

First Edition-October 2013
10 9 8 7 6 5 4 3 2 1

Printed by:
Lightning Press
www.lightning-press.com

To cozy mystery readers-and those who aren't. Yet!

ACKNOWLEDGMENTS

Thanks to our husbands and families for their patience during the lengthy writing and editing process; Sergio Gonzales for the insights regarding character, Franky Alvarez and to Michele Lewis for allowing us to use Hye Point Centre in Kansas and her horse Hye Mister Man, in our cozy mystery and information on horses and stables.

Thanks also to Amy and Karen Herr, Christie Kerns and Kelly Elsmore for their suggestions and encouragement.

Thanks to Matthew and Jonathan Kerns for their graphics expertise

Thanks to Loren and Kayla Pruitt for their input on the expressions of our characters in the first twenty five chapters.

Thanks also to the management of Favorites, who allowed us to use the OTB in our book. Thanks also to Jimmy Ryan and Sal, for sharing their knowledge of horse racing and handicapping.

Thanks to all our friends in the VIP seats for their encouragement and to our friends behind the bar, Dominick and Christine for their support.

Special thanks to Gisela Bly, an extraordinarily talented artist, whose original artwork graces the cover of both of our cozy mysteries.

THE SANDCASTLE MYSTERIES:

CATCHMEIFYOUCAN

AMEA LAKE

PROLOGUE

Friends help you move. Real friends help you move dead bodies.

Last night's quarrel played over and over in Laura's mind. She stayed in bed listening to the morning sounds outside the guest room window: horses whinnying in the stables, birds splashing in the bird bath and stablehands' voices calling to one another. After a few minutes, she sat up and assured herself, "Well, we'll have to act like two adults tonight and talk it out."

Laura waited for Jonathan to get his horses loaded into the trailer and head out for Monmouth Park Racetrack before she left the room. Usually, she went with him but she needed time to cool off. She finally heard the unmistakable sound of his truck as it left the yards.

Wearing her favorite jeans and riding boots, Laura took an apple, two cubes of sugar and a carrot from the kitchen counter and went to check on her horse, Another Foxy Lady, whose foal would soon be birthed. Laura was excited. She'd been running names through her mind for weeks now. As she walked to the stall where her horse was kept, she heard a man's deep, harsh voice, "You'll do as I tell you; you have no choice." Laura stopped outside the door and heard another man reply in a low voice but she couldn't understand his words. She walked into the barn and saw three men standing near Another Foxy Lady's stall.

"What's going on in here?" she asked. The men turned and looked at her, startled by her entrance.

"I asked you a question," Laura repeated. She looked at the men, pointed her finger and said, "You," adding in a shaky voice, "I'm calling Jon. . . ."

Laura turned away, took two steps and fell face down onto the dirt floor. One of the men stood over her holding a muck rake while another man quickly bent over her figure. He checked for a pulse but found none, stood up and looked at the man holding the rake.

"What were you thinking? She's dead!"

"I didn't mean to kill her. She was going to call her husband."

"What the heck are we gonna do now? Call 911?"

"No, you idiot, we gotta get rid of her."

"Okay, so let's get her out of here. Go get the truck." He turned and spoke in a menacing tone to a third figure standing near the stall, "This doesn't change anything. You know what you have to do on Saturday Franky. If you don't follow orders, you know exactly what will happen to you."

***

Tall pine trees gave off a fresh scent as they swayed in the light breeze. The two men leaned over their shovels and stared at the mound of dirt at their feet.

"Who'd think that someone so small would be so damned heavy," mumbled one of the men. He wiped his face with his sopping shirtsleeve.

"Is that all you can think about dimwit? You killed her!" responded the man standing next to him.

"Listen, you jerk. You were there too and don't you forget it. We're all in this together."

"Do you think anyone will notice the extra digging here?"

"Nah, after we put the sod back down nobody'll notice nothin'."

The men climbed back into their truck, and the driver drove the F 150 slowly back a dirt road and circled around the cranberry bogs. He turned left onto Route 537. The laborious job of burying a body, and the adrenalin that had been coursing through their systems since the murder, left them deeply drained.

The driver finally spoke, "I need a stiff drink and something to eat. I know just the place where we'll fit in."

Fifteen minutes later, he pulled the Ford into the graveled parking lot across the street from the Cassville Tavern in Jackson, New Jersey. He parked his truck near the other pick-ups in the lot. The two men crossed the street and went directly to the bar. They ordered JACK straight-up. The strength of the whiskey brought them out of their fog.

Several other men at the bar were watching the sports network on the TV mounted over the bar and most of the tables in the room were filled with customers. No one paid any attention to the two men.

"Sweetie, can I get a menu over here?" A waitress, standing at the end of the bar, handed the men a menu and took them to a corner table outside on the porch.

"I'll be back in a jiff," she said as she went to wait on another customer.

The man sitting in the chair facing the parking lot spoke first, "It wasn't supposed to be like this. It started out as simple bribery and then ended up in murder. Murder, can you believe it?"

"Shut up and stop whining like a sissy. We need to figure out what we're going to do now."

CHAPTER 1

Running makes every day a good day.

Susan Jeffries parked her white Mercedes C 300 in the private parking lot and walked the short distance to the beach to go for her daily run. Running helped erase the memory of her husband Mark's death, and she needed the exercise to get rid of the effects of snacking on too many M&M's-her favorite candy. A light thrum, thrum, thrum sounded each time Susan's bare feet padded on the wet sand. It had a trance-like effect on her; the only time her mind returned to the present was when the ocean waves washed over her feet. The adrenalin rush she experienced made her feel like an eighteen-year-old lifeguard again, in control of her life and her destiny.

Susan slowed her pace and looked up and down the pristine Manasquan beach. Sand dunes paraded along the shoreline and were joined by Main Street, the roadway that coursed through the coastal town of Manasquan, New Jersey. The sun's rays were brilliant and the sand glistened. The ocean movement was lake-like with a few lapping waves disturbing its calm. She extended her arms toward the blue sky and noticed there wasn't a puff of a cloud anywhere. Seagulls circled about looking for food scraps on the sand. Many of the tourists or *bennys,* (residents of Bayonne, Elizabeth, Newark, and New York as locals called them) had returned north to their homes. School was in session and now a handful of sun worshipers captured the warmth of the rays on the beach.

Susan jogged back to her car, grabbed her purse and briefcase, and walked to the path that led to the shops lining the main street, a shopper's alley for the elite residents and the tourists who frequented the shore area during the sweltering summer months. The shopkeepers encouraged business and catered to the eye of their customers too.

It was early and very few people were out and about. Her neighbor, Sal Catalano, wearing his straw fedora, was busily adjusting the awning at his café next door. The café had a red-striped awning over the entry and large palm trees in rustic wooden planters on either side of the doorway.

"Good morning Sal," Susan called out waving her hand. "That was some rain and wind last night."

"Susan, I no see-a you coming," he said as he returned the wave. "It looks-a like I've got some sweeping up-a to do this morning before I open. The awning, she comes-a loose by the wind; it'll need fixing a bit. I no usually worry-a about it when I leave-a for the day."

Susan smiled. Sal's night school classes had improved his conversational ability, but he still had strong traces of an Italian accent.

The Manasquan Café was one of the best dining places in the beach town and Sal Catalano was its noble proprietor. Local customers, as well as tourists, applauded his genuine, friendly nature and the café's good food. Every dish he served featured the delicate spicing Sal knew so well.

Sal had established the café when he came to the Jersey Shore from the Tuscany Valley in Italy with his wife, Bella. He was rarely seen in town without his fedora, and his easy-going manner made up for his lack of a bulky stature. His upper lip held onto a small moustache but he kept his chin shaved at Bella's request.

Susan looked forward to chatting with him every morning. "Yes, Sal, there's always some work to do. I've thought about putting an awning in front too, but for now I think I'll just settle for window film to keep the sun from fading my books. Don't work too hard; you'll have it fixed in no time. Have a good day."

Susan's auburn hair bounced on her shoulders as she walked past the café. She held her head high; her green eyes sparkled. The early morning sun warmed her face. Susan responded to the warmth as she hummed, *"It's a beautiful morning. . . ."* She felt more carefree than she had in a long time and approached the shaded front door of the Sandcastle Bookstore-her very own shop. She silently reminded herself to buy a new WELCOME mat to cover the cracked bricks on the sidewalk in front.

    The bookstore was sandwiched between the Manasquan Café and Chang Lee's Laundry and Dry Cleaners, which offered wrought iron bench seating as a shopper's reprieve. These two shops were prime examples for the other establishments on the street. Susan hoped that her bookstore would become a showcase as well.

CHAPTER 2

All my friends wave their pages at me when I walk into a bookstore

Susan's Sandcastle Bookstore had bustled with activity during the summer. She wasn't sure, though, if it was her store and all the current reads that drew in the crowds, or if it was the notoriety that her husband's murder investigation had given her. Either way, once customers came in, they came back. She had scheduled a few book signings with local authors to be held in the fall. In addition to the signings, Susan planned a book reading by a local group of authors, who used **AMEA LAKE** as their pen name. She knew such events lured readers in.

Susan unlocked the door and reached in quickly to turn off the alarm before it sounded then stepped inside and clicked the lock shut. Nicky, her cherished African Grey parrot, perched on the hemp rope swing in his cage next to the front door.

"Good morning, good morning," Nicky squawked as soon as he saw her. "I wanna grape."

Susan had to smile. She was so pleased to have someone greet her every morning even though that someone was just a parrot.

"Good morning back," she called out reaching in the snack jar to give the parrot some cheese nibbles. She usually opened up about 10:00 a.m. since things had settled in her life; this gave her a few moments to tidy up the way she liked and put the coffee on. Susan acknowledged to herself when she opened up each morning that she might not have returned to caring about the business of her bookstore if it hadn't been for the encouragement of her assistant, Chelsea Keating, who had such a fresh outlook on life. Opening her shop each morning, Susan mentally thanked Chelsea for all the boosts in confidence that she gave her.

Susan stood looking at Nicky's cage. "Today, I have to clean out your house before customers come in," she said to the bird, "and then . . . I have to call Ryan Brewster. Don't you let me forget."

Nicky flapped his wings wildly in response. Seed shells showered to the floor. "Don't you forget."

"Oh, I hope I brought the right papers with me so I can ask Ryan some final questions about buying the laundry next door, Nicky, my pal." Nicky tilted his head listening to her. Susan placed her purse on the counter by the register and searched in her red leather briefcase for the forms she had filled out the evening before. "Nicky, today's my new beginning. I'm forging ahead. I've worked so hard to start the best darn bookstore on the Jersey shore."

Nicky squawked again. "Good grief, like I wanna grape."

"You sound just like Chelsea." Susan laughed as she tucked her hair behind her ears. She went to the back of the store and quickly showered in the tiny stall shower in the shop's equally small bathroom. Feeling refreshed, she looked at the stacks of books that had arrived the evening before. She had been too tired last evening to open the boxes, but now she was anxious to see if the new cookbook series by Chef Jon Locke had arrived. She thought about the nice job Chelsea had done with the cookbook series back in the spring and hoped that she would use her creative talents in arranging these as well.

Susan took a handful of grapes out of the refrigerator and went back to Nicky. "Here you go, like, do you think I would forget you?" Susan stopped and realized that she sounded like Chelsea too.

After Nicky ate his fill, Susan swept out the scattered seeds and damp cornhusk gravel on the bottom of his cage. She glanced at her watch and saw that it was 9:45 a.m. The chimes on the front door played as Chelsea unlocked the door and breezed in. She wore her usual black jeans and tee shirt, but looked different today. The pink stripe was gone from her jet-black hair and her hair appeared softer.

"Like, good morning, Mrs. Jeffries. Good morning, Nicky. I hope you have good news for me today, Mrs. Jeffries. Did you sign the application for the new addition? Are we going to expand the bookstore?"

Susan closed the door on the bird's cage and waved toward the rear of the store. "Come in the back for some coffee, Chelsea, I'll fill you in."

Chelsea followed Susan to the back of the store. While Susan poured the coffee, Chelsea got out the cream and sugar. They seated themselves to chat at the glass-top bistro table Susan had brought in from her home.

"Boy did I ever have a strange dream last night," Susan said as she poured Coffee-Mate into her coffee.

"Like, what was it?"

"Well, I was still the owner of a bookstore, but it was right on the water. In fact it was sort of a house boat, with docks attached to it where the boats could pull in and order books or tea. And I had kids-twin girls. And I had them dressed in little dresses with bows in their hair and earrings in their ears. There didn't seem to be a man in the picture, but I felt happy then I woke up. What do you think it means?"

"Oh that's easy, Mrs. J. You're all involved setting up the tea room. Don't you see that in your dream everything was finished. You even had your family. Like I think that dream's a good omen. I think everything's going to be wonderful for you from here on out."

"I certainly hope you're right." Susan finished the sweet coffee. "I've had enough problems in my life, thank you very much."

Chelsea laughed and adjusted her tight-fitting top as she stood up.

"Now we've got to get down to business. I'm meeting my attorney, Ryan Brewster, tonight to sign the final papers for the addition. Chelsea, it's so exciting! The crew I hired will be ready to start right away when the last papers are filed." Susan clapped her hands together ready to share her plans. "Chels, there'll be a lot of work these next few weeks. We'll have to put up with dust and workmen coming in and out."

"That's okay. Like, I'll take up man watching if we have any down time," said Chelsea grinning widely.

"Yeah, I bet you would," Susan winked.

Susan stood up, washed her coffee cup and turned toward Chelsea. "I really hope my mother doesn't interfere. Every time she hears that I'm trying something new she wants to put in her two cents."

"What do you mean?"

"Oh, she thinks I need more than one person here working with me. I really think she would like to be included in my business and my success."

"Do you suppose you'll hire more help especially once the tearoom is up and running?"

"Definitely, we'll need more help."

The door chimes rang and both women heard Nicky squawk.

"Hello there, dearie. Ch-ching!"

They walked to the front of the store; their work day had begun.

CHAPTER 3

Although winning isn't everything, losing has little to recommend it.

JUNE 2012

Catchmeifyoucan, the prize Thoroughbred owned by Fox and Hound Stables of Colts Neck, New Jersey, had won the Kentucky Derby and the Preakness and was expected to win the third and final leg of the Triple Crown at the Belmont Stakes. To the shock and surprise of the crowd attending, another horse, Have Faith, came in first.

As soon as the Belmont race was over, Jonathan Fox, owner of the Fox and Hound Stables, approached the jockey, Franky Alvarez, as he rode Fox's horse, Catchmeifyoucan, toward the groomer.

"What the hell were you doing out there? My whole life was tied up in this race. You rode my horse for wins at the Derby and Preakness. He was a sure thing today, and somehow you managed to screw it up and keep him from winning. Why were you riding the rail? You know Catchmeifyoucan hates it. I'm asking you again, what the heck were you doing?"

Franky dismounted. His slight five-foot frame dripped with sweat and his dark brown hair clung to his head. He looked at Fox. "Mr. Fox, I gave this race everything I had, so did Catchmeifyoucan. The horse just didn't settle. It wasn't in the cards for us today, sir. Walsh's horse, Have Faith, had more power."

"Well, the two of you lost me a ton of money. Clear out. I don't want to see your face on my property again. You'll get whatever's coming to you and that will end it between us."

"Mr. Fox, you can't mean that. I've always done my best for you and I've won you lots of other races. Don't do this to me."

"Get out. That's my last word!" Jonathan Fox stormed off toward the VIP tent.

"Ay dios mio," Franky whispered as he walked toward the stables. He was stunned by Fox's words. "What am I gonna do now?" he mumbled. He felt empty, he was sweating profusely and his heart pounded in his chest. "Everyone's going to know I've been fired. They'll laugh at me."

News of Franky's dismissal as a jockey for Fox and Hound Stables would spread quickly. Franky had some good friends at the stables, although there were a few guys he neither liked nor trusted. Tonight he couldn't bear to say goodbye to any of them. When he entered the changing room, he didn't speak to or look at the other jockeys who were there. He folded his silks and placed them on the upper shelf of the locker, collected his personal belongings and walked outside to his Mercedes.

"Hey Franky, where ya goin'?" someone called from the yard. Franky didn't respond. He opened the car door and mopped his face with his handkerchief. He couldn't get the voices of the crowd cheering Have Faith out of his head.

When Franky arrived at his condo, he took a bottle from the refrigerator and settled in his red leather lounge chair deep in thought. I've never been fired before. Why did I agree to do that? It was a dumb thing to do.

He sat hunched in his chair not realizing that it had become dark. His recall of the day's events was so intense that he was unaware of anything else. When the sun finally rose, he walked into the kitchen, pulled out a pad and pen and began to calculate his earnings and losses.

Franky was broke. He played poker on a weekly basis. It was his favorite pastime, but the stakes always made others richer. He had always managed to have enough money left to send home to his family, but now he had nothing left. His flamboyant lifestyle would have to change. Maybe it was time for him to go back to Florida.

CHAPTER 4

When I am in a bad dream, I can't wake up.

Jonathan Fox was enraged. He felt a throbbing at the back of his head. He walked into the stables and approached Jake, an old friend and one of his stablehands, who was mucking a stall. "Hey Jake, drop that pitchfork and come with me to my office."

"Okay Fox. Hey, what's up? You don't look so good."

The men walked into the office. Each grabbed a beer, pulled up one of the nicked-up wooden chairs and sat at the table. Jonathan took a long swig. "I can't believe what happened, Jake. It's like a bad dream. Everything was in order. All that was left to win the Triple Crown was the Belmont Stakes. I had the best horse and the best jockey, but somehow it wasn't enough. What part of this picture did I miss?"

"Beats the heck out o' me! I don't know what went wrong. I noticed Franky's been acting nervous for the last couple of days. He didn't seem to have his usual confidence, but I figured it was big race jitters."

Jake eyed Jonathan and thought, damn it. I hope Fox isn't stroking out. Fox's face was flushed and his eyes looked crossed. "Hey man, you okay?"

Jonathan forced himself to focus at the sound of Jake's rough voice. "Yeah, but I've got to get some answers soon. You better get back to work, Jake. If you hear anything, be sure to let me know."

As Jake walked out the door, Jonathan grabbed another beer and sat back down thinking, where are you Laura? I wish you'd been here today. You would've handled Franky much better than I did. Jonathan took a long swig of his beer and thought about the last time he saw his wife. "What should I do?" he said aloud. "I wonder. . . Annie Somers!" He unsnapped his cell from his belt and punched in her number. He waited for three rings before he heard Annie's voice. She sounded breathless and anxious.

"Hi Laura, I saw the race on TV. Sorry about *Catch* not winning. And sorry I couldn't be there with you. The doctors wouldn't let me travel to New Jersey. You both must be heartbroken. I was going to call you . . . is everything all right? Laura are you okay?" She stopped talking for a moment and then heard Fox's voice.

"Annie, it's me, Jonathan. Tell me Laura's there. Please don't tease me. My life is pure hell without her."

Annie's voice was hesitant, "Jonathan, you're calling here for Laura? No, she's not here. You mean she's not with you?"

"She's not here. We had a fight a couple days ago and she left. We seldom argue about anything, but Laura told me that someone was stealing from me. I couldn't believe it. None of my people would do that. I got so angry I almost hit her then she stormed off to the guest room and locked the door without a word. She didn't even answer me when I called her name and pounded on the door. I don't know where she is. I was hoping she might be with you. I know she's worried about your heart surgery. I figured she went to see you to cool off. I was sure she would come back in time for the Belmont. You're the only person I can think of to call."

Annie tried to make sense of what Fox was telling her. "Have you called the police? Laura would never go away this long without telling someone. She might have had an accident."

"No. I haven't reported her missing yet," Jonathan said. "Do you think she would have gone to her sister's? I know that Laura hasn't spoken to Virginia in a while."

"Not on your life," Annie replied. "You better call the police. Get back to me as soon as you can and let me know what's going on."

"Okay Annie. I've got to go now." Jonathan ended his call. I have no choice but to call the police, he thought. And I know the publicity will be huge; newspapers will have a field day commenting on my horse losing the race and my losing Laura.

CHAPTER 5

An argument is like a country road, you never know where it is going to lead.

Fox called the Colts Neck police and then watched a rerun of the race on television while he waited for them to arrive. He didn't wait long. When Detective Tommy Walker entered Fox's office, he shook Jonathan's hand and introduced him to his partner Officer Smith. Both tried to put Fox at ease.

"Why don't we sit down?"

"Nice office you have here. Take your time; tell us about your wife."

Fox drummed nervously on the table and stumbled through his story. He told them about the argument mentioning that Laura told him one of his men was stealing from him. The officers looked at Fox quizzically at the mention of the word argument.

"It was a big blowout," Fox said sadly. "Laura was annoyed that I didn't take her more seriously. I became worried when she didn't show up for the Belmont Stakes. That's not like Laura. I have no idea where she is," he added with his head down and shoulders slumped.

Detective Walker asked Fox a few more questions: "Do you have a list of her friends? Where are some likely places she might go for a few days?

Have you checked to see if any of her clothing or jewelry is missing?" Fox looked stunned for a minute. "Go up to your house, check out your wife's things, and we'll meet you in a few minutes over there."

Fox headed off to his house to search the bedroom that he and Laura shared. He looked through her drawers and her closet. Laura's belongings were all in place. The monogrammed, chestnut leather overnight bag he had brought her last Christmas was still in the closet. Her jewelry box was locked.

Fifteen minutes later, Detective Walker and Officer Smith entered the house. "Officer, I checked upstairs and didn't find anything missing." Fox sat down at his desk.

"Well, we talked to some of your men and took down their statements. They didn't have much to say. We'll come back in the morning to complete a missing person report. If you think of anything that may be of significance, give the station a call. They know how to reach us."

Fox was sweating profusely and grabbed a fistful of tissues from the top drawer of his desk to wipe his face. "I can't make any sense out of this," he muttered. His rapid heartbeat and the pounding in his head made him feel sick.

CHAPTER 6

Stop caring what others think and have some fun.

People knew Jonathan to be a narcissistic and proud man, often using his own last name in the names of his Thoroughbreds. One afternoon Jake had been playing poker with him and three others when he asked Jonathan with a wink, "How come you never named any of your horses after Laura? You must think pretty highly of yourself."

If Jonathan hadn't had a winning hand, he would have turned the table over in anger. "Who do you think pays the bills anyway? I'm the one taking the risk. I pay the trainers, the vet, the jockeys and the guys mucking the stalls. So Jake, pay more attention to the game, 'cause I have four of a kind- and your money." They tossed their cards on the table and called it a day.

Jonathan knew what others thought of him. Some people even hinted he might be bi-polar because his disposition would change quickly from one extreme to another. But he felt comfortable with himself as a self-made man and ignored all the talk.

In 2010, at the annual Fox and Hound Stables employee picnic, Jonathan appeared to be having a good time talking to everyone. Later in the day, though, he became so dismayed over losing a game of horseshoes to Jake that he threw a steel shoe in the air in disgust. One moment, he was the happiest kid on the playground licking an ice cream cone; the next he was the kid staring at it in the sandbox.

***

Jonathan thought again about Laura as he leaned back in his leather chair and held his head in his hands thinking, if only she would contact me. This is her get-back at me; I know it. I thought for sure she was with Annie. Where else can she possibly be?

Jonathan picked up a framed photo of Laura and himself standing together in front of the bronze statue of Secretariat in Lexington, Kentucky, and thought, what a wonderful vacation we had that summer at Kentucky Race Park. Fingering the picture, he felt anger rising as he imagined Laura was laughing at him. He threw the picture across his office, hitting one of the small statuettes of Catchmeifyoucan. It tumbled to the floor. "You didn't win the Belmont for me," he yelled. "That's where you belong."

CHAPTER 7

Mothers and daughters with strong personalities see the world from very different points of view.

SEPTEMBER 2012

The Sandcastle Bookstore was open and waiting for business. Susan's cell phone rang in her jacket pocket. She flipped it open and checked the caller ID. "Mother, this is a surprise. How are you? It's been a while since you called me." Her mother's calls always made her feel exasperated.

"Yep and you haven't called me either."

"Well mother, I'm busy too. What are you calling about?"

Susan took a sip of coffee and listened to her mother for a few minutes, then interrupted her mother's prattle. "But mother, I haven't spoken to Aunt Laura in a long time or even thought of her, actually. I haven't seen her since the last time we had a family reunion. You remember that time when the two of you had that huge argument and you almost came to blows."

Susan shifted her weight on the stool beside the work table and continued talking, "Let me get this straight. No one has heard from Aunt Laura in months? How do you know this?" Susan punched the 'speaker' button on the phone and placed it on the counter.

Virginia McGovern replied, "A long-time friend of Laura's, Annie Somers, called me the other day. She had major heart surgery and Laura had promised to visit her toward the end of May. But Annie hasn't heard anything from her and is quite concerned. When Jonathan called Annie after the Belmont Stakes, he was far from being forthcoming. She said he seemed anxious and told Annie that Laura had been missing for days. Annie thinks something is seriously wrong. She and Laura have been friends since they were kids and it isn't like Laura not to get in touch with her. Annie called me to see if I've talked to her. That's a laugh! So, since Laura lives in New Jersey and you live there too, I thought you could look in to what's going on."

"Mother . . . who's Jonathan?"

"Why, Laura's husband. She got herself a rich one this time. He owns the Fox and Hound Stables."

Susan was a bit surprised. "I didn't realize she had married again and is living here in New Jersey. They own the Fox and Hound Stables?" She listened a few more minutes and said, "Mother, I'll see what I can do but I'm pretty busy these days. I'll call you later, okay? . . . Yes mother, I'll do my best."

Susan hit 'end' on the phone and walked out to Chelsea who had taken the shipment of cookbooks to the front of the store to set up a new display. Susan let out a frustrated sigh. "Mothers! Can you believe it Chels? My mother wants me to drop everything and try to find my Aunt Laura. I haven't seen her since there was a family rift, which I believe was entirely my mother's fault anyway. Now here I am, ready to renovate my store, and she wants me to take time to take care of this. She still only thinks of herself."

"Mrs. Jeffries, what did you say about a stable?" Chelsea blushed a little when she saw Susan raise an eyebrow at the obvious eavesdropping confession. "It's okay Mrs. Jeffries, I won't tell anyone about your call."

"Mother told me Aunt Laura married a Jonathan Fox several years ago, and they own some really great Thoroughbreds at the Fox and Hound Stables located in Colts Neck. They have horses running at Monmouth Park Racetrack all the time."

Chelsea looked pensive for a moment and scrunched up her face with a questioning look. "Mrs. Jeffries, that name sounds so familiar. Let's check out something on the computer."

"What are you talking about Chelsea?"

Chelsea tapped the side of her head and said, "I remember hearing some guys talking in Sal's café one day when I was picking up lunch. Like, they were making jokes really because of the name of the stables and the names of some of the horses. I remember someone mentioned something about a missing woman."

Chelsea led the way back to the counter. She was a whiz on the computer and quickly did a search of the **Asbury Park Press** archives. "There it is: **Laura Fox Disappears.** I remember her name being mentioned that day at Sal's."

Both women scanned the first paragraph. **Prominent stable owner Jonathan Fox reports his wife as missing. Police find no apparent evidence of foul play after a thorough investigation. Some reports speculate that there may have been a lover's quarrel.**

The picture at the top of the article showed an attractive and youthful blonde woman standing in the Winners Circle at Monmouth Park Racetrack with her horse, Little Foxy Lady.

Susan studied the picture. "I'm going to talk with Ryan tonight Chels. I don't have a lot of time to do investigating on my own and he might know of a private detective I could hire. I'm committed now to looking into this, not only because my mother asked me, but for myself. I always liked Aunt Laura and was disappointed when she cut all ties with the family after the argument."

In her next breath, Susan asked Chelsea, "If you haven't any plans on Sunday, how about a road trip?"

"A road trip? Where?"

"Why don't we head out to Monmouth Park Racetrack and watch the races? Maybe we'll get a chance to meet with Jonathan Fox. I could start there."

"Like way cool, Mrs. Jeffries, way cool!"

Nicky screeched in the front of the store. "Hello, what's your name," as a woman entered. Susan went out to greet her while Chelsea continued scrolling through the article about Laura Fox.

The customer purchased one of the new cookbooks and Susan returned to the back.

"Oh by the way, Mrs. Jeffries," said Chelsea. "The article I read said there was no reason for Laura Fox to walk away. Do you think Jonathan has something to hide? Could there be another woman? You know the saying about trading a fifty-year old for two twenty-five year olds."

"Come on Chelsea, that's unfair to say but I know you meant it as a joke. It sure looks bad, but there's no reason to jump to conclusions. There'll always be rumors where there's wealth and fame. According to the article they worked together and loved horses."

Chelsea rolled her eyes. "Jonathan Fox may love horses, but I'm sure he loves the money they make for him even more."

"Chelsea you're a little cynical this morning."

The chimes rang again on the front door. Chelsea exited the web site she had been browsing and Susan went to the front to assist a customer. The work-day went by quickly and Chelsea completed the Jon Locke Cookbook display.

"Wonderful job, Chels," Susan said as she looked at the finished work. "Say, it's four o'clock, and I have to get over to Ryan's office. Would you be a pal and close up today? I'll pick you up at 10:30 Sunday morning. We'll continue our detective work then."

"As I said before Mrs. J, like cool!"

Susan climbed into her Mercedes and thought, wow what a day! The phone call from my mother surprised me. Mother never spoke kindly about Aunt Laura when we talked about her, Susan thought. Someday I'll figure her out.

She pulled into the parking lot of Brewster, Brewster and Brown, Law Offices.

CHAPTER 8

Lawyers pride themselves on their professional craft.

Ryan Brewster motioned to the chair facing his dark mahogany desk and asked Susan to sit down. "This is the cushy seat I reserve for my favorite clients," he said with a boyish grin. He cleared his throat and immediately said, "I have all the applications ready for you to sign, Susan. I'll file everything necessary for you to get the renovations started on your bookstore."

"Thank you so much Ryan. I've planned this for so long, I can't believe it's actually happening and I appreciate all your help. By the way, I have something else to ask you if you don't mind."

Ryan put his pen down and moved his chair away from his desk. He leaned back and cupped the back of his head with his hands. "Okay, ask away."

Susan sat on the edge of her chair and straightened her skirt. "My mother called and told me that my Aunt Laura has been missing since June. You may be acquainted with the case. She's the wife of a very well-known stable owner. Her name...."

"Are you talking about Laura Fox? Don't tell me she's your aunt!"

"Yes, she's my mother's younger sister."

Ryan gave a long low whistle. "Sure is a small world. I've been interested in the case too. It seems strange to me that a well-known person like that could just disappear. I've heard the police still have no clues?"

"That's what I've read. I promised my mother that I'd look into it as she apparently doesn't have the time. But I'm no detective, of course." Susan looked down at her skirt and picked at a speck of lint.

Ryan detected a harsh tone in Susan's voice. "Okay. I'm not sure I can help you but I know of a good private investigator. His name is Joe Boulder. He has an office in Brick Township. He's done some work for me off and on and we've golfed together. He's a fun guy too. Do you want me to call him?"

The name sounded familiar to Susan. "I think I've seen his ad in **The Press** a few times. Among other things I seem to recall, he does background checks and pre-employment checks. So you think he would help me find my aunt?"

"Oh yeah, Boulder's trained in all sorts of investigative work and has licenses in New Jersey, New York and Pennsylvania. I'll try to make an appointment for next week and then give you a call. Is that okay with you?"

"That's great Ryan. I'm worried about Aunt Laura and this eases my mind a bit. I hope he's free.

Oh, I'll pay him of course," Susan said as she stood up.

Ryan grinned at her reply and continued, "Let me ease your mind a bit more and take you out to the Bonefish Grill for some dinner. I'll bet you could use a glass of wine and some food after a long day."

"Thanks for asking, Ryan. Dinner will have to be quick. I've had a busy week and tomorrow's my day to run errands while Chelsea minds the store. I'd really like to get home early tonight."

"Okay, but promise me you'll relax while we eat," Ryan said with a broad grin.

They left the office in their own cars and arrived at the Bonefish Grill at the same time. The restaurant was crowded, but they dined leisurely and lingered over dessert. Susan's request for a quick dinner was quickly forgotten. Finally Susan reached out and patted Ryan's hand.

Instead of shaking her hand goodbye, Ryan kissed Susan on her cheek and said, "We'll do this again sometime soon."

As she drove home, Susan thought about Fox and Hound Stables. Where had she heard about them before her mother called her? She decided that, after her errands the next day she would go to the stables in Colts Neck to walk around and take a look.

CHAPTER 9

Nothing is better for the inside of a man than the outside of a horse.

Susan drove through the heavy, white wooden gate at the Fox and Hound Stables the next day. The gate reminded her of the entrance to the South Fork Ranch on the television show, *DALLAS*. There were two other cars parked in a small lot on the side of the first barn. Susan put her car in the lot but kept the engine running. It's so quiet-nobody's around this side anyway, she thought. After a minute, she turned off the ignition and stood outside the car. She sniffed the odor of the horses in the morning air and wrinkled her nose.

As Susan walked closer to the center barn, she noticed that the door was spiked open with a large stick and a man stood in the doorway. She turned 180 degrees and watched as another stablehand lead one of the most beautiful horses she had ever seen across the yard. Gosh, I miss the horses Dad had on the farm in Maryland, she thought. Worried that the guy standing in the doorway would approach her, Susan felt her stomach clench and decided to walk back toward her parked car. She noticed that he had left the doorway and was now at the side of the barn kicking up stones with his boot.

His whole demeanor frightened her for some reason. Next time I'll bring Chelsea with me, she thought.

Susan drove back through the gate and headed home. Aunt Laura, she thought, where on earth are you? Please come back to us safe and sound.

CHAPTER 10

The only difference between a tattooed person and a person who isn't tattooed is that a tattooed person doesn't care if you're tattooed or not.

Sunday at 10:30 a.m., Susan pulled into the driveway outside Chelsea's apartment complex on Route 70. The apartment buildings were clad in whitewashed brick but had no visible charm; they resembled army barracks. Chelsea's apartment was the last building on the right. The location of the complex was convenient for Chelsea's mom who worked in Toms River, and for Chelsea who attended Monmouth University. Chelsea was waiting at the curb.

Except for our age difference, we could almost pass for sisters, Susan thought as she watched Chelsea walk to the passenger side of her car. Chelsea's appearance had changed during the two years that Susan had known her. At first Chelsea had been very Gothic: every stitch of clothing she wore was black; her hair color changed from pinks to greens depending on her mood; her tattoos were not the girly pink butterfly type; and she usually wore large chunky silver jewelry. But today, Chelsea's hair was a deep chestnut brown with auburn highlights. Welcome to maturity, Susan thought with approval.

"Good morning Chels, you look chipper."

"Mrs. J. I hate to tell you, but no one says chipper anymore," she said with a smile.

"Okay Chels, keep me current. I like that. And while we're at it, call me Susan. 'Mrs. Jeffries' makes me feel old."

"Okay, like, I'll try." Chelsea buckled her seat belt.

Both women were dressed in jeans with black fitted tee-shirts and light jackets. Susan grinned as she looked at Chelsea's feet. Chelsea sported huge yet Victorian-looking Doc Martens boots. Although Susan could never see herself wearing shoes of that kind, or getting any kind of tattoo, she still felt a kinship with Chelsea.

"Which way are we going to the track?" Chelsea's tone of voice indicated that she had her own idea of how to get there.

"I was thinking of taking the Parkway unless you have a better idea."

"Well, like, usually I take the back roads to Monmouth, and the track is not too far from there. Like besides, I want to tell you what I found out about horse racing," Chelsea replied as she opened the backpack she brought with her.

"Okay co-pilot, show me the way. Did you get the information off the internet?"

"No, I was surfing the channels on cable when I landed on this documentary about horseracing. I love the educational channel, don't you? I figured, what with our taking this road trip and all, I'd give it a shot."

"You like the educational channels?" asked Susan, realizing she didn't know as much about Chelsea as she thought.

"I do, and the geographic ones too. I like, love the fact that they tell you so much about what's going on, like, in the shore area too."

"I know that horseracing has become very popular," Susan said as she reached over and turned off the radio.

"Yeah, you're right," Chelsea continued. "Did you know that Thoroughbred racing started with the breeding of three Arabian stallions with stable horses from England in the eighteenth century?"

"Arabian? Like, in Lawrence of Arabia?"

"Who?" asked Chelsea, squinting her eyes and tilting her head to one side. Susan turned and looked at Chelsea. "Never mind, it's not important. It's an old movie my mom used to drool over. What else did they say?"

Chelsea looked down at her notes. "The Arabian stallion was given the swiftness of the wind and was struck with a star on its forehead to indicate the blessing it received. Racing was the sport of kings and aristocrats in Europe."

"That's pretty interesting," Susan said. "Do you know when racing came to the United States?"

"Umm, it came when the British came to the colonies. First, it was only on the east coast, but later the rich colonialists purchased farms in Kentucky to breed and raise Thoroughbreds. They became family-owned businesses for generations."

"My grandparents owned racehorses in Maryland. I bet that's where Aunt Laura learned to love them. But my mom hated anything to do with the country. My dad loved the shore-could be that's why I grew up there."

"Listen to this. The early race tracks were owned by very elite groups, and when the tracks failed to make money, the individual owners covered their losses with personal funds to keep them going. Betting was finally opened to all people, not just the rich and famous."

"Well, we're almost there. Anything else we need to know?" asked Susan.

"Yeah, apparently there have been a lot of changes in the past twenty years. Now the emphasis is on money rather than the horses themselves. Corporations are purchasing the horses for investment. Off-Track betting is replacing the trip to the track. So the tracks are losing their appeal as well as money and they're beginning to deteriorate." She folded her notes and stuffed them inside her backpack. "Whew, like I'm finished."

"That was pretty educational," responded Susan. "Wonder how many horses Fox and Hound Stables race?"

Susan pulled into the parking lot at Monmouth Park Racetrack.

"Over there's a spot. That car is pulling out. Boy is it crowded," Chelsea said grabbing her backpack and opening the door.

The two women got out of the Mercedes, walked toward the grandstand area and saw signs pointing to the stables. A security guard was standing near a wrought iron gate at the end.

"Do you have a pass?"

Susan gave him a broad grin. "I'd like to see Jonathan Fox before the race starts to wish him luck. I'm his niece."

"What's your name?"

"Susan Jeffries."

The guard pulled out his phone. "Fox, there are two women here to see you. One tells me she's your niece. Do you want me to send them back? . . . Right I'll tell them."

Susan turned toward Chelsea and winked. "I wonder if Jonathan will be curious to see who his niece is," she whispered. Both women laughed.

The guard, squinting in the bright sunshine, stepped aside. "Go round to the far end of that first group of stables. Mr. Fox is usually right outside the stable. He can only see you for a sec."

Susan and Chelsea walked toward the stable the guard had indicated. A man, clad in tan pants and a navy jacket, leaned against the rail by the stable with papers in his hand. He had a pen clenched in his teeth.

The women approached him. "Jonathan Fox?" asked Susan.

"That's me," he said, taking the pen out of his mouth.

"I'm Susan Jeffries and this is my friend, Chelsea. My mother is Virginia McGovern." Susan did not detect any changes in Fox's facial expression as she continued. "I'd like to talk to you about my Aunt Laura."

"Well, well, well. So you're my niece, eh? Nice to meet you."

"Yes. My mother told me my aunt is missing."

Jonathan looked at the two women. "Come to my office. It's a short walk; we can talk there."

Susan and Chelsea looked at each other and Susan agreed. Jonathan led the way to his office. When the women entered the room, they saw a conference table with six captain's chairs and a paneled wall with original oils of 'Seabiscuit', 'Man O' War' and 'Foxy Lady' in gilded frames.

Fox saw their admiring glances and said, "Did you know that 'Man O' War' was a great Kentucky Thoroughbred and the greatest racehorse in American history? He won every one of his 21 races except one. He lost to a horse named Upset, believe it or not." The women were impressed.

Fox motioned them to the table. "Have a seat, ladies. Can I get you something to drink?"

"Thanks Mr. Fox, water will be fine."

Susan and Chelsea sat down at the end of the table. Fox poured two glasses of water from the water cooler in the front corner of the room.

"Tell me again. Why are you here?"

"Like I said before; my mother is your wife's sister. She called me and told me Aunt Laura is missing."

"I remember Laura mentioning she had a special fondness for her niece. That would be you, no doubt."

"Yes. I was fond of her too," said Susan. "Aunt Laura and my mother had an argument some time ago and they haven't spoken since. I haven't kept in touch either. Is she really missing?"

Jonathan frowned. "Yes, Laura's been missing for a few months. The police investigated and came up with nothing. I hired a private investigator who hasn't been able to find out anything either. The media covered the story in the beginning, but I guess they found another fish to fry," he added cynically. "There's not much more information I can give you."

"Mr. Fox, I'd like to help. Maybe I could hire another investigator. Perhaps someone new looking into her case can come up with something. Do you have any idea where she might be? Do you think any of her friends might know something?"

"Susan, the police looked into all of those things. They took her computer to check her e-mails but didn't get any answers there either. As each day passes, I miss her more and more. I'm afraid I'll never see her again." Fox bit his lip, lowered his eyes and began to pick at a knick at the edge of the table. "I'm at a loss for any more information to give you." He glanced at his watch and said in a rushed voice, "Sorry to cut this short but I have to go back out to the track and make sure Red Fox is ready for the race."

"Of course, we don't want to hold you up, but maybe we can talk again. Like I said, I really want to help if I can." Susan stood up and gave Fox a card from the Sandcastle Bookstore. "Here's my address and e-mail. I want you to know that you're not alone now. I'll talk to a private eye recommended by my lawyer. We'll see if he can help. Don't worry, we'll find her," she assured him.

Susan and Chelsea walked back through the gate and bought tickets at the ticket office. Before they entered the stands, Susan looked back and saw a man with deep-set eyes. He was carrying a blanket with the Fox and Hound monogram on the corner and was walking toward the barn where they first met Jonathan Fox.

"Hey Chels," Susan said. "See that man over there, the one with the blanket?"

"You mean that kinda creepy guy?"

"Yeah, I'm getting a weird feeling that I've seen him somewhere before. And I agree; he's creepy looking."

CHAPTER 11

The ocean breezes still the voices in my head.

The view from the southeast side of Susan's living room was glorious. The sun created a mystic glow over the ocean. Susan often sat in her soft leather recliner next to the windows to soak in the sun, relax and organize her thoughts. Her decision to purchase the two-story house was a sound one. Susan arranged her furniture so she could enjoy the view of the water and hear the surf as it splashed against the shoreline. She could see the sea gulls as they hovered over the beach, hoping to find a morsel of food.

It was Monday morning and, as Susan sipped her coffee, she thought about her road trip the day before. The ride to Monmouth Park Racetrack had gone without a hitch, but the meeting with Jonathan Fox left Susan confused. Chelsea talked incessantly on the way over but on the return home she was quiet and subdued. I don't have enough information about Jonathan and Laura to form an opinion about them at this point, Susan thought. I have to find that old box of family pictures that Mother gave me. It's been years since I looked at them. I hope I can find them. Surely they might help me . . . at least a little bit.

It had been two days since Susan had looked at the **Asbury Park Press** website. Although she remembered the previous information concerning her Aunt Laura, she hoped there would be something she had missed. She logged on her computer but found no additional information. Susan finished her coffee and decided to contact Bud Thorne, the reporter who had written the article for **The Press**.

Susan called the newspaper office and the call was forwarded to Thorne's extension. "Mr. Thorne, this is Susan Jeffries from The Sandcastle Bookstore in Manasquan. How are you?"

"Great, Ms. Jeffries, what can I do for you?"

"Well . . . I'm interested in discussing the article about the disappearance of Laura Fox that you wrote for **The Press** back in June. I read it on the website and I'd like more information. You see, Laura's my aunt."

"Oh yeah, I remember the case. She disappeared, right?"

"Yes Mr. Thorne, that's why I'm calling."

"Okay ma'am," Thorne replied in a cool tone of voice.

"Could we meet sometime soon to talk? I have several questions, and maybe you can answer them." Susan tried to sound as casual as she could.

"Sure. Where and when?"

Susan swallowed a lump in her throat. I didn't think it would be this easy to get in touch with him and schedule a meeting, she thought as she gripped the phone. "How about this coming Thursday? We can get together at the Manasquan Café. Do you know where it's located?"

"Sure do. Is 12:30 okay?"

"It sounds good to me, Mr. Thorne. I'll be waiting for you inside."

Hmm, this broad has definitely got my curiosity piqued, thought Thorne. He hung up the phone and drummed his fingers on the desk.

***

A tall, meaty man, Thorne knew that he was not what most women thought of as handsome. His hair was sparse, his ears protruded and his body was lumpy and ungainly. In his almost fifty years, he had learned to project a tough demeanor. As a writer, he was demanding and thorough. The **Asbury Park Press** management was glad to have him. His articles provoked thoughtful comments from the readers and his extensive research was reflected in his writing. His bosses never had any reason to worry about legal repercussions from his work.

Susan clicked her smart phone shut, pleased with herself and anxious at the same time. To quell the butterflies in her stomach, she decided to get out the box filled with family pictures and letters and sort them on the large dining room table for a better view. She placed those taken of Laura in a separate pile. She worked for a few minutes then looked at her watch. Oh, my gosh, she thought. I have to get going. I'm late opening the store. When she arrived a few minutes later, she saw that Chelsea had already opened up, fed Nicky his grapes and made one book sale.

"Good morning, Chels. Sorry I'm late. So glad to know that you've been taking care of business," Susan said, giving her a smile

"No bother Mrs. J., like I know you have things on your mind. How're things this morning anyway?"

"Well Chels, I need to talk with you about taking care of the bookstore in order to free up some of my time to handle this Laura Fox situation. I'll give you whatever schedule you think will work. Your classes come first. I don't want you to fall behind."

"Hey like Mrs. J., that's easy. I'm taking late afternoon classes this semester. Like, if I have to get up early I'd rather come here first. I'm down to four this semester and the late ones have labs which, like, the profs teach at dinnertime. Don't ask me why they don't want to go home to eat instead."

"You're such a friend, Chels. I'm so lucky. Let's see, is there anything else to go over before business picks up?"

Susan poured coffee for the two of them and smiled at her assistant. Chelsea took a drink and said, "Jonathan really looked upset when he spoke about Laura yesterday. I think I'll take another look on the web and try to find articles from other papers."

"Good, Chels! Also, be prepared for more road trips. You have to help me sort things out. I really need you."

"Need you. Need you too!" squawked Nicky. He was sitting on the top of the world globe which Susan displayed in the history section of the store.

When Susan returned home at the end of the day, she put on a pair of skinny jeans and a light sweatshirt. She wasn't hungry but she needed a glass of wine to relax; there were so many thoughts floating in and out of her mind. Taking the wine into the dining room, she sorted through the photos again, leaving out on the table only those of the McGovern family. Some of the old pictures were taken at the horse farm in Maryland. Hmm . . . there are several group pictures taken with horses. Dad looked happy with Star; Mother's not smiling. I remember Dad and Laura were always talking or joking while grooming, cleaning and feeding the horses. Perhaps Mother was a bit jealous, Susan thought. She sat down at the table. The phone rang and interrupted her thoughts.

It was Ryan Brewster. "Hi Susan, I located that private detective I told you about and he's available. His name is Joe Boulder. He's fast and efficient, so I'm told, and I think he'll get you some answers. I'll give him your number?"

"Thanks Ryan, that's good news. Have him call me to set up an appointment. I'd prefer that he call before coming over."

"You got it Susan. Give me a buzz after you meet him and tell me what you think."

Susan felt good for the second time that day and returned to studying the photos.

***

On Thursday afternoon, Susan met Bud Thorne as planned. He entered the Manasquan Café and spotted her when she waved. There were a few other patrons at 12:30 but the dining rush didn't usually start until happy hour. Sal Catalano looked up from the register and saw his new customers. He crossed to their table.

"Buona sera, Susan." Sal kissed her on both cheeks and handed the two a menu. "It's nice to see you again. Can I get you a little vino?" He motioned for the lone waiter to bring over some wine. "It'll be my treat."

"Thanks Sal. I'll leave the choice of appetizer to you, too, if that's all right with you Bud. May I call you Bud?" Susan asked.

"Sure thing," he replied. "I don't mind at all-on both counts." Bud Thorne settled back in his chair and Sal hurried to the kitchen.

Susan spoke up in her soft voice, hesitant at first.

"Let me tell you my story. My mother called me a short time ago and told me my Aunt Laura Fox is missing. She wants me to find her, or at least get some more information if I can. I went on line to see if I could find any information and saw the article you wrote in **The Press**. Perhaps you can share your thoughts with me?"

"Ms. Jeffries, I've filed my notes from the article regarding Mrs. Fox. My report was short and to the point. I followed the police investigations for a while and I remember there were no leads regarding her disappearance. Without more evidence, the only conclusion released was that there apparently was no foul play."

Thorne looked past Susan as Sal brought the appetizers out and placed them on the table.

"Enjoy, Ms. Susan. May I recommend Chicken Cacciatore a la Sal? Tell me when you are ready and if you want more vino."

Susan and Bud arranged the napkins on their laps and silence hung over the table. A dour expression covered Thorne's face. I can't waste any more time on a dead case, he thought.

They finished lunch and declined Sal's offer of dessert. The conversation lulled and neither brought up the subject of Laura again. They gave in to small talk about the weather and local news.

Thorne looked at his watch and said, "I hate to run but I have a meeting at 2:00 and it's 1:45 already. I'll look in my files, see what additional information I might have and e-mail it to you. Or better yet, I'll give you a call."

"That's fine Bud. I'll watch my inbox and wait for your call."

Thorne put out his hand. Susan shook it. His skin was cool and clammy.

Susan shivered.

CHAPTER 12

A balanced diet is an M&M in each hand.

Susan left the café and went next door to her bookstore. Chelsea was waiting on a customer and when she finished, she said to Susan, "Hey, like, I'm in control. Why don't you go home? The construction crew is due back from wherever they went and it's real quiet today."

Susan thought about the offer. "Thanks a lot, Chels. I really had a tense lunch hour. Maybe I will go home if you're sure you don't mind."

"Like, go," Chelsea said. She waved a hand as if dismissing her.

Susan took a handful of M&M's out of the candy dish on the counter and hurried out the door.

"Bye, bye," Nicky sang as he clung upside down to the top of his cage.

Susan went home and decided to call Jonathan Fox to arrange another meeting with him. She waited through four rings and on the fifth ring, Jonathan answered.

"Hello Susan, nice to hear from you again. This caller ID is terrific!"

Susan noted a particular friendliness in his voice. "Hello Mr. Fox. Say, I know you're busy; this'll take only a minute. I'd like to set up another meeting with you. Perhaps we can dig a little deeper and come up with more information on Aunt Laura. I'd really appreciate it."

Jonathan coughed, clearing his throat. "Well, I'd like that but I'm busy trying to purchase another Thoroughbred. I've scheduled myself for several meetings already this week. How about next week?"

"Fine with me. Thanks Mr. Fox, I'll look forward to it."

"Good Susan, but please call me Jon-my friends do," he said.

"Let me know the time and place; you've got my e-mail," Susan said as she clicked her phone shut.

Now I have to call Mother and find out what she remembers from the pictures I sent her yesterday, Susan thought. She began to notice a tightness creep in the back of her neck. Stress, that's what it is, she thought. She went into the kitchen to get a glass of wine realizing this was becoming an afternoon habit. "Well, at least it's late afternoon," she giggled to herself. She poured the wine then dialed her mother's number on the kitchen phone. She stretched the cord back to the table and sat down.

"Hello, Mother. How are things going in sunny Florida?" Susan took a sip of Chardonnay and tried to sound cheerful.

"Susan, I'm glad you called. Have you found out anything new about Laura? Tell me everything you know."

"Hold on Mother, and I'll tell you what I've done. I met with Jonathan Fox a few days ago, but he had nothing to add about Aunt Laura's disappearance. He seemed genuinely concerned though and we'll meet again next week."

"Concerned? I don't believe for one minute he's concerned. Laura always did whatever she pleased."

"Wait, Mother. How do you know this? You haven't spoken to Aunt Laura for many years. Is this just your opinion?"

Susan's mother was silent.

Trying again to open the conversation, Susan said, "Mother, I found the box with old pictures from the farm. Have you checked your in-box? I've sent some of them to you."

Again, there was an icy silence.

Susan shifted her feet and shook her fist in the air. "Mother, turn on your computer and, when you take a look at the pictures I sent, check out the one where Aunt Laura is standing with a man at the corral gate. Who is he? What's his name? When was this picture taken?"

After another long silence, Virginia responded. "I already looked at them Susan. That's the first man Laura married. I never liked him. He had such a controlling nature. When I told her how I felt, she became upset and angry; we argued for quite some time and exchanged hostile words. She left my house and I never saw her again. She hurt my feelings."

"Mother, do you remember his name?"

"No," she snapped.

Susan slowly poured another glass of wine and said, "Okay then. Maybe it'll come to you. Keep looking at the pictures. I'd like to know when and where they were taken. And there are other people I can't identify. Give me a call soon. I think whatever you remember may be helpful. After all, it was you who asked me to look into this. Think about it, please? Talk to you later."

Susan hung up the phone and stared out the window. I hope she calls me back, she thought.

CHAPTER 13

To see the wind's power, the rain's cleansing and the sun's radiant life, one needs only to look at a horse.

Jonathan Fox logged off his computer, swiveled his chair and glanced out the window. His days always started the same way ever since Laura's disappearance. He got up at 5:00 a.m., drank three cups of coffee, skipped breakfast and sat in his home office checking his in-box. The office, designed by Laura, was located on the second level of their home and overlooked the entire stable yard.

Jonathan and Laura had owned the Fox and Hound Stables since their first wedding anniversary. They bought the sixty-five acres of land after some wheeling and dealing, and designed a professional set-up. The larger yards had a gallop, good trails, horse exerciser and living quarters for two on-site groomers. The property had paddocks with run sheds, an equipment building and a barn with hay and shaving storages and twenty box stalls, each 12 feet by 13 feet. Jonathan prided himself on his architectural abilities and had designed an indoor arena, 100 feet by 200 feet. He encouraged riding shows and promoted competitions between local horse enthusiasts.

Now, as the sun rose higher over the barn, Jonathan watched Scott, one of the trainers, in an outside ring as he attempted to calm the new yearling, Tara's Dreams. That horse sure is spirited, he thought. The lunge lead pulled taut as the horse resisted Scott's efforts. "He'll get her broken soon," Jonathan muttered to himself.

Fox had bought Tara's Dreams in a Claiming Crown event in 2010. Later in the year, he bought a second Thoroughbred registered as Tim Buck Too. Scott had a lot of work ahead if these two horses were to bring in good-size purses.

Chester Fox, Jonathan's dad, had instilled the love of horses in him when he first saddled him on his prize Shetland pony, Miracle, back in Harper's Ferry, Maryland. Jonathan was only three years old. Since his childhood days, the workings of the horse business were dear to his heart and today he owned his dream. He lived by his dad's words, "Time, money, quality."

Jonathan was tall and lanky as a youth but now at the age of 55, he sported an overhang at his belt. His hair, a showcase on top of his head, had the beginnings of a salt and pepper sprinkling; lines formed across his forehead and wrinkles crimped the skin around his eyes. His facial expression was tense and taut and his jawline was as straight and level as a carpenter's tool.

When Fox met and married Laura, he was taken in by her spell. She pleased him with her kitchen skills, cooking comfort foods and living a healthy lifestyle. Laura worked alongside him in the stable business. She was his computer expert and logged all the business information in files, on spread sheets and in Quick Books. Jonathan was devastated when she disappeared and he had grown lonelier with every passing day.

Suddenly, Jonathan slapped his desk with both hands. Got to get going here, he thought. He went downstairs to the kitchen, grabbed a day-old muffin, shoved it in his mouth and went out the back door. He smelled the odor of manure that wafted in the morning breeze. Ahh, nothing like that perfume, right smack in the nostrils, he thought. The scent reminded Jonathan to order another manure cart to handle the output of his eleven horses.

Jonathan kicked the dirt in the dusty yard as he walked to the tack room on the left side of the barn. Cody O'Shea, his favorite stable boy, was hard at work inside repairing some harness straps.

"Morning, Cody. Nice out today."

"Sure is, Mr. Fox. Just like I like it. It's not too stuffy in here either with the breeze blowing through." Cody had propped the door open with a horse-chewed boot.

Jonathan grinned. "Say man, this afternoon a guy's coming over to fill me in on the auction that's coming up later in the fall. They're selling a new Thoroughbred almost ready for racing. I'd like to get some information on him. It seems like this one might bring in a big purse someday if I'm lucky enough to buy him."

"Hey, that's good news," Cody said as he hung the harness over the back of the bench. "Mind if I tag along when you have a look-see? I enjoyed our trip to get Catchmeifyoucan. I need to watch you buy a few more horses so I can get the hang of it and buy my own someday."

"I'll keep that in mind, Cody. Think about doing some training with him if I buy him. By the way, you do a good job here."

"Thanks Mr. Fox." Cody's face reddened and he brushed a lock of red hair back from his forehead.

"Oh. The new Thoroughbred is registered as Hye Mister Man. He's from the Hye Pointe Centre in Kansas. How's that for a name? Catchy don't you think?"

"Yep, it sounds like he's all grown up."

Jonathan walked past Cody and went through a door into the stall area. "I need to pick out a nice box for this new guy," he called back over his shoulder to Cody.

On his way back across the yard twenty minutes later, Jonathan noticed several of his stable employees gathered in a training ring near the first paddock. He saw something dark lying on the ground, and as he walked nearer, the group separated to allow him to walk closer. Tim Buck Too was down on the ground; the lunge lead was wrapped around his right front leg. The horse twitched his head, while making an attempt to stand up.

"Whoa boy," Scott, his trainer, whispered at him.

"What's going on here?" Jonathan asked. He kept his voice low to avoid startling the horse.

"I dropped the lunge lead for just a minute," Scott answered. "Boss, he's gonna be okay, but I think you should head over to your house. I heard a loud noise over there; I'm not sure what it was. I heard it just as I brought your horse to the ring."

Jonathan looked past the barn and saw the back screen door hanging loose on the top hinge. "You're sure everything's okay here? Have the vet come over and check that leg."

"Will do, Boss. He's fine though."

"Well, I'm going back to the stables to check on Red Fox, I'll check back with you on the way over to my house. That hinge on the back door has been loose for a long time."

Red Fox was being saddled when Jonathan entered his stall. "Good looking horse there, Jim. Give him a work out."

"Will do, Boss."

Fox left the barn and went toward his house. He examined the loosened door. I don't think anyone would try to get in here in broad daylight. I'd better check though; anything can happen these days, he thought. He cautiously entered the kitchen. Things looked undisturbed and he found nothing in the remaining areas downstairs. He moved toward the stairs leading to the second floor. There wasn't a sound on the second level.

Jonathan checked all the rooms and then walked into the study. He noticed the computer screen had been turned on. I'm sure I turned it off when I left, he thought. He discovered that a drawer in his top file cabinet was ajar. "What the hell's going on?" he mumbled. "First, Laura's family shows up out of nowhere and hits me with questions and now someone wanders into my house." Jonathan turned off the computer and checked the drawers in his desk. They were locked. Frowning, he went downstairs and walked back out to the stables to check on Tim Buck Too.

The veterinarian was examining the horse when Jonathan entered the barn. After he finished, he stood up and said, "Sure is a beaut of a horse. He's fine." He picked up his bag and left; Jonathan felt relieved. "Okay, let's get back to work."

Jonathan walked slowly back to the house and Laura re-entered his mind for the second time that morning.

CHAPTER 14

A horse perseveres with his heart and gallops with his lungs.

Cody O'Shea walked into the stables later that same day, chatted with Scott for a few minutes then made his usual rounds to check on the other horses and left. On his way home, he thought of the day's events and, because he had no plans for the evening, he headed to Toms River about thirty minutes away. He had heard about Favorites, a new off-track betting parlor located on Route 37, and decided he would try it out.

When Cody entered, he noticed everyone was smiling and calling one another by name. He grabbed a stool at the bar, put down a ten dollar bill, caught the pretty bartender's attention and ordered a Sam Adams draft. After taking a long, cold swallow, he stared at one of the television screens over the bar for a minute. "That's one grand horse racing tonight," he commented in a low voice. He looked around the bar again and noticed the intensity on the men's faces. *He kind of reminds me of Fox's horse. Gee, I wish things had turned out differently for him,* he thought.

***

Cody had delivered a supply of monogrammed mugs to Fox and Hound Stables, a promotional item that Jonathan Fox had planned to give out after his horse won the Triple Crown. Fox had groomed a beauty of a grey, with a silver mane and tail, and it looked as if he was going to win it. Catchmeifyoucan had already won the Kentucky Derby and the Preakness and, facing the Belmont Stakes, Fox had believed that Catchmeifyoucan was the best of all the contenders.

Cody had arrived at the stables and noticed a pick-up truck with two men in it, heading south out of the gate. He had a lot on his mind at the time and the appearance of the vehicle only registered as he drove further into the yards. The truck could have come from there. He'd mentioned it to the police when they questioned him later but he didn't think anything came of it since there wasn't much information to go on.

Cody had told the police that he'd put the promotional mugs in the storage area and walked over to the stables to check the horses. He loved Another Foxy Lady and had wanted to check on her since she was with foal. He'd brought her some sugar and a carrot. Nothing had seemed amiss at the stables. Also, there had been no sign of Laura.

***

Catching the bartender's eye as she stood by the taps, Cody motioned for another beer. There was a buzz of conversation and a clinking of glasses. The atmosphere seems like that television show *CHEERS* that was on a couple of years ago, he thought. Cody felt comfortable. He left the bar to place a few bets on the Thoroughbreds. Back at the bar, Cody pictured Laura's face in his mind and thought, where could she have gone? I can't believe that Laura would have left Mr. Fox for another man. What could have happened to her? Was there foul play? Why haven't the cops been able to find any trace of her?

Cody finished his beer and checked his tickets: one winner and one loser. He stood up, surveyed the bar, the outer circle and the television screens for the umpteenth time; he knew he would come here again. Cody slapped a hefty tip on the counter and winked at the bartender.

"See you soon," he said as he patted the money.

Back in his vehicle, Cody headed home with thoughts of Fox streaming in his head. Mr. Fox was definitely devastated by Laura going missing and Catchmeifyoucan placing second at the Belmont Stakes. "He hasn't been the same man since," Cody said aloud in the stillness of the cab.

Cody turned into the parking lot of his apartment and thought about the Belmont Stakes.

Funny, I haven't seen Franky Alvarez since a few days before the race. He's a good jockey and Mr. Fox thought the combination of his horse and Franky was a sure winner. But that 20-1 long-shot named Have Faith beat him by a nose. Mr. Fox sure was wrong.

It seemed odd to Cody that he hadn't seen Alvarez back at the track or even heard about him lately. Hmm, wonder what's up with Franky, he mused.

CHAPTER 15

Life is good, horses make it better.

Franky was born in Havana, Cuba, and given the name Franky Benito Alvarez Gonzalez. Franky and his parents were among the many Cuban refugees in 1979 who had settled in Miami, Florida. Franky's family was sponsored by a second cousin who had been living there for several years.

Franky spent most of his childhood and youth in Miami. He was small for his age and he loved horses. He watched horse races, drew pictures of horses, read every book he could find about horses and constantly begged to own a horse. When Franky turned sixteen, his parents allowed him to join with a trainer at the Hialeah Race Track outside Miami. Because of his size, he was an excellent candidate for jockey.

A few years later, on the advice of a friend, he moved to New Jersey, where he became apprentice rider at Monmouth Park Racetrack. That's where he met Jonathan Fox, who was so impressed by Franky's enthusiasm and spunk that he hired him to work for the Fox and Hound Stables.

***

Franky sat on a bench near a tall royal palm tree, one of the many lining the walkways of Miami's Tropical Park. His left leg bounced nervously on the ball of his foot and he smoothed his pants with sweaty palms. He could see the children in the playground kicking their legs to make the swings go faster. A scout group was picking up trash and a young mother pushed a baby in a stroller.

Franky was in a foul mood and he kicked at a small gecko that scurried past and ran up the leg of a table nearby. His thoughts went back to New Jersey. I had no choice; it was an offer I couldn't refuse. That wasn't about money. It was personal. When I got fired from the stables, I didn't care about my friends. Besides there was nothing they could do. I never done anything like this before. I was just so darn scared.

"You by yourself?" boomed a voice behind Franky.

Startled, he looked around. A tall man with broad shoulders and a barrel chest stood menacingly over him. His eyes were deep-set and he had a heavy brow. He was no youngster as could be seen in his receding hairline and greying temples.

"Yeah, what are you doing here?"

"The boss thought I should find you. He said you're asking for more money now. We had a deal, Franky, and that deal didn't include any more dough."

Franky fidgeted nervously with his hands. "Yeah, the money was okay at first but now I want more."

"Are you trying to blackmail us, Franky?"

"You can call it whatever you like. You'll have to pay me if you don't want any trouble."

"Oh there'll be trouble all right. The boss isn't an easy man to deal with. You'd better watch your step. This isn't the end, you little squirt. I'll tell him what you want then we'll see what kind of song you'll be singing. I'll be in touch."

Franky began to sweat as he watched the tall man walk away. There was no easy solution. That loser uses people. That's what he does, Franky thought. And now he sent his ape around trying to scare me. Well, it worked. I am scared and I don't know what I'm gonna do if they don't get me that money.

Franky stood and walked slowly toward 40th Street, his hands in his pockets and a haunted look in his eyes.

CHAPTER 16

Unsatisfied desire needs a strong psychic force to enable it.

VENEZUELA 2011

Paul Thomas leaned back in his chair and looked out his office window. In the distance were the uninhabited emerald slopes of Avila National Park rising above the city like an immense green wave, forever on the verge of breaking. The **El Globo** newspaper on his desk was open to an inside page.

SAN FERNANDO DE APURE, Venezuela (AP) – At the blast of a whistle, a half dozen horses plunge into the Apure River and set out for the distant shore in a unique annual spectacle commemorating a historic battle.

Thousands of cowboys and their families gather to watch each year on the anniversary of an 1819 battle fought by soldiers led by independence heroes Simon Bolivar and Gen. Jose Antonio Paez.

Paez and about 150 soldiers swam across the river alongside their horses, then attacked and defeated a force of more than 1,000 Spanish troops who had been sent to quash their rebellion.

Today, only the horses do the swimming, as competitors in canoes guide them across the river.

Paul thought about what glorious creatures horses are. The idea of glorious creatures led his mind along other heavenly avenues, and his mental images led him to picture Susan Jeffries. It had been almost a year since he had managed to escape to Caracas after fleeing the United States on a money laundering charge. The moment I saw her, I wanted her, he thought. But she didn't want me. I promised myself that one day I would return. Now might be the time. Since there is a warrant for my arrest, I can't go back as Paul Thomas, but as a master of disguise I can pick another personality. Who will it be this time?

Paul's eyes wandered to the paper on his desk and became riveted to another article. This weekend there would be races both Saturday and Sunday at La Riconada, Venezuela's oldest and largest racetrack. Racing! Of course! Paul loved betting on the horses and whenever he was in New Jersey, he spent a lot of time at Monmouth Park Racetrack.

He had become friends with a young man named Cody who worked for one of the stables in the area. Their friendship began when Cody followed Paul's advice and they bet on a 50-1 shot and won a bundle. I still have Cody's cell number, he thought. Maybe I should call him and get a job at the stables where he works. Stable owners are always looking for someone to do menial labor. This will certainly be below my standards, but at least it might get me to New Jersey, give me a place to stay and give me time to figure out my next move.

Paul picked up his cell and punched in Cody's number. "Cody, is that you?" he asked. "It's Paul. Do you remember me from Monmouth Park Racetrack? We bet on that 50-1 shot and . . . well, good, I'm glad you took my tip about the horse too. Listen, I've got a funny kind of favor to ask you . . . ."

CHAPTER 17

A disguise cannot conceal love where it exists.

Paul Thomas had accomplished his mission. He had perfected a disguise as Pete Carter, ponytailed and bearded. He had been hired as a stablehand by the Fox and Hound Stables. He knew that Susan Jeffries lived in Manasquan, which was not far from the stables, so he'd be able to look her up or maybe run into her accidentally sometime. There was no rush. There was something else on his mind. I like Jonathan Fox, he thought. And I'm impressed by his business, his stables and his stablehands. But there's some mystery about the disappearance of his wife. And I've heard several whispered conversations that lead me to believe that some of Fox's employees might be embezzling funds from him, or at least up to no good.

Pete looked around furtively. All the other stable employees were with Fox in the training ring looking at the downed horse. This might be a good time to do some investigating on my own, he thought. Pete knew that Fox had his office in his house and decided to start his search there. "I don't know what I'm looking for, but nothing ventured, nothing gained," he told himself.

The Foxes never locked their house when they were at the stables, so getting inside was easy enough for him. Pete found nothing of interest on the first floor, so he went up the stairs to the second level and found the study which was wood paneled and very clearly the office of a horseman. Pictures of winning race horses covered the walls, and a tall glass case was filled with trophies and ribbons. A desktop computer on the table behind a large mahogany desk drew Pete's attention. He pressed the power button and watched as the screen brightened. He looked at the prompt for a username and password. He tried several combinations that didn't work then looked around the room again.

A tall mahogany file cabinet was Pete's next focus. Maybe I'll find the passwords in there, he thought. Pete opened each drawer and looked at the labels on each folder. In the bottom drawer, he found two files: one labeled, Financial Reports and the other, Employees to Watch. Pete selected both of them and was about to sit down to look at them when he heard the sound of someone approaching the front of the house.

Pete stuck the files under his arm and ran down the stairs and out the back door. As he dashed out, the screen door banged loudly against the wall of the house and one of the top hinges fell to the porch. "Damn," he said in a low voice.

Pete furtively walked back to the bunk house and hid the folders under his mattress before anyone saw him. He wiped the sweat from his face and sauntered out to join the stable hands. I can't wait to see what's in those files, he thought. But I've gotta get to work now.

Pete dragged a hose over to Red Fox's stall and began to hose it down. "Good thing I've got these boots on, I can't let this horse manure get on my skin; it's already getting on my nerves." Pete looked around to make sure no one heard him mumbling. He turned off the hose and tried to pick up on the conversation in the barn. The most he heard was men laughing at the jokes that Jake spit out. Pete hung the mucking rake and the muck bucket on a side wall. Fox runs a tight stable and, boy he is a son-of-a-gun. Everyone gets along real well here but there's something going on with Fox, he thought.

Pete replaced some of the bedding in Red Fox's stall and went to the cabinet in back of the stable and took out the brushes. He arranged his grooming tools inside his work sack and started toward the back door. Once outside, he glanced across the yards and looked at the back of Fox's house. I didn't find much in Fox's office and I didn't expect the back door hinge to give way either, Pete thought. Boy, what a chance I took! The computer wasn't an easy-enter and it was hard to make sense of the files in the short time I had. Pete continued across to the next barn. It was time to check out the new Thoroughbred.

Pete was deep in thought as he wandered over to look at the horse. I had intended to keep a low profile right from the start of my employment here. After all, I have my own mission and don't want to owe anything to anyone. I'm still trying to get the hang of being a stablehand. It's demeaning. Where was my mind when I tripped into this trap? I hate mucking out the stalls; it's hard labor compared to the work I did back in Venezuela. Scouring down walls during the heat is exhausting. The air reeks from the stench of horse manure and my throat is always raw. "There's no way I can get used to this," he muttered.

Cody walked into the stables to check out Krypton Bay. "Look at that proud stallion, Pete, isn't he magnificent? Horses are the noblest animals in the world for sure!"

"They certainly are. Say Cody, let me buy you a beer when we're done here, okay?"

"Sure Pete, let's head to the OTB in Toms River and get a few there. I want to place a couple of bets. Jack Walsh has a new filly running tonight at Charlestown. I'd like to watch her run."

"Good idea Cody. I'll place a few bets myself. I'm going in to clean up a little; meet you by the truck in about fifteen minutes."

Carter walked back to his room pondering about what he knew about Laura's disappearance. The police don't have anything to go on. I want to talk to Cody about that day. Maybe I can find out something that no one else has thought about to help Fox and by doing so get back into Susan's good graces, he thought.

Cody and Pete had their racing forms with them as they walked into Favorites and headed directly to the bar. Pete's eyes took in everything as they placed their orders with the friendly bartender. He handicapped a long shot at Parx and wanted to get his wager in. The odds still looked great as he put down $20.00 to win on him.

Back at the bar after placing their wagers, Pete asked Cody, "What do you remember about the day Fox's wife disappeared?"

"Well, I took an order of championship mugs that Fox had me pick up over to the stables that morning. I told the police that there was a truck that passed me as I was driving through the main gate. My mind was on the Belmont and our winning the Triple Crown and I didn't notice anything else."

Pete persisted. "What did you tell the cops about the truck?"

"Just that it was an F150 and it was black. There was nothing else to tell. I think there were two men in it."

"Did you notice anything about the truck that

was different: any dents, decals or bumper stickers? What about the plates? Were they from Jersey or some other state?"

Cody finished his beer, ordered another and watched the race he had bet on. After crumpling up his losing ticket, he turned to Pete, "There was a decal on the side window I'm sure. I'd have to think about it some more, but the plates weren't from New Jersey. Now that we're talking about them, I remember there were light colors on them. A friend of mine had similar plates and he was from Ohio. I probably should tell someone about it. There was something vaguely familiar about that decal. It'll come to me I'm sure."

Pete thought a minute then said, "Listen Cody. I want to nose around a little bit. Don't say anything just yet and keep trying to place that decal. I want to know what happened to Laura Fox too."

The long shot at Parx came in and Pete went to cash his winning ticket. The horse paid $132.40 to win. I've still got the gift even though it's been awhile. Geez, I'm such a good handicapper, he mused.

Pete walked back to the bar thirteen hundred dollars richer. He ordered another beer for the two of them. While bantering with the pretty bartender, he noticed the camaraderie among the patrons.

"Let's order some food to go with the beer, Pete," Cody suggested. They ordered burgers and fries. Pete pored over his racing form and checked out the tracks that were running. I'll try for another good one and this time share with Cody, he thought. Tomorrow, I might check out Jack Walsh and his stables. Maybe I can find out a little more about this feud with Fox. Pete let the ideas sink deep in his mind. The two men decided to head back to Colts Neck; it was almost 11 p.m.

Once back at Fox and Hound Stables, Pete closed the wooden door to his small bunkroom, pulled the two folders from under his mattress and sat down on the narrow bed. Poring through the financial reports, he noticed there were several discrepancies between income, expenses and profits. Someone had circled the notes with a red marker. It looks like that at least $3000.00 of income each month is not accounted for. Now why wouldn't Fox have stopped this? Laura was the bookkeeper so she must have seen that there was something wrong here. Pete snapped his fingers. Maybe this has something to do with her disappearance!

Pete grabbed the other file and flipped through the papers. There was a file for each employee giving their starting date, job title and salary. There were various notes indicating: good worker, greenhorn but learning, this one's a keeper. But the most curious note indicated: this one needs watching. Is there a connection with this guy and the missing money, he thought. I better keep my eyes and ears open, Pete decided. I've got to find out who's involved. Maybe I should ask Fox if I can help him.

CHAPTER 18

Your mind and heart will tell you when you are overwhelmed.

The past few weeks had been busier than ever for Susan and she hadn't spent much time in the bookstore. Her attorney had filed for the construction permits necessary to begin her tearoom and she had met with the architect recommended by Gig Giovanni, contractor from the construction company.

Susan had used her inheritance money to establish herself as a bookstore owner. She contacted the New Jersey Health Department to obtain several licenses enabling her to serve pastries, tea and coffee in the tearoom. She obtained a food vending license and corporate and federal tax identification numbers. She confirmed that Sal Catalano, who was supplying the baked goods from his baker, was registered with the Food and Drug Administration. She still needed to come up with ten thousand dollars to make upgrades to the septic system and the grease traps that existed in the former laundry.

I feel so overwhelmed, she thought as she started her car. Even though it's still early, maybe I'll let Chelsea sleep in today. I'll give her the day off and tell her tomorrow about my plans to hire someone to help in the store. I've got so much to do and it will free me up a bit. Susan took out her cell and punched in Chelsea's number. The phone rang several times before Chelsea picked up.

"Hello." Her voice sounded groggy with sleep.

"Good morning, sleepyhead. I just want to let you know that you can go back to sleep. I'm on my way to the store and plan to stay all day."

"Great Mrs. J, I have lots of classwork to do. It all needs to be completed by tomorrow. What a drag. I'm so tired of studying!"

"Chels, are there any important issues that I need to focus on in particular?"

"Like, I can't focus on anything except getting back to sleep. Everything's in order for you. Bye now."

Susan drove to work and pulled into the parking lot. As she unlocked the door of the bookstore, Nicky squawked, "Feed me, feed me."

"Okay, okay. Have you forgotten how to say good morning? You sound very pesky today."

"Nicky need grapes."

Susan gave the bird some cheese nibbles and then walked around looking at the progress made on the store's expansion project. So much work had been done since she had wandered through a week ago. It looked like it would be completed in just a few more weeks. Suddenly, there was a knock at the door followed by two sharp raps. Susan left the new addition to answer it.

"Good morning Mrs. Jeffries. I'm Joe Boulder. My friend Ryan Brewster called me and said you're looking for the services of a private investigator. Well, here I am!"

Susan was stunned by his obvious boldness. She didn't expect that he would show up unannounced, especially after she had asked Ryan to have him call first. "Hello Mr. Boulder," she said in a cool tone. "I was expecting a call from you."

"Sorry about that. I located your bookstore online so I thought I'd drop in to speak with you today. Is my timing bad?"

"No, no. I just got here myself." Susan glanced out the door window as it closed behind him. There was nobody on the street outside.

Joe Boulder stood six feet tall and was impeccably dressed in dark brown pants and a tan micro-suede jacket. His cream-colored shirt had an open neck which showed off wispy chest hair. He had a rugged skin tone with pock marks on his chin, and greying hair with long side burns. It was apparent to Susan that he spent time outdoors. His wide shoulders suggested that he enjoyed physical workouts too.

Susan remembered Ryan's advice to ask for credentials although she knew Ryan wouldn't recommend someone who might take advantage of her. Ryan had told her that Boulder was a former police officer and had taken the criminal justice course at Stockton College in South Jersey.

Boulder handed Susan his license and she quickly looked at it.

"Mr. Boulder, I don't have much information to give you about my aunt. This is about her disappearance and things are sketchy to say the least. I only have this early picture of her. I made you a copy."

"Thanks. I remember reading about Laura Fox. Sorry that her disappearance hasn't been solved," Boulder said.

"I know there were some articles published in **The Press**. A reporter, named Bud Thorne, wrote the article and may have some notes. I met my uncle, Jonathan Fox at the Monmouth Park Racetrack last Sunday and we talked for a short time. He didn't have much to say."

Susan moved toward the counter and Boulder followed. His bulky frame made his footsteps sound heavy on the bookstore floor. "Sit here," Susan said, motioning to him to sit at the worktable. "Would you like some coffee?"

"No thanks ma'am. Been up since five and have had four cups already."

"Well then Mr. Boulder will you work for me? I really need some help."

"Mrs. Jeffries I'm at your service," said Boulder smiling broadly.

"What do you charge?"

"My retainer fee is $500.00. I charge $55.00 an hour when I work on the case plus expenses.

"Do you have a contract with you? I'd like to sign it today and get started as soon as we can." Susan was satisfied with Ryan's choice and anxious to move forward.

Boulder opened a worn, black leather portfolio, took out papers and placed them in front of her.

"Will you make a list of your expenses for me? I'll need them weekly, if you can do that."

"Sure thing Mrs. Jeffries. I'll keep a tally for you."

Susan took time looking over the contract then signed her name. She went to the back of the bookstore to make a copy.

While Susan was in the back, Boulder meandered through the store. He wasn't much of a fiction reader but found the cookbook display interesting. He turned back toward the worktable.

"If you had given me a call, I might have had a little information for you," said Susan on her return. She handed him the papers.

Boulder's face reddened a bit at Susan's remark. "That's all right. I'll get started and get back to you." He held out his hand, shook Susan's hand

and turned to the door. As he stepped onto the new doormat, he turned and waved a thumbs-up. *I didn't expect to sign papers so soon* he thought. *Ryan must have filled her in on my credentials and my work. She seems like a sharp lady.*

Susan felt an immediate sense of relief flow through her as she closed the door, but there were still some doubts edging back into her mind.

CHAPTER 19

The only circle of trust you should have is a donut.

Susan stretched her arms, yawned and turned the alarm clock off. It was seven o'clock the following morning, and she had to get to the bookstore to talk with Chelsea about her plans. She showered, dressed and grabbed a glass of orange juice and a granola bar for breakfast. It had started to rain so she didn't plan on running on the beach. Yesterday she had hired Joe Boulder to help investigate her aunt's disappearance. Today she would take the next step in her hiring plan.

When Susan arrived at the store, she saw the stack of newspapers outside on the curb. Chelsea must not be in yet, she thought. Minutes later, Chelsea walked in lugging the newspapers by the jute twine that held them together.

"Morning Mrs. J. You beat me today."

"Hi Chels, I bought some doughnuts on my way here. They're in the back room. Enjoy."

"Thanks. I'm starved. I skipped breakfast since I woke up late."

Susan went to the back and drank a cup of coffee while Chelsea ate two of the gooey, chocolate doughnuts. She set her cup on the table and said,

"Chels, I want to talk to you about a change I'm making."

"Change? What's up?"

"I'm meeting a friend today for lunch and hope to hire her."

"Are you letting me go? I mean, you know, are you angry with me?"

"Oh heavens no, Chelsea, I love your work and definitely want you to stay. I'm thinking about a second person to work here with you. I'm finding myself swamped with tearoom preparations and trying to find my aunt. Also, it will soon start getting busier what with the holidays coming and all. Besides, this will give you more time to yourself when you need it."

"Well, I suppose I could use more time to study."

Susan chuckled and said, "That's exactly what I thought."

"Like can you tell me more about this new person? Is she my age and just as beautiful?" Chelsea laughed and patted her auburn hair.

Susan poured another cup of coffee, grabbed a doughnut with sprinkles and smiled. "Well, her name is Millie Larson. She worked in a flower shop for years. That's where I met her and we started up a friendship. We get along fine even though she is twenty years older than me. Her husband died in his thirties and left her and their daughter, Ingrid, well off with a large insurance policy and a sizable savings account. She lives in Toms River now with her Schnauzer dog, Buttons. She's attractive, tall and slender and has a quick wit. Sometimes she gets her words mixed up. She could be accused of being a 'Mrs. Malaprop'."

"She sounds like fun, I guess." Chelsea wrinkled up her nose and grinned. "Have I ever seen her?"

"Maybe you have. Millie adores her precious granddaughter and has come in to buy her picture books from time to time." Susan sat back and thought for a second, Millie will be good to work with seniors who don't appreciate Chelsea's expressions and background rap music. Aloud she said, "First, I have to catch the 'possum before I make 'possum soup, Chels, if you know what I mean. And second, I have to tell you some funny things but don't repeat this. Sometimes Millie is a little quirky, like the time she opened her front door wearing big bunny slippers to greet guests who came to dinner. Another time, she climbed to the top of the fifty-foot fire truck ladder at a local fair. Oh yes, she used to drive her JEEP around town decorated with Christmas lights. She's an honest person and well-read but known for some unusual ways."

"Well, she sounds like rad to me. After your lunch date, you'll have to tell me more."

The morning went by quickly and Susan looked forward to meeting Millie for lunch. It had been months since she had last seen her. When Susan parked her car in the parking lot, she heard a beep. Millie was sitting in her JEEP next to the handicap sign, waving a red hanky with white lace out the window. Just like Millie, Susan thought.

"It's so good to see you Millie." They gave each other a huge hug.

"Me too. Say I've never been to the Bonefish Grill before. You sure it's good?"

"I come here often, Millie, don't worry."

After ordering lunch, they laughed over old times. Then Susan asked, "Millie, have you ever thought about going back to work? I mean would you want to work in a nice quiet, social, non-pressured job?"

"Where's that-in a library?" Millie said with a smirk.

"I'm thinking of a bookstore."

Millie stared at her for a moment and then spoke. "I'd love to work in your bookstore," she said realizing she knew what Susan meant.

"We can talk about your responsibilities, hours, and pay later on. But I'm thrilled you'll be coming to my store. Let's have another drink to celebrate."

Millie looked at Susan and held up the red hanky. "One thing Susan, does that quirky girl who says 'like' all the time still work there?"

"Yes, she sure does." Susan smiled to herself. I guess quirky is in the eye of the beholder, she thought.

CHAPTER 20

I am always late and have no excuses; maybe I need a new watch?

Millie Larson rose earlier than her usual time of seven-thirty. The weather looked as if the prediction was wrong. It was bright and sunny, not cloudy with a chance of rain. Millie checked her Mickey Mouse watch to see if she had enough time to go to the post office. "Good," she muttered. "I'll have plenty of time before I'm expected at the store. Perhaps I should switch watches for my Big Foot watch. That will make customers curious." Millie spotted her red velvet hat on the rack. She grabbed it and placed it on her head. "Nah, I don't need this today," she decided. Millie always had the habit of talking aloud to herself and to her dog Buttons.

Millie gazed into the mirror above her hallway table. "Welcome to the Sandcastle Bookstore. May I help you? What books are you interested in?" Millie practiced. As she continued her imaginary greetings, her thoughts changed. I hope that college girl, what's her name . . . Chelsea, that's it, will be a little civil. She cracks gum, likes loud music, talks my ear off and doesn't speak properly what with all her likes, ya knows, and uhs between words. The last time I saw her, she was wearing that ugly top with big polka dots on it and worn-out jeans. That top makes her look like a Dalmatian!

At 8:25 a.m., Millie parked her JEEP in the parking lot across from the bookstore. Chelsea was in the store waiting to greet her.

"Like, nice you got here early. I came in at eight to open so I can start to show you around. Susan's not going to be here today."

"That's fine with me," said Millie eyeing her up and down.

As Chelsea led her to the far side of the store, she asked, "Do you know how to use a computer?"

Millie pulled her eyebrows together and in an indignant tone of voice, answered, "Do you think I'm from the Stone Age? Of course I do!"

Chelsea smiled and thought, I don't want to go there. Millie will think I'm rude. She turned toward the work table and said, "This computer does sales and inventories our books as well as logging new books and other store items. One thing we do as soon as we arrive is to wrap up all the newspapers that didn't sell and put them outside the door. Lunch break is whenever you grab it when you're alone, but if Susan or I are here you can go out."

Millie took out a small red notebook with a metal spiral which had sprung off its end and wrote some of the instructions down. She looked at Chelsea and grinned, "I imagine the TV is for the customers, but not for the homeless, if you know what I mean. Maybe you can discourage them by putting on a channel about getting a job."

"Mill . . . we're really getting away from your duties, if you know what I mean. There aren't many people who come here just to sit." Chelsea continued and Millie followed her jotting down do's and don'ts.

"Remember, if people want help they'll ask you. You're not selling a used car, like don't push. Susan told me you go to the library a lot so you know where the books go on the shelves. We divide our books the same way-fiction, non-fiction like you know."

"Nicky's hungry, Nicky's hungry!" Chelsea walked over to the bird's cage and handed him a sesame cracker.

"Is he part of my job, too?" asked Millie.

"Oh yeah, like unless you don't want to hear, 'Nicky wanna grape' a dozen times. He gets louder each time he calls out." Chelsea watched Millie's eyes following Nicky. She's more of a bird than Nicky, Chelsea thought. She acts quirky so she can get attention. I'll have to throw her a compliment once in a while so we're not at each other's throats. I don't want Mrs. J. upset with me.

Millie roamed around the room checking out the Halloween decorations. She smiled thinking of her granddaughter and the delight she would have seeing the festive orange lights and posters of Jack-O-Lanterns.

The door chimes rang and both women turned toward the door. Chelsea's eyes widened and she greeted her mother. "Hi Mom, it's nice to see you. Why're you here? Did you get lost or are you just checking up on your daughter?" She reached her arms out to give her a hug.

Chelsea's mother laughed and remarked, "Neither. I came by to meet the new woman you'll be working with and to look for a cookbook, HOLIDAY FAVORITES. As she turned toward Millie, she said, "Hello, I'm Autumn. You can guess I'm Chelsea's mom. By the way, I love the small stars on your fingernails."

"Thanks. Nice to meet you," Millie said extending her hand.

Chelsea tilted her head slightly and said, "I'm sorry, I should have introduced you both."

Millie smiled and thought: what an interesting name. Here is a person I can connect with. She seems very gracious. The women continued conversing as Chelsea went to get her mother a cup of coffee and a vanilla crumpet.

When she returned, an elderly couple entered the store, with their Great Dane on a leash. "Hi. Come in and look around. By the way, is that a service dog? Otherwise, we must insist dogs stay outside," said Chelsea.

"Maximillian goes where I go," the customer retorted.

"Well you see, the Health Department won't allow dogs where food is served. The Tea Cup Room is adjacent to the bookstore."

"How come you have that parrot in here then?"

"He's confined in his cage and he's not near the food either."

The woman looked at her husband and said, "Joseph, let's find a bookstore where the people aren't so rude. Come on Maximillian; Mommy loves you even if these people don't."

Chelsea bit her lip and suggested, "Why don't you tie it up outside on the bench?"

"Maximillian is a 'he', so don't call him an 'it'."

Millie stepped forward. "May I pet Maximillian? I have a Schnauzer, named Buttons, and I love dogs. Let me take him for a walk. That way you can look around."

The woman looked apprehensive at first but then gave in.

Thirty minutes later, after the couple bought several books and the last Curious George hand puppet in the store, they left.

Chelsea gave Millie a hug. "Thanks so much for handling the situation. You're going to work out just fine."

CHAPTER 21

Temper gets you into trouble. Pride keeps you there.

Joe Boulder decided to tackle the first thing on his mind after Susan signed the contract for his investigative services: Bud Thorne at **Asbury Park Press**. It was noontime the day after Susan hired him. Even though Susan had gotten nowhere in her meeting with Thorne, he was determined to do better.

When he arrived on the second floor of the newspaper building, he saw a door slightly ajar with Thorne's name on it. He tapped on the tempered glass window. "Hello Mr. Thorne, I'm Joe Boulder, a private investigator." He pulled out his ID badge. "I'm here to talk to you about that piece you wrote on Laura Fox's disappearance a few months ago."

Bud Thorne had developed a short temper as a newspaper journalist over the years. He pushed back on his rolling desk chair and tossed his pen onto the desk. He didn't like PIs but he swung around to face Boulder. He remained seated.

"Well, what do you want to know? Sit here." He motioned to the chair beside his desk.

"I've read your article on the web concerning Mrs. Fox," said Boulder. "I'm representing her niece.

Have you heard anything more about her disappearance since your article?"

Thorne turned back to his work on top of the desk and said in a sharp voice, "I talked to that woman, Jeffries, the other day and told her that the investigation has been on hold. I can get my folder and check my notes, but right now I'm busy. You should have called for an appointment. We'll have to discuss this another time."

Boulder shook his head. "I'm busy too, man. Can you just give me a few minutes to ask some questions? I know you met with Susan Jeffries."

"I have a deadline in an hour." Boy, he's a horse's butt, Thorne thought. He stood up and walked toward the door. "I'm not sure I have anything that will interest you. You know, I submitted my story. It got edited and what was left got published. I'm afraid I don't have anything more to say." Thorne's voice reflected that he was annoyed and he held the door open.

Boulder took the hint that it was time to leave. "Well, if you find some time to review your notes, email me." The men exchanged business cards then Boulder put on his 'newsboy' hat and left. As he went back to his car, Boulder thought, this isn't the end of tackling this guy-the pompous so and so.

CHAPTER 22

Horses make a landscape beautiful.

Boulder was annoyed with his not-too-friendly meeting with Thorne, he agreed to meet with him later. He put Thorne's card in his pocket and slid into his car. He's blunt. It seems as if he didn't want to let me in on any information he might have. Oh well, that was a long shot anyway. Looks like I'm in the same boat as Susan. I'll head over to the Fox and Hound Stables and check things out, he thought. Maybe the guys have heard some talk.

Boulder was familiar with the Fox and Hound Stables. He attended races at Monmouth Park Racetrack and knew some of the jockeys, owners of the Thoroughbreds and many of the stablehands who worked there. On several occasions, he had gone to a nearby pub with them after the races.

When Boulder arrived at the stables, he took some time to watch the Thoroughbreds grazing in the field. The yards looked neat and clean and the horses were well-groomed. He walked inside the stables and saw several stablehands at work. As he approached them, he introduced himself, "Howdy guys. I'm Joe Boulder."

"Well, you needn't introduce yourself, man. How're ya doin'?" a grizzly bearded man yelled from across the barn.

"Is that you Jake under that beard?"

"Sure is me, you son-of-a-gun. It's been a long time hasn't it?"

"Yep, and you guys are still here every time I drop by," Boulder laughed.

Boulder looked around at the men and spotted Scott and the old man, Jim. He exchanged glances with a tall man who looked somewhat familiar. As he walked toward him, Jake introduced him as Pete Carter. Boulder extended his hand and felt a firm grip although he saw a grey-haired man with scores of wrinkles on his face and neck and dark rings under his eyes. "Howdy, nice day." Boulder turned and nodded his head to the right. "Who's that young guy over there, Jake?"

"That's Cody O'Shea. He's been here a few years. He keeps to himself and's not much of a talker. Takes care of the harnesses and pretty much does a little of everything. So how's it goin' for you Joe? Win any big bets at the tracks lately? You were always a big winner."

Boulder hadn't spoken with Jake in at least six months; his time was spoken for by clients in three states. It's good to hear Jake's deep, raspy voice and laughter again, he thought.

The two men walked through the barn and Boulder looked at a few Thoroughbreds in the nearby stalls. His eyes rested on the name Red Fox.

He walked toward the stall thinking, this must be Fox's new hope for a win in the next race. What a beauty.

Jake interrupted Boulder's thought. "We're hoping Red Fox beats Walsh's horse next time."

"Who's Walsh?"

Jake walked away from the stall and motioned for Boulder to follow him. "Jack Walsh is Fox's rival. Everyone who hangs out at the tracks knows the story."

"Sounds interesting. Tell me about it," said Boulder.

"Well, Walsh is a good-looking, big time gambler and yeah, liked by the ladies. One night in a high-stakes poker game, he wagered his ranch in Texas against the Shore Thing Racing Stables in Cream Ridge and a horse named Big Blue. They were both owned by Charlie Ayers who was a friend of Jonathan Fox. Well, when the cards were laid on the table, Walsh's ace high straight flush in spades beat Ayers' ace high straight flush in hearts. Ayers was inconsolable."

"Damn, what are the odds," Boulder said.

"Several days later, Ayers committed suicide. Fox blamed Walsh for his friend's death and that started a feud between the two."

"Does Walsh still own 'em?" asked Boulder as he walked beside Jake.

"Well... Walsh loved Big Blue. The horse had become a big money maker: he won several races and had the highest stud fees on the east coast. All the colts and fillies he sired paid off well. Walsh treated Big Blue like a family member. When the horse died suddenly from an infection, everyone understood his wanting to bury Big Blue and not sending him off to a glue factory."

Boulder took in this information, all the while pondering if there might be something else going on between Fox and Walsh. He tuned Jake out for a moment and thought, maybe this feud has gone in other directions. Wonder if Fox's wife might have liked him too. Maybe I should look at that angle.

Jake peered at Boulder and saw the blank look in his eyes. "Hey man, whatcha thinkin' 'bout?"

"Oh, got a lot on my mind. I'm doing some work for someone who knows Fox, a lady in fact."

"She anyone I know? I've been around here for a long time," Jake volunteered.

"Nah, your story about Big Blue got me to thinking."

Boulder pulled up the sleeve of his jacket and checked his Rolex. "Wow, it's almost time to call it quits for the day, isn't it Jake? Say man, it's been nice talking to you. I'll stop by again soon. If you remember any more stories let me know."

"Nice to see ya 'gain, Joe. Enjoyed our talk." Jake crossed the dusty lot beside the barn and went inside.

Boulder stood for a moment, looked over the horses in the nearest field and thought, oh yeah, I'll be back.

Boulder walked across the yards to his car parked on the side of the first barn. He stood by the rear fender, bent down and wiped off a layer of dirt that was smeared on the bumper sticker. It read, "PI's are the Good Guys." Now I have to visit Fox. There wasn't anything unusual that I could see in the stables-only the two new guys, he thought. He slid into his MINI Cooper, drove back through the main gate and over to the circle drive in front of the house. The lawn was beginning to thin out in spots, a certain sign of the fall season.

He walked up the steps two at a time, rang the doorbell and rapped once on the door. He heard footsteps sound on the hard floor and as he raised his hand to knock again, Fox opened the door.

"Hey, I'm Joe Boulder, PI."

"I thought you'd be stopping by one day. My niece told me she hired you. Come on in. Want a drink?"

Boulder noticed Fox had a crystal tumbler in his hand with about three fingers of dark liquid inside. "Sure. Give me what you've got."

"Bourbon it is." Fox led him down the hallway into a small, softly lit den. The walls were lined with mahogany bookcases filled with an array of books and knick-knacks. There was a red brick fireplace on the back wall and a white sheepskin rug on the hearth in front.

"Sit down, sit down, man. What's up?"

Boulder settled in a burgundy-colored overstuffed Benjamin chair and started to nurse his drink. "Mr. Fox, I need to talk to you about yourself and your wife. Susan hired me to help investigate her aunt's disappearance, so mind if I ask a few questions?"

"Shoot. I've probably answered all of them for the police months ago." Fox went over to an antique side-bar and refilled his glass.

"Well, I'd like to know who her friends are. You know, anyone she spends a great deal of time with?"

Fox laughed, "Little Foxy Lady, her prize horse."

"Besides her horse is there anyone special?" Boulder wiped the bottom of his glass with his hand and perched it on the arm of the chair.

"A . . . she has a friend, Annie Somers, in Maryland. They don't see each other a lot but they yak almost daily on the phone."

"Anyone else? Anyone she goes riding with or someone from the stables?"

Fox shook his head. "Nope, she's my right hand. Laura spends most of her time between the house and the stables. She's so beautiful and she has many admirers especially when she volunteers at the children's wing at Jersey Shore."

Boulder watched Fox's brow furrow and the shadow of sadness creep into his eyes.

"Well, what about money? Does Laura have a stash somewhere, like savings for a rainy day? Money she would use if she wanted to leave?"

"No, we share everything. She keeps the books so she has access to whatever she wants."

Boulder continued with another question looking directly at Fox. "Did you and your wife have a fight?"

Fox picked up his glass of bourbon and finished it before he answered, "Just the night before she disappeared. I'm sorry we never got to work it out. She told me that one of my hands might be stealing from me, and I yelled at her. That's it; I told the police the same thing. They've gotten nowhere; she's still missing."

Fox stood up, walked over to the fireplace, put his hands on the mantle and stared down at the rug. "Any more questions?"

"One more thing, what's your relationship with Jack Walsh? Known him long?"

"Yeah, he's got some stables over in Cream Ridge and likes to compete with my horses. Wants only the best and tries to get ahead of the game from all angles. We don't get along and never have."

Boulder raised his eyebrows. There was bitterness in Fox's voice and Boulder saw him clench his jaw. "Well Fox, do you mind if I check out Laura's computer and your phone records? I know the police checked the e-mails but sometimes they miss things."

"Follow me. It's upstairs in my office." He led Boulder up the front stairs and showed him Laura's password, which was logged in a mini-address book he took from his shirt pocket.

While Boulder sat at the desk scrolling through the emails in the delete files, he watched Fox. Fox stood staring out the side windows; his shoulders were hunched and his hands were tucked in his back pockets.

Ten minutes later, Boulder stood up and exercised his fingers. "Well Fox, I didn't find anything unusual in your wife's personal e-mails either. Thanks for allowing me to look at them. I imagine the police told you the same thing."

"Yes. Then they mentioned the fact that someone could have threatened her or wanted money from her. Several people know that she does the books for the stables. The police asked me if there was anyone who lost a race to one of my horses who might want revenge...."

"Was there anyone else?"

"Not to my knowledge."

"Well, I won't take up any more of your time. I've got to get going now. If you think of anyone I should talk to let me know, will you?"

"I'll do that but right now I'm wasted. I can't think straight about any of this."

The men shook hands and Boulder said, "Take it easy. We'll keep in touch."

CHAPTER 23

One picture is worth a thousand words.

Susan sat at her dining room table squinting her eyes as she tried to focus on one of the faded family photos taken years ago at the horse farm in Maryland. She held a magnifying glass on the image of a man standing at the corral gate. The man was quite handsome despite having a scar on his left cheek that extended to his cleft chin. His six foot frame sported a body builder's physique. Susan noticed an eagle tattoo on his left arm. A woman Susan recognized as her aunt, stood next to him holding his hand. Aunt Laura was a beauty in her own right, Susan thought. They made a stunning couple. They looked like they were in love.

Susan remembered that her mother had told her that Laura's husband was very controlling. He questioned her on her whereabouts, finances and her choice of clothing. He harped endlessly about which of her friends he didn't like. After several years, they divorced. Laura never trusted any man after her first husband. She never wanted to marry again, that is until she met Jonathan Fox.

Looking at the picture, Susan decided to call her mother. Maybe she can answer some of my questions, Susan thought. She grabbed her cell, found her mother's name in her contact list and pressed the call button.

After several rings, a voice said, "Hello, who's this?"

"Mother, it's me, Susan. I called to get some answers about Aunt Laura."

"What? No hello? Just questions?"

"I'm sorry, Mother. Hello. I'm anxious about Aunt Laura," Susan replied. "Did you find anything at all about her disappearance? Oh, and do you know her first husband's name?"

"His name was . . . um blank."

"Blank?" asked Susan.

"Oh no, my mind is blank."

"Try to remember his name and if you do, call me back." Susan's voice betrayed the irritation she was feeling.

"No, wait. I think it was . . . Fred, no Ed, maybe Ned." After a short pause, she said, "It was Ted . . . yes, Ted Watson."

"Are you sure Mother?"

"Of course I'm certain, because now I remember a scandal about him."

"What was that about?"

"Ted was a very bitter and vengeful person after the divorce. He began following Laura everywhere. Finally, she couldn't take any more and had the police serve him a restraining order. I knew all along he wasn't a good choice for her. Of course, she didn't appreciate my judgment."

"Mother, why didn't I know any of this about Aunt Laura?"

"Who wants to hang out dirty wash?"

"But it wasn't Aunt Laura's fault she was stalked."

"Yes it was. She made a bad decision in picking out the wrong man to marry."

Give Aunt Laura a break mother, Susan thought. Sometimes bad things happen to good people. She rolled her eyes in disbelief as she concluded her conversation with her mother. "Thanks for that information about Ted. I'll call you back if I find out anything more about Aunt Laura. Bye."

Susan's mind swirled with the name–Ted Watson. She also realized now that her mom probably thought it was Susan's own fault that she had gotten involved with and married Mark Jeffries, another control freak. Well, now I know that, too, she thought.

Susan had an hour before her appointment with Bud Thorne. I hope that he can give me additional information about my aunt, she thought. She called Chelsea to see if she had any concerns or problems at the store.

"Everything's like super, Mrs. J. I sold two of the cookbooks we just got in, and Mrs. Wright bought one of those cute stuffed owls with glasses for her granddaughter. I also stacked the newspapers we didn't sell from yesterday. Millie took over the register and I got a chance to read a few chapters in philosophy for my class too."

"Good. I'll talk to you later, Chels. I have an appointment now."

When Susan drove into the parking lot at Bud Thorne's office, she recognized Joe Boulder's yellow MINI Cooper. It's so strange that a big man like Joe would buy such a small car, she thought.

Boulder was just leaving the building and greeted her as she got out of her car. "Hello Susan. Are you here to see Thorne?"

"He asked me here. I didn't invite myself. And we both want all the information we can get on my aunt, right?" she said with a grin on her face.

"Don't expect too much. For a person who's supposed to gather news like an anteater gathers ants, he doesn't fit the stereotype. This is my second time here and I still haven't gotten any answers. Good luck."

"Keep in touch with me, Joe. Take care." Susan didn't want to hear such negative rambling and she inhaled deeply. She entered the building and smiled as she saw all the workers in their cubicles on computers. It reminded her of her days in a high school keyboarding class. She went up to the second floor and found Thorne's office.

"Come in Susan," he said, looking up from his

work. "May I get you coffee or something?"

"I'll take bottled water if you have that. Incidentally, I met Joe Boulder outside."

"Yeah, I just talked to him, but not as much as he wanted."

When Susan repeated to Thorne what her mother had told her about her aunt, he nodded his head in agreement.

"Susan, I knew about the stalking and the arrest of Laura's ex-husband but I used discretion in keeping that out of my story. Too many times the media is accused of drawing conclusions about a person's guilt or innocence before an indictment or a trial. I'm sure the detectives and police are privy to this information. Joe Boulder should already have all this information."

A man was trying to get Thorne's attention. Susan sighed and placed her hands on the arm of the chair as if she were about to stand up.

"You know, Mr. Thorne, you haven't shared any information with me about my aunt. This is a bit more frustrating than I thought it would be. Perhaps I should just let Boulder be my source."

"You can do what you want. I didn't know Boulder was showing up today too and he really interrupted my work. I never had a chance to get back to my notes on the computer. Why don't we just scrap today and set up a meeting for the first of the week?"

Susan looked at Thorne. I bet you won't have anything then either, she thought. "Okay. I'll come in the first of the week. I'd like your full attention because I've got to get some answers and soon."

Thorne stood up to offer his hand, but Susan had already turned away.

She left the building and retraced her steps to her car. Aunt Laura has been missing these past few months and her disappearance is still as much a mystery as day one, she thought. I've talked to Bud Thorne, Joe Boulder, Jonathan Fox and Mother and I still don't have any answers. Joe's the expert in finding missing people, but he seems to be coming up cold too. Should I try to find Aunt Laura's ex? I wonder if he could help. Yep, that's what I'll do and Joe can do the foot work to find him. Surely Ted might be easier to find than Aunt Laura.

Susan got in her car and immediately called Boulder. It might be a long shot, but I'm getting desperate for any help I can get, she thought.

"Susan, what's up?"

"Joe. I'm glad I got hold of you. Your line is always busy."

"Not only is my line busy, but I'm also busy," he said, laughing at his own joke.

Susan grimaced after hearing his corny joke and didn't laugh. "Seriously Joe, I have someone for you to look into. His name is Ted Watson."

"Yeah, Laura's ex. How'd you figure he might

help? Don't forget, she had a bad experience with that marriage years ago."

"That's my point. He might have been harassing her on the internet."

"This might cost you a little more. After all, you want me to find two missing people now," he joked.

"Oh come on Joe. This is part of the same case; stop being so facetious."

"Okay Susan, I'll try to find Ted Watson and see what he's been doing. I'll call you soon." Ted Watson, he thought when the call ended. I don't know much about him except the little bit Susan had to say when she showed me the picture of her aunt standing alongside him at the horse farm. Guess their marriage didn't last long.

Boulder headed to his office. "Might have to look into this. Marriages go sour and this guy could be long gone," he mumbled.

When he arrived in his office, he discovered that his earlier attempts to get information on a job candidate's credit background hadn't produced any good news. I'm sure my friend at the local community bank won't think much of him let alone hire him, he thought. I'll write up my report tonight and tackle the search for Ted Watson later.

CHAPTER 24

Sometimes a strong scent can tell a good tale.

On Saturday, Susan clicked the garage door remote and parked her car in the garage. Inside parking was a definite must-have at the shore; otherwise her new car would take a beating from the sand and salt in the air.

She went into the front foyer and was hit with the pungent odors of rotten onion, sewage and wet newspapers. Has the sewer backed up or is there a dead animal somewhere in my house? she wondered. Susan walked carefully throughout the house looking for the cause of the odor. Nothing in the living room, she thought. Nothing in the dining room either. Susan looked under the table and went to the half-bath in the hall. Fine here too, she mused.

As she walked to the back of the house however, she detected a stronger odor. The kitchen was clean, although she hadn't remembered to put her morning coffee cup away. Tiptoeing into the tiled Florida room just off the kitchen, she almost gagged. An offensive odor seemed to be rising from a huge pile of rags and clothes lying on the floor. Susan held her breath. By now, she was more shocked than repulsed and spoke aloud. "Is it a person or an animal and is it dead? It certainly smells that way. How on earth did 'it' get here in my house anyway?"

Susan went back to the kitchen, got a broom and a 16-inch cast iron frying pan and poked at the pile on the tile floor. She heard a loud grunt and felt something grabbing the broom handle. Susan let out a piercing scream and dropped the pan and the broom.

"What the hell?" grumbled a deep voice from the dirty pile of rags. Then Susan saw deep chocolate eyes and a smiling Cheshire mouth.

"Oh, hi, Babe!"

"Tony! You scared the you-know-what out of me. You really stink."

"Good to see you too," he laughed. "How about a kiss?"

"I don't want to get any closer until you've soaked in bleach or a close cousin to it," Susan shot back. "What are you doing here and why didn't you call?"

Tony looked at the pan next to him. "A frying pan? Really? That's what you use for an intruder? Where's the gun I gave you?"

Susan frowned. "It's in the safe. I'm just not comfortable with a gun," she confessed. "And since I don't use the pan for anything else, it seemed like a good choice."

Tony shook his head and mumbled, "What am I going to do with you? Sorry about scaring you. I'm still undercover nearby, so I thought I'd stop by. I miss seeing you. I had to sneak in so no one would see me."

Susan backed away. "Good thing my house isn't really close to the neighbors; otherwise they wouldn't have had to see you, they would've smelled you. I thought you were in the city. Throw your clothes away, take a shower and then we can talk. I don't know how you can stand yourself."

"You get used to it. It sort of grows on you." Tony stood up and his jacket dropped to the floor. He gave Susan a playful grin. "I can't throw them away; it would blow my cover, but I could shower and put on a pair of your sweats while I'm here. I would've done it sooner, but I didn't want to go snooping around in this get-up to find things. Then, since you were late in coming home, and since I haven't had a decent sleep for nearly two months, I laid down in here so I wouldn't dirty anything. That was the last thing I remember."

"How did you get in here?" Susan questioned innocently but then realized how adept Tony was at picking locks. Tony had been the lead detective on her husband, Mark's murder case and she knew he had many talents.

Susan went back to the garage and returned with a 30-gallon plastic bag. "Here, put your clothes . . . in here," she said as she turned her face. "You know," she said with a smirk. "Some homeless people do go to the Laundromat."

"Okay, okay. I'll put them in one of those machines later, before I leave." Tony headed for the bathroom, turned on the shower and stood with the hot water pouring over his body. He scrubbed with Susan's favorite Dove soap bar, relishing its scent even though he preferred Irish Spring. The scent of any soap after months of dirt is good, he thought.

Susan found a pair of stretched out sweats that would fit him. "Guess he'll have to go commando," she giggled to herself. Susan opened the bathroom door and, amongst the fog-like steam, she saw Tony standing by the sink with a towel wrapped around his waist. He wiped the mirror and looked at the reflection staring back at him. "I look like a cross between a hermit and a lumberjack."

Tony Russo was usually clean-shaven and sported a manicured razor-cut hair style. Now he had a full-grown, six-inch, black, scraggly beard and looked like a hippie from the 1960's.

As Tony eyed the changes this assignment made on his head, Susan eyed the changes it made on his body. He was always fit, but now he had a leaner, more muscular build. He had rippled abs that even one of those guys on infomercials might envy.

"See anything you like?" Tony asked as he noticed Susan's stare.

"Maybe," she flipped back.

Tony looped his towel around Susan, quickly pulled her to him and surrounded her with his arms. He hungrily kissed her welcoming lips, picked her up and carried her into the bedroom. He gently laid her on the bed, his eyes never leaving her face. Carefully, almost methodically, he undressed her, bringing her closer to him with every move. He hadn't realized how much he had missed her but now he wanted her to know just how much that was.

It had been almost four months since Susan had last seen Tony. She was glad that he had gone on assignment because she needed to sort out her feelings without his influence. Their dating after Mark's death had started suddenly and had become intense. Susan wanted to be sure that their attraction was genuine and not because she had been vulnerable.

Now, as she lay in his arms, wrapped in his embrace, there was no doubt, she needed to be as close to Tony as possible.

Susan awoke to the smell of freshly brewed coffee. Tony stood by her bed lightly wafting the steam from the cup toward Susan. She opened one eye and Tony laughed.

"Thought you were dead. It's morning, Sunshine. Time to get up. Or would you rather I join you?" Tony asked with a playful glint in his eye.

"Hmm, what a dilemma," Susan teased back. She reached for the coffee he handed her, "What time is it?" She looked at him thinking how much he looked like Paul Bunyan with his wooly hair and bushy beard.

Tony sat on the edge of the bed admiring Susan. Even waking from a deep sleep, she looks beautiful, he thought. "It's seven o'clock. I've already showered, been to the Laundromat and even picked up breakfast. C'mon sleepy head rise and shine."

"Why are you up so early? That was the best sleep I've had in months." Susan smothered another yawn.

"I wanted to get things done so I can hang with you for the rest of the day. Besides, I don't want anyone to see me out and about, and since it's Sunday I figured you'd be free. I know the bookstore's closed. Do you have other plans?"

"No, not really. Tell you what, let me go shower and dress. I'll meet you downstairs and tell you what I've been up to."

"Sounds intriguing. Need any help in the shower?" Tony's eyes twinkled with mischief.

"I think I can handle it," Susan quipped over her shoulder as she grabbed the cup and headed for the bathroom. "By the way, who do you think would recognize you looking like Paul Bunyan?" she teased back. As she washed her hair she wondered, why on earth did I think that time away from each other would be a good thing? She grinned to herself and realized how much fun she had when she was with him.

Susan went downstairs wearing denim jeans, a tight, light blue, long-sleeved tee shirt and her hair tied back. She wore no make-up; she knew that was the way Tony liked her best. He called her a natural beauty, unlike the way her husband used to speak to her.

Tony was wearing jeans and a sporty, light-weight black hoodie-his choice of relaxing clothes. He looked up from the table and smiled at Susan.

"I picked up some clothes to leave here too, if that's okay. I put them in the spare closet next to the den. I'll be able to find them when I come back. Here dear, sit down and have a bagel. Tell me what you've been up to and, when you're finished, I'll tell you about the undercover job I'm on. . . well, at least as much as I can."

Susan and Tony sat at the table and Susan told him all she knew about her Aunt Laura and her disappearance. She filled him in on Chelsea and the bookstore, describing the new renovations and her ideas for changing the décor. "I've hardly had much time to do any of it though. Chelsea has worked harder than I ever could have imagined. I rely her completely."

"So, you had lots of spare time. Maybe

spending time with someone else?"

"Stop it, Tony. Nothing like that. My time is consumed with the disappearance of my Aunt Laura." Susan told Tony about the telephone call from her mother and about hiring Joe Boulder.

"You're investigating on your own again aren't you?"

Although Susan knew Tony spoke teasingly, she became a little upset with his question but decided to let it go. She knew how important Tony's assignment was to him; she didn't want to burden him with too many details.

"I'm involved with my family. It seems that all the dirty laundry is out of the hamper and hanging on the line. I've become acquainted with a family member I had never even met before. Tony, the only bit of investigation I'm guilty of is meeting with Jonathan Fox at the Monmouth Park Racetrack.

"Be careful. Don't jump to conclusions, Susan. Keep your eyes and ears in constant alert mode. Sometimes if you're lucky, things will fall into place for you. If not, then you'll need to work harder to find leads. At this point, as in any investigation, you must be patient."

After lunch, Tony told Susan about the undercover operation that started as a sting for narcotics, but turned to investigating the harvesting of body parts from homeless people. Luckily for him, this work led to the central New Jersey area.

Rain started to tap against the kitchen windows with a steady rhythm, and the two sat and sipped coffee while they talked, turning the afternoon into a lazy day.

"You know how much my career means to me," Tony continued. "I can't afford to mess up in any way."

"Tony, what's your part in this?"

"Susan, the homeless are targeted to sell their organs for cost; this is called organ harvesting. I'm checking it out."

Susan stood up and walked over to the other side of the table. She placed her arms around Tony's shoulders. "I've missed you so much and I worry about you."

"Don't worry. You already saw me at my worst: grubby, smelly and exhausted. I'll be going back to work this evening disguised as a homeless person." Tony stood up, took her into his arms and looked into her eyes. "I'm a big boy and can handle it. Believe me."

The remainder of the afternoon and into the evening both relaxed. They lightened up their conversation and enjoyed the warmth of their closeness.

As soon as darkness settled in, Tony stood up, gathered Susan in his arms and gently kissed her. "I've got to go," he murmured in her ear.

"Oh Tony, I know you do. I'll leave a key for

you so you can clean up and rest properly the next time you come," Susan said with a grin.

Tony kissed her again and went out the back door.

"Be careful Tony," she whispered softly. "I worry about you."

CHAPTER 25

May the Lord give them a limp so you can see them coming.

After Tony left Susan, he walked with a disguised limp for three blocks, turned right and climbed into a battered Chevy pick-up. Once inside the cab, he shifted uncomfortably on the worn passenger seat with many of the springs exposed. The two men were silent as the driver started the motor. The only good thing about this dilapidated wreck is the motor, he thought.

About fifteen minutes later, the driver stopped at the Lakewood Bus Terminal, dropped off his passenger and left promptly. Tony went inside, checked his locker and took out his cell phone, which was lying alongside his laptop. He exited through a side door and walked toward the railroad tracks.

As Tony approached his assigned location there were few people milling about. He scrutinized the surrounding area putting his photographic memory to use.

Two days later, Tony returned to the bus station, took his laptop and remaining belongings from the storage locker and hopped into a blue truck.

"Movin' up are you?" Tony said to the driver.

"No worn-out springs here that I can see. I haven't sat on anything this comfortable in a long time." They both laughed.

The duo arrived at Police Headquarters in Brick and, once inside, the Captain spoke to Tony in detail. "Russo, there's been a change of plans arranged for you. Take a couple of days off after you file your reports today."

Three hours later, Tony emerged from the station. "Glad that's over. Think I'll give Susan a buzz."

CHAPTER 26

Whatever you say, whatever you don't say; whatever you do, whatever you don't do. Believe me, you pay!

"Susan, I'm missing you lots."

"I've been missing you too, Tony."

"If you've got the evening free, can I bring you over some Chinese food?"

"You must have read my mind Tony. I'll put up a pot of tea and throw together a pineapple upside-down cake for dessert."

Later, as they tidied up the kitchen together, kissing the crumbs off each other's lips in between chores, Tony mentioned that the guys at the station were dying to meet her; his friend, Ron, in particular, had been most persistent.

"Ron, Ron," Susan murmured. "Why does that name ring a bell? Oh!" she suddenly recalled, "Isn't he the guy who you told me beats up on his wife?"

"Well, yeah. But, other than that, he's an okay guy."

"Other than that. . ." Susan repeated numbly. "Tony!" she responded.

"Hold that thought. . ." Tony answered over his shoulder as he went to answer the doorbell. "Oh, by the way, I forgot to mention that I ran into Ron and his wife at the Chinese place earlier and suggested they drop by for a drink after the show they were heading for. Hope you don't mind."

Susan rolled her eyes and prepared for her, as far as she was concerned, uninvited guests.

After the introductions, Ron and his wife seemed friendly enough. Ron, in particular, could even be classified as charismatic. Maybe Tony was mistaken in his evaluation of Ron, she thought.

The subject of sports came up in conversation, and both Ron and Tony started discussing an upcoming football game to be played nearby the following week. The guys agreed that attending the game with the wives and girlfriends would be a fun outing.

"I hate to sound like a wet blanket, guys, but I don't think so," Susan chimed in. "I'm not really into football."

"Oh, come on," they pleaded. "You'll love the fresh air, the crowd, the whole atmosphere. We'll happily explain what's happening on the field, if that's your concern." Reluctantly, she agreed to the group outing.

✽✽✽

On the day of the game, the weather was crisp and sunny. Spirits were high and thoughts of murder and intrigue were shelved for a few precious hours.

The game began and the crowd cheered and booed as the players tossed the ball and it was caught or fumbled by another player. In short order, the scoreboard reflected the current score in large neon lettering.

As Susan sat in the bleachers, she thought, I care nothing about the outcome of the game or the various maneuvers leading up to the outcome. But I do admit enjoying breathing in the fresh air and relish taking a well-needed break from the last stressful weeks. And, of course, my heart flips seeing Tony obviously enjoying himself.

After the game, someone suggested unwinding at a local restaurant. The men sat Monday-morning-quarterbacking the game for a while, and then, during a temporary lull in the conversation, one of the women mentioned a recent episode of *Desperate Housewives*. I really like watching that show with a glass of wine. It's my one indulgence, Susan thought. Finally I can contribute a thing or two to the conversation.

Then Ron piped up with, "Only stupid people watch soap operas."

The utter rudeness and unsociability of his statement stunned everyone into complete silence, except for his wife's one-word comment, "Ron-ald!"

Susan cleared her throat and calmly said, "Well now, Ron, let's examine that statement a bit, shall we? I think it's fair to say that soap operas involve a little bit of give-and-take, a social interaction among civilized human beings; a process you, Ron, obviously know very little about." Snickers and squelched laughter were heard around the table. "On the other hand," Susan continued, "Let's see what happens at a football game: a bunch of guys kick a ball back and forth across a field and everyone jumps up and down in sheer joy or else punches the air in pure disgust. Now, is this the mark of intelligence, or what?" The snickers escalated into belly laughs and spontaneous applause.

"Hey Ron," Tony exclaimed as he gave Susan a big hug, "You're dealing with my gal now!"

"Typical female drivel," mumbled Ron.

"What was that?" Susan piped up as she cocked her ear in Ron's direction. Susan had come across lots of 'Ronalds' in her life. All the stories she had heard about Ron, as well as memories of her deceased husband, Mark, came flooding back to her conscious mind: all the intimidations, all the put downs and that machismo, holier-than-thou, know-it-all attitude.

But Susan wasn't the obedient schoolgirl any more. She wasn't the dutiful housewife. She certainly wasn't a defenseless female. She was a mature, confident business woman who had already gone through a lot in life, including running a successful bookstore, helping to solve her husband's murder and being involved in the investigation of her aunt's disappearance. I'm not about to be put in my place by anyone, she thought; certainly, not by the likes of a wife beater.

"You know Ron," she spaced her words carefully, "if there's such a thing as fairness in this life, and reincarnation in the next, there's no doubt in my mind but that you are going to come back as a female." She paused and then added slowly and emphatically, "And I hope I'm around to see it, 'cause I'm going to laugh my butt off."

"Way to go Susan." Tony exclaimed with a huge grin as he gave her a high five.

"Oh, do you believe in reincarnation?" Ron managed to ask changing the subject.

Susan calmly locked eyes with him. Then, as she popped an olive in her mouth, said, "Enjoy the rest of your meal. Ron, I know I will."

CHAPTER 27

Winston tastes good like a cigarette should.

Boulder inhaled the smoke from his Winston cigarette as he sat in front of his computer. He smoked what he called "frustration sticks" only when he felt a sense of discouragement.

His office was located at the end of a row of retailers on Main Street in Manasquan. He'd been there since 1992 in his single practice in the same small, cramped space. This suited him fine: a desk, a computer, a phone and a coffee pot. When his work was done for the day, he'd drive over to Spring Lake, where he lived in Boulder Mansion left to him by his grandfather.

Now as he sat alone in his office, he drummed on the computer keyboard not bothering to turn it on. I'm not getting anywhere with this Laura Fox business, he thought.

Boulder had the usual information: Laura's name, age, date of birth and her social security number, but that was what a rooky private investigator would have in the beginning of an investigation. He picked up a black leather pocket notebook and flipped it open. He had written nothing at his meeting with Bud Thorne and hadn't put in any notes from the visit to Fox and Hound Stables. He closed it and shoved it into the middle drawer of his desk.

Boulder pushed back from the desk and swung his feet across the top. "My trip to the Fox and Hound Stables was interesting though," he muttered aloud. "It was great seeing those guys again especially Jake. Gosh, his beard is something else."

Boulder thought about Jake's story on Jack Walsh and the ongoing feud between him and Fox. Jake had told him about remarks Walsh made after one of their poker nights: "Ya know Joe, that Walsh guy constantly criticized Mr. Fox. He didn't like any of Fox's choices of Thoroughbreds. He especially didn't like how his trainers got them race-ready. Fox just kinda let his remarks slide most of the time. He really resented them. Fox told me that Walsh would get his due one day. Walsh wanted his own horse, Have Faith, to be the best. He ran his horse against Fox's horses in the big three and was determined to win by any means he could."

Boulder thought about that conversation and the reference to stables owned by Walsh and then turned on his computer. He waited for the screen to come alive. He **Googled**: Shore Thing Racing Stable. When the web page appeared, he saw that the stables were owned by Jack and Marie Walsh. He clicked **About Us** at the top and read further that, in addition to owning the 40-acre farm in Upper

Freehold, their primary interest now centered on the Thoroughbred breeding industry. They currently had four stallions and kept fourteen mares year round. They bred, raised and sold Thoroughbred horses to stables in Ohio and Maryland. "Interesting," Joe muttered. He continued his search and clicked on **Racing News**. On April 9, 2011, one of Walsh's horses, Do It Again, won at the River Downs Racing Park in Ohio. He brought in $1 million dollars in a grade one race. One of his horses, Meet Me, which he later sold to John and June Lamont, won in Laurel Park, Maryland, stamping the ticket for entry in the Kentucky Derby in 2012.

    Boulder let his thoughts wander for a moment as he took a drink from his now-warm Poland Spring water. He tried to digest the facts he found regarding Walsh. Looks to me like he built himself quite a business, he thought. Boulder shut down his computer and glanced at his Rolex; it was 9 p.m. "Where to next?" he mumbled. He grabbed the notebook out of the desk drawer and shoved it in his jacket pocket. "Family next," he said. He had found information earlier on Laura in the database, which he subscribed to on the internet. It gave him basic information and listed her sister, Virginia McGovern, in Florida. I'll fly down tomorrow and pay her a little visit, he thought.

    A few minutes later, Boulder drove toward his home in Spring Lake. He thought about the other stablehands at the Fox stables. Jake had mentioned that he and two others lived year-round on the stable grounds. I wonder how well they get along with Fox. Hmm, I wonder if Laura got along with them, he thought, as he drove onto his driveway.

CHAPTER 28

Some questions tempt you to tell lies.

It was unusually warm at 9 p.m. Boulder stopped to pick up his mail at the end of the drive and then opened the front door of his home. He really appreciated the central air in Boulder Mansion as the cool air greeted him. He threw his keys and the mail onto the entry table, grabbed a beer in the kitchen and looked out the window.

Boulder fingered his greying hair absently and thought about which angle to work on first. I can't get my head around these relationships in Susan's family. Laura Fox is her aunt, but they haven't been in touch for years. Maybe my best bet is to start with Susan's mom. If I can get her answers to some of my questions maybe I can get more leads into Laura's disappearance.

He grabbed his cell and punched in the number for his travel agent. "Hey Amelia, I need to get down to Tampa ASAP. Can you get me a flight from Atlantic City tomorrow morning?"

"Sure Mr. Boulder, that shouldn't be a problem. I'll get back to you." Amelia had scheduled Boulder's flights for the past twenty years.

Boulder clicked his cell shut, fixed himself a sandwich and grabbed another beer. He sat down in the den to figure out his strategy. Boulder's online sources indicated that Virginia McGovern lived in Indian Rocks Beach, Florida-a small town on the gulf coast between St. Petersburg and Clearwater. He searched yellowpages.com, where he found Virginia's street address and her phone number. "Great," he whooped. "That's one hurdle past me." He picked up his cell and called the number listed for Virginia McGovern.

"Yes?" a pleasant, low-pitched female voice answered.

"Virginia McGovern?" he asked.

"That's me. Who's this?"

"I'm Joe Boulder, a private investigator. Your daughter hired me to help her find your sister." Boulder rubbed the back of his neck. "I'm going to be in your neck of the woods tomorrow and I wonder if you'd have time to talk with me."

"I suppose so," she replied hesitantly, "But I don't know what help I'll be."

"I don't either but let's see if we can fill in some blanks in my investigation together."

"Okay, I guess that will be all right. I'm working until five but I could meet you after that. There's a great seafood place called Crabby Bill's near the Holiday Inn."

"That sounds great! I'm a seafood lover. I'll find the place. See you at 5:30?"

"Okay Mr. Boulder, I'll be there."

Boulder shut his cell and went to the kitchen to get another beer.

Amelia called with his flight information: Spirit Airlines, leaving Atlantic City the next morning at 10:35 and arriving at Tampa at 12:56 p.m. Boulder packed a bag, called the Borgata Casino and booked a room for the night. If I'm going to be in AC, I might as well have a little fun before I have to meet Mrs. McGovern, he thought.

***

The trip to AC had been profitable-$400 profitable! As Boulder got on the plane, he smiled at the flight attendant and then settled down to catch up on the sleep he had lost over the past few days.

The flight was smooth and arrived on time in Tampa. Boulder rented a car and drove to Indian Rock Beach. It was too early to meet with Virginia, so he found his way to the Holiday Inn and parked the car in the large lot. Boulder checked in at the front desk, then went to the bar and ordered a Sam Adams. He had a little time to wait before he was scheduled to meet Susan's mother.

At 5:15 p.m., he got back in his rental car. The concierge at the hotel had given him directions, and he pulled into the parking lot at Crabby Bill's. There was a huge red crab on the roof, and a fresh fish store on the left side. It was a very casual-looking place, with picnic benches inside and out, and a large outside bar. Boulder walked through the front door.

Virginia had told him to ask any of the wait staff for her when he arrived. She was one of their regulars. Boulder asked the petite, curly-haired young woman who greeted him, "Say, is Mrs. McGovern here?" She pointed to a booth in the corner and smiled.

"Thanks hon," he said giving her a wink.

Boulder saw a thin woman in her 50's, with greying blonde hair pulled back with a scrunchy, drinking from a tall mug of beer. She put the drink down and looked up at him. "Hi," he said, "that young lady told me you're Virginia McGovern."

"That's right."

"May I have a seat?" Boulder slid into the low red leather seat and looked around for the waitress.

"The beer here is good." Virginia said. "A local brewery supplies it."

"Interesting. You come here often?"

Virginia looked up as the waitress approached the table and didn't respond to the question.

Once the waitress had taken his order for a YBOR GOLD, Boulder leaned forward and looked at Susan's mother. "What can you tell me about Laura? Her husband is worried about her disappearance, and the police haven't come up with any leads. I've been trying to look into areas the police might not have explored. But first I need to know a lot more about her. I imagine you're concerned too."

"Well, you probably already know that she's my sister and that we've been on the outs," Virginia began.

"I know a little. Susan sort of filled me in. From what I've been told Laura didn't like hearing negative things about her husband."

"Right, that was her first husband. The marriage went sour, as I knew it would, and that made things even worse. Laura hated being wrong about anything. Then she met this one, this Jonathan Fox. I don't know anything about him, but she probably made the same mistake."

The waitress came back to the table. "You need another beer?"

"Yeah, thanks. And I'd like to try some of those Gater Tots, too," Boulder said.

"Oh, they're real good. Lots of folks like them. Anything for you honey?" the waitress asked Virginia and at the same time gave Boulder a grin.

"Not right now thanks." Virginia took a long swallow of her Coors Light.

Boulder moved the floral display aside and leaned over the table. "I'll tell you what I know. There's been no evidence of foul play," he began. "None of Laura's clothing is missing according to the police report. One of the stablehands told them the couple had always worked well together. She kept the books, and apparently Fox depended on her a lot."

"Well, how do you think I can help?" Virginia asked, her voice a little louder than necessary. "I haven't heard anything. I'm down here. How would I know anything?" She used her napkin to wipe at the ring of condensation on the table.

"I'm not sure. Tell me why you haven't kept in touch since Laura's marriage to Jonathan. Do you know him? Have you ever been to New Jersey to visit them? You've got to tell me if you know anything at all; it might give us a lead. Your daughter is now involved in trying to find your sister. If Laura's dead, I need to find out. If it's murder, others might be in danger. I've been in this business a long time and I smell a rat!"

"Boy you're sure asking a lot of questions," Virginia said as she shredded her napkin into tiny pieces.

"If you have any information, you need to tell me. It can stay between us. You have my word that I'll keep it secret. But if it might help in this investigation, you know I'll have to tell the authorities."

The waitress placed the sizzling nuggets of alligator meat in front of Boulder and plunked down his second beer. She looked at Virginia with raised eyebrows, "Do you want a refill?" Boulder saw Virginia give her a slight nod.

When the waitress left the table, Boulder looked at Virginia. "So what gives? What can you tell me about Laura?"

Virginia took another swig of her beer and answered him with a question. "Laura? What do I really know about my sister?"

This isn't Virginia's second beer, Boulder thought. There's no telling how many she had. I'll just start with simpler questions and see how that goes. He took two alligator nuggets on his fork and popped them into his mouth.

"How long has it been since you talked to or saw Laura?" he asked with his mouth filled with food.

"How long?" Virginia repeated. She gazed out toward the bar.

"Yeah, how long?"

"Can't remember."

"Is there anything you can tell me about your sister's disappearance?"

"No, not really."

"What is it you want to tell me?" Boulder pleaded.

"No, I don't think I want to tell you anything. I don't even know you." Virginia's speech had slowed down considerably.

"Why did you agree to meet with me if you weren't going to tell me anything?" Boulder put his fork down on his plate and leaned closer. "I feel like I'm wasting my time with you."

"Why are you asking me anyway? You should be talking to Annie. Annie Mc-er, Somers." Virginia began to slur her words. "She was the one who Laura thought of as a sister anyway. She knows everything 'bout Laura you wanna know."

"Where does Annie Somers live?"

"Why did she call me anyway. I never liked her. She was trouble when she went to see Laura. Why would I know anything about Laura?" Virginia hiccoughed and covered her mouth with Boulder's napkin. "Now I've gotten Susan into this."

"What about Susan?" Boulder hoped that Virginia would keep talking but he couldn't make much sense of what she was saying.

Virginia looked at him blankly and signaled the waitress to bring her a menu and another Coors.

Oh well, Boulder thought. Boy, she really didn't answer my questions but this wasn't a complete waste of time. For sure there are hard feelings in the family between Virginia and Laura. I guess I'll call Annie Somers and see what I can find out from her.

Boulder signaled the waitress for the check. When she returned, she had another beer for Virginia, put it on the table and took the empty glass. "Are you from around here? I haven't seen you in here before," she asked.

Virginia scowled and spoke sharply, "No he's not. If you want some peace, leave him alone. He's just snoopin'."

Boulder stood up. Nothing more for me here, he thought. He reached out and patted her hand. "Take care, Mrs. McGovern. Get home safe. I've got a plane to catch." He smiled at the waitress and gave her a wink. "See you around."

CHAPTER 29

The tool you need is always missing.

Gig Giovanni and several construction crew members picked up the last of their finishing tools at the Sandcastle Bookstore and placed them in their van. The building inspector from the Manasquan Borough shook Gig's hand and put his copy of the final inspection in his portfolio.
"I'll give Susan her copy," Gig said. "Thanks a lot." The inspector went outside and Gig walked over to the counter in Susan's bookstore.
"Well, work's done." He gave Susan the paperwork and shook her hand warmly.
"Thank you Gig," Susan smiled. "I'm so glad I finally have my tearoom. You've done a great job; now Chelsea and I can get started moving in. I'd like to be able to contact you if I have any questions in the next few days. I think I'll be okay though."
"No problem ma'am, my crew is moving up to Asbury Park. There's some big renovations going on in a couple of old hotels there. We've got a lot of work to do, thank God. You can call my cell number; I'll be there with them."
"Well, good luck Gig. This is a good day."
Giovanni left and Susan motioned for Chelsea to follow her into the new addition.

"Chels, now we can move in. I'll contact U-Store-It and set a date for them to deliver the tables and other furniture we've stored. I'm glad Gig suggested that we have The Tile House put in terrazzo flooring. It almost looks like we have an outdoor patio. Now it needs a woman's touch."

"Like, it's great Susan. Who gets to serve the first cup of tea?"

"We'll see. Let's go in the back to get out the tea pot and our cups. This is so exciting!"

Both women walked past Nicky's cage on their way to the back of the store.

"Break time, break time, darlings," the bird squawked.

While Susan and Chelsea were celebrating over a cup of tea, the mailman entered through the front door and placed a stack of mail next to the register.

"Hello Susan, mail's here. Do you have anything outgoing?" he called loudly.

"There's a couple of bills on the counter for you to take. They already have stamps on them."

"Okay, thanks. See you tomorrow." As the mailman walked out the door, Nicky called, "Bye man, see you later."

Susan and Chelsea sat for fifteen minutes and, after finishing her tea, Chelsea grabbed her backpack off the extra chair.

"Gotta go to class. I have a late lab today. Do you mind closing up by yourself Mrs. J?"

Susan laughed, "Do you think I'm out of practice? Go ahead. I'll manage to count the money today. See you tomorrow."

After Chelsea went out the door, Susan grabbed the money bag from under the counter and totaled out the register. She spotted the stack of letters the mailman had left and was curious about a large manila envelope under the stack. She glanced for a return address, but there was none. This is strange, Susan thought. She carried the envelope to the back of the store and sat down at the table to open it. Inside there was a single, full-size white paper. "There's no letterhead," she mumbled. Susan turned the paper over, then back again. "There's no signature either." Susan read . . . **We know you're looking for your family member. She did not leave. Check out Big Blue. Be careful.**

"This has to mean Aunt Laura. Did somebody do something to her?"

Susan sat for a few seconds then stood up. Her knees were wobbly and she had difficulty walking back out to the counter. "I've got to call someone about the letter. The police? Boulder? Tony?" Susan spoke in a whisper that even Nicky couldn't hear.

It was five o'clock, and Susan was too confused to leave the store. She went to the front and turned the sign over to CLOSED. As she looked out the large center window, she saw a woman standing outside. The woman was rocking side to side and stretching her neck as if to peer inside the bookstore. Hmm, she doesn't look familiar. I wonder if she's been here before. I hope she goes away, thought Susan. She backed away and put the cover over Nicky's cage.

"I wanna grape," he snickered.

"Quiet now. You've had your share of grapes today; now it's time for sleep."

Susan went back to the register. "Maybe I should call Tony about this note," she told herself as she reached over and nudged it off the money bag where she had laid it. Maybe I should call Joe Boulder first though. This is the first clue we might have in Aunt Laura's case.

Susan shook her head trying to clear the muddle in her mind. When she looked up, she noticed a movement outside the store by the door. It's that woman again, she thought.

The woman saw Susan and started pounding on the front door and yelling. The noise and commotion caused Nicky to screech, "Who's that" and flap excitedly in his cage.

"Oh Nicky, do be quiet," Susan said. "I just can't ignore this anymore. Hold your horses!

Where's the fire? I'm coming!" she yelled as she walked toward the door and unlocked it. She could see the woman more clearly now. And what a sight she was. A tall light-skinned woman with disheveled hair that was colored yellow, green, pink and blue looked at her out of hazel eyes heavily lined with black eyeliner. She wore a multicolored cape that looked homemade. A huge pink and white polka-dotted tote bag hung on her shoulder.

"Oh Lady, thank you so much," she gasped. "I need your help. My cell phone's flat and I've got a dead tire. . . . Oh, I mean my cell phone's dead and I've got a flat tire. I need to call AAA and get some help. Could I use your phone please?"

"Okay, I guess so. But please don't take too long. I have to be somewhere. The phone's over there." Susan pointed to the phone near the cash register and. sighed, I'm always a pushover for someone with a problem. But I'm a little nervous about letting this strange-looking person into my shop. She looked out the door to be sure there were no other people lurking about and left the door open so she could run to Sal's if she sensed any danger.

"Thanks again. I'll just be a jiff. By the way, my name's Wanda. What's yours?"

"Susan."

"Okay Susan, I'll just make that call now."

Wanda walked over to the phone and picked up the handset. After connecting with AAA and giving her location, she hung up the phone. She walked around toward Susan, but stopped suddenly. Susan had left Bud Thorne's newspaper article on the counter and Wanda stared at it.

"Susan, why do you have this article here?" she asked.

"Well, it's about my aunt who disappeared a while ago. I'm trying to find out what happened to her."

"She's dead," Wanda said in a flat voice.

"No, no," Susan replied, horrified. "The police don't know where she is. There's not been any evidence that she died. The police don't think there was foul play."

"Oh there was foul play all right. Very, very foul. She's dead and she's not alone."

"Wait a minute. You barge in here, use my phone and tell me my aunt is dead. I think you better leave right now or I'll call the police. Get going."

"Listen Susan, I can help you!"

"Why should I believe you? I don't even know you."

"I have psychic powers. The Freehold police department calls me in when they're stumped on a case. Sometimes I can help. I'm not always 100% right but I can see enough to really help move a stalled investigation toward a solution. And today I have a really strong sense that your aunt is deceased and that somehow she's not alone. I'm not getting any more than that, except that I'm seeing a blue aura around this picture of your aunt in the article. That might be something, or maybe it's just the lighting in here. I can see that you're upset and skeptical. I'll leave you my card. If you think I can help, call me. Thanks again for the use of your phone. Wouldn't you think I'd be able to sense that I needed to charge my cell!" she mumbled in exasperation.

Wanda handed Susan her card and left. Susan locked the door again and looked at the card. **Wanda Lubowski, Psychic Medium.** The card included a phone number, website and email address.

It was getting darker. Susan went back to the small kitchen area in the back of the bookstore. Rain started pelting the roof. The entire building needed a new set of shingles and Susan often thought about what a disaster it would be if there was a water leak. But . . . this was not what she had time to worry about now.

Susan picked up her cell and scrolled in her contacts in search of Joe Boulder's number. I have to do something. I can't call Tony, she thought. He has enough to do and, even though he has his cell in his pocket, it's not fair to get him involved in this. . . Susan pushed call and waited. After five rings, she heard the voice message instructing her to enter her name and number and give a brief message. "Just when I need to talk to you, you're not available," she said into the phone-before the beep. Once she heard the beep, she said, "Hello, Mr. Boulder. You haven't checked in with me. I need to talk to you as soon as possible. Call me."

Susan's eyes welled with tears. I haven't seen Aunt Laura for years except for the newspaper article, she thought. "I really think something terrible has happened to her," she whispered.

CHAPTER 30

Find your best friend somewhere on this planet.

Joe Boulder hailed a cab at Reagan International the morning after his interview with Virginia. He gave the driver an address and sat back in the seat to look at the file he had pulled up on his computer the evening before.

Annie and Kirkland Somers lived just outside Washington DC. They had been married for 27 years and had no children. Kirkland had been a naval pilot then a Jag Officer in his early career and later had been assigned to the Pentagon. He had retired in 2011. Annie had been an attorney who worked for the government. The file did not say where or in what capacity. She also had retired in 2011.

This trip to the Somers' home is taking longer than I planned, he thought. I'd forgotten about the constant construction on the beltway. This road will never be finished. Thirty minutes later, the cab pulled in front of a well-kept, three-story brick townhouse reminiscent of the brownstones in New York City.

Wow, nice digs, Boulder thought as he paid the driver. He walked up the five steps to the stoop and turning around he could see a portion of the

Capital Dome in the distance. He had called Annie before leaving for the airport to set up the meeting and was lucky she was available on short notice. She had suggested that he come to her home; they would be able to talk more comfortably there. Boulder rang the doorbell and turned to take another look at the view.

    Kirkland Somers opened the door. He was six feet, four inches tall and sported about 180 pounds of solid muscle. His hairline was receding and he had a bit of grey at the temples. He smiled. "You must be Joe Boulder," he said in a low baritone voice. "We've been expecting you. Annie is in the back." He led Boulder down a hallway which had an extensive collection of art work on the walls.

    "Someone dabble in art?" Boulder asked.

    Kirkland shook his head. "No, it's a collection from our travels."

    "These are nice pieces," Boulder said as he walked behind him.

    Annie stood up as the men walked into the room. "Oh, you've seen my collection," she said as she shook Boulder's hand. Annie was five feet, seven inches tall with black hair and clear blue eyes. She was dressed in a light peach, long sleeved tee with black jeans and appeared to be about 125 pounds. She's drop dead gorgeous and except for using a cane and having a slight, ashy skin tone, I would never think she's ill, Boulder thought, let alone has a bad ticker.

"Come on in," she said with a lilt in her voice. "Kirk, offer Mr. Boulder a drink."

"That's okay, I'm good," Boulder said holding up his hand.

Kirkland stepped toward the doorway. "Since you two have a lot of things to talk about, I'm going to grab a beer and go into the den to watch the Nationals. Do you want anything before I leave Hon?"

"No dear."

Kirkland grabbed the beer from the small refrigerator bar, kissed Annie on her forehead and left the room.

"So, what is it I can do for you Mr. Boulder?" Annie asked frankly.

Boulder sat down in a chair across from Annie, told her about his investigation to date and concluded, "I need more background information about your friend, Laura. Virginia McGovern told me that, since you're more like a sister than she is, you would be the one to ask."

"Oh, that attitude doesn't surprise me." Annie shook her head. "But that was no one else's fault but hers."

"How did you two meet?" Boulder asked.

Annie's thoughts flew back in time to when she and Laura were children. . . Laura and Annie had been BFF's since childhood, though a more unlikely pair would be hard to imagine. As a fifth grader, recently transferred from parochial school, Laura had been alternately teased and ignored by her classmates for being a goody-two-shoes and an obvious teacher's pet. She developed a hang-dog expression and secretly couldn't wait until sixth grade, when she hoped that somehow a different set of classmates would magically shoot her popularity up a few notches. In the meantime, the teasing continued and she was always the last one chosen to be on a team. Laura Bora was one of the kinder names she was called. Though the teachers hadn't a clue, she knew the kids were taunting her for being boring. She cried in her pillow every night.

One day mid-term, Laura's teacher introduced a new girl, Annie, to the class, who had been transferred from a school across town. Rumors soon began to fly that Annie was a problem child and had been given a second chance by her parents to shape up or go to reform school.

Out of sheer loneliness, the two gravitated to each other. Laura became less prim and proper and more down to earth. She had a calming effect on Annie and offered to help her make sense of the teacher's lesson of the day thereby improving Annie's grades and boosting her self-esteem. Annie, knowing that she was a street-smart tomboy-type by nature and had a bad-girl reputation, whispered to

Laura one day, "Watch the kids start eating honeymoon sandwiches." Laura looked at her new friend quizzically. "You know," Annie explained with a wink, "lettuce alone." They giggled co-conspiratorially. Each girl secretly suspected that being part of a group would have been nicer but, hey, having one really good friend was darn nice too and sure made life bearable. Their friendship continued down through the years. . . .

"Earth to Annie, earth to Annie. Where'd you go?"

"Oh, I was just thinking back. Laura and I became close friends in grade school. We were both on the outside looking in. We were kind of gawky and nerdy and spent a lot of time in the awkward stage," she said smiling. "Virginia was on the cheerleading squad, class vice president and so pretty. She certainly never wanted to be associated with Laura at the time. Laura was more into reading and studying. Did you know Laura graduated second in her class? I never knew anyone who was as good with numbers as she. Virginia always wanted to get out of Maryland even as a child. She hated the farm, although it was the one thing that allowed her the privilege of going to school in Pennsylvania. Her parents made good money. As soon as she could after she graduated though, she married and left everything behind."

"How about Laura, did she want to leave also?" Boulder nudged.

"Laura went to the University of Maryland on a full academic scholarship. When her dad got sick, she moved back to the ranch but still managed to get her degree. She took care of the books and managed the stables. Laura loved the horses. I went to visit her on weekends when I could. I went to the American University here in DC and the track team took up a lot of my time in school, so there were weeks when I couldn't make it. Later, I met Kirk. He was a runner for Annapolis and I spent even less time with Laura, but we still kept in touch by phone at least weekly."

"Didn't Laura marry about then too?"

"She fell head over heels for Ted Watson. He was a so-called trainer at the stables."

Boulder settled back against a cushion. How much more forthcoming Annie is compared to Virginia, he thought. "Annie, I'd like to find out about her youth, her friends and her marriage to Ted."

"I can't tell you much about her friends but I can tell you about my observations of Ted. I'll start at the beginning."

Annie placed her feet on the footstool and looked down remembering Laura and Ted. She folded her hands together and began, "Ted worked on his father's dairy farm when he was growing up.

Their farm was about ten miles away from Laura and Virginia's parents' horse farm."

"Did they know each other in their earlier years?"

"No, but I do remember her telling me about this dreamy guy she met at the 4-H Club Square Dance. That was the beginning of their romance. He became interested in horses when he found out about the Y's Horse Farm. Y stood for the family's last name of Young. It was two years later when she went off to college that Mr. Young hired Ted as a trainer at the stable."

"Did they continue their relationship during her college years?"

"Yes, and she commuted on the weekends so she could be with him. Laura told me that Ted wanted to own a stable with prize horses. That's what he kiddingly called them instead of Thoroughbreds. I suppose he wanted to be a gentleman horse farmer," she said sarcastically.

"Sounds as if he had big ideas," Boulder remarked.

"Before they married . . ." Annie said. She stopped and called, "Kirk, would you please get me a glass of water? My throat is dry from talking so long."

Kirkland re-entered the room with Annie's water, "Here you are my dear. It's also time for your next pill." He handed her a large white capsule and a glass of water, then turned to Boulder and said, "I could tell you a few things about Ted, but my wife's doing fine." He winked at Annie. "May I get you a drink now, Mr. Boulder?"

Boulder shook his head and said, "No thank you. I'm finding this story very interesting, but if you want to stop...."

"Oh no," Annie said, "I want to make sure you know what a scoundrel Ted really was."

"Why did Laura find him so compelling? It sounds as if she was the brains and he was the brawn."

"Before they were married," Annie continued, "He was the perfect boyfriend: always polite to her parents and never lost his temper. He gave her nice, thoughtful gifts. He had everyone fooled."

"What about Virginia? Did she like him?"

"Oh, she thought he was beneath Laura's status."

"Was that because Laura went to college and he didn't?"

"Maybe, but I think it was more than that. Laura was classy, charming and diplomatic. Ted was crude, impulsive and egocentric. I think their love of horses, his plans for the future, his handsome looks, physique and sense of humor made her think he was her perfect catch. You know the old saying that opposites attract."

Boulder leaned over a little closer to Annie as if he didn't want to miss any part of the story.

"As I said before, they married after she graduated from college. She was a young 20 year old. Laura asked me to be maid of honor for her wedding, and not Virginia. There was bad blood between Laura and Virginia. She didn't even invite Virginia to the wedding. I wonder if Virginia would have attended even if she did get an invitation," Annie said as she cupped her chin in her hand.

Boulder continued to ask Annie a volley of questions. "Was Ted still working as a trainer at the stables? Where were they living after they married? Did Laura work?"

"Not so fast," Annie said and then smiled.

"They lived near her parents' farm so Ted could work as a trainer. Laura was a math teacher in the high school. She was the real breadwinner since she had a CPA and also did bookkeeping for some of the farms in the area. I think Ted's confidence dropped since she was making more money. He was very jealous. Arguments started when she stayed longer at work than he thought she should."

"It seems as if you didn't like him very much."

"Nope, I always felt he was after the farm. But Laura could see no bad in him. I think she really deserved someone better. Virginia was right about that."

"Virginia mentioned that Laura had told her that Ted wanted the farm," Boulder said. He leaned forward and continued. "Virginia also said that she thought Watson was controlling, and that she and Laura didn't speak because Virginia thought that her own husband was having an affair with Laura."

"Well, Laura had become quite striking as she became older." Annie continued, "After Virginia gave birth to Susan, she didn't feel as pretty as she once did, although it wasn't true. So, when Susan's dad showed Laura any attention, Virginia got angry. Susan's dad loved Virginia, but Virginia didn't always see it that way.

"Laura and Ted had been married for only two years when Ted started fooling around with other women and running up gambling debts. He was controlling and wouldn't let Laura do anything or see anybody. He even tried to hit on me and tried to keep Laura and me apart. Laura put up with a lot."

"What happened when he made a play for you?" asked Boulder.

"Well, I told Kirk, and he never did it again."

"So if it wasn't the women or gambling, what finally made Laura leave?"

"She didn't leave; she kicked Ted out. She found discrepancies in the books where he had taken money from the farm. He stole from her parents. That was the last straw. She told him to get out and I filed the papers for her. She told him she would see him in jail if she ever saw him around the farm again."

"Do you know where he went?"

"Not really. Rumor was he went to Ohio to work at some stables there."

CHAPTER 31

The most successful person is the one who has the best information.

While Boulder sat in Annie's rustically decorated enclosed porch, he felt the vibration from his phone inside the leather pouch on his hip.

"Just a minute Mrs. Somers, I've got to see who buzzed me. I've been on the road these past few days and everyone's trying to reach me."

Boulder checked his phone to see who had called. Ahh . . . Susan Jeffries. I guess I'd better call her back soon, he thought.

"Mrs. Somers, I appreciate your time. Is there anything else you can tell me about Laura? Virginia seemed quite hesitant to discuss anything concerning Laura's first husband. I got the sense that she really didn't like him from the get-go and didn't want to divulge much information. I hope she's doing okay down there all alone in Florida. She doesn't keep in touch with Susan."

"Oh, she has some problems from what Laura has told me. They might not have talked to each other a lot these past years, but Laura has ways of keeping in touch."

"Anything else come to mind about Laura?"

"Not really, Mr. Boulder. But I'm sure you'll talk to others."

"Well many thanks for your hospitality Mrs. Somers and for your time but I have to go now." Boulder stood up, shook Annie's frail hand and looked into her eyes.

"Any time I can help, just let me know," Annie said. "By the way, I know some government people in investigations if Laura's case develops into one of Federal interest. The FBI unit in Newark, New Jersey would be the likely unit to get involved. But you already know this."

Annie Somers turned her head away from Boulder. Tears flooded her eyes and she started to sob. Kirkland walked through the doorway just as Boulder reached out to calm her.

"Annie dear, you know your doctor wants you to take it easy. It's hard not knowing where Laura is, I understand, but please. . . ."

Annie began to shake uncontrollably. Her face was ashen. She gave a small cry before she collapsed.

"Call 911," Kirkland yelled.

Boulder's pulse pounded as he punched in the numbers on his cell. "Is your wife okay?" he managed to ask as he handed the phone over to Kirkland.

"Oh, she'll be okay. It's just stress. Let me talk to the dispatcher. They know her real well."

The paramedics arrived in the next few minutes. They placed an oxygen mask on Annie's face and lifted her onto a stretcher. Boulder heard them reporting Annie's vital signs over their phone to a doctor at the hospital. They reported that she was awake, but slightly confused and unable to answer their questions. He heard them say their ETA would be in eight to ten minutes.

Perspiration sat in the creases on Boulder's forehead as he watched the paramedics prepare for departure. Kirkland climbed into the back of the ambulance.

"Sorry to end our conversation like this," he said waving his hand toward the stretcher.

"I hope she'll be okay, Kirkland."

After the rig pulled away, Boulder called a taxi to take him back to the airport.

Forty minutes later, he sat in the Fly Rite Bar. He had two and a half hours before he would board Spirit Airlines for his flight back to the Atlantic City airport. I need something to calm the anxiety surging in my veins, he thought. I hope she's okay. She looked like she lost her only friend. Boulder lifted the Scotch and water to his lips; his right hand shook spilling some of the liquid onto the table. Damn, I haven't picked up any useful information from either of these women, he thought. Should Ted Watson be my next source? Where do I look for him? Wonder if he's in Ohio like Annie said. Boulder signaled the bartender for a refill then reached inside his jacket pocket for his cell and called Susan's number. "I'd better let her know where I am," he mumbled.

Susan answered after one ring; her voice was hesitant and shaky. "Hello Mr. Boulder. Are you in your Manasquan office? Can you come over to the bookstore? A lot has happened that I think you should be aware of. Why don't you . . . ."

Boulder cut her short. "Wait a minute Susan, what's your rush? I'm sitting here waiting for my plane in DC. You sound upset. What's going on?"

"I don't know what to do. I received a letter today with nothing written, I mean, no one signed it and . . . . " Susan took a deep breath then continued, "It says something about Big Blue, whoever that is. There's more but . . . ."

"Okay, okay. Give me a few hours. I'll be at your bookstore when you open in the morning. I can't make it any sooner."

Susan sighed. "Mr. Boulder, I'll open early and make some coffee; you bring breakfast." Susan shut her phone and grabbed her purse. "I need to go home where it's quiet and I can think clearly," she mumbled,

Boulder clicked his phone shut, gulped the last of his Scotch and walked to the terminal seating area. Big Blue? That was the name of Walsh's horse, he thought. At least this might be another avenue to explore. Good. At least my entire day hasn't been wasted!

CHAPTER 32

One is amazing who has psychic powers.

Susan didn't sleep well the night of the psychic's visit. Next morning, she dragged herself out of bed and went down to the kitchen to brew some strong coffee. As the water dripped through the Arabica blend, she sniffed the heavenly aroma then poured the brew into the cup and took her first sip. "Oh, that's so much better," she murmured aloud. "I can almost face the day now."

Her mind was filled with loose ends: the note that said Laura didn't leave and to check out Big Blue; the psychic who told her Laura was dead but that she wasn't alone and the blue aura the psychic saw on Aunt Laura's picture. Susan sat down at the table and pulled a notepad toward her. She wrote down five bullet points: Didn't leave, Big Blue, Dead, Not Alone, and Blue Aura, and stared at them hoping to get some kind of inspiration. Did the blue aura have anything to do with Big Blue? What, or who, was Big Blue? Who sent me that note? Am I in danger? I might have some leads, but I have no answers, she thought.

Susan switched on her laptop and **Googled**: Big Blue. There were tons of hits. Big Blue could be a 1988 film, a California bus, a New York Giants fan, a drink, a computer and a multitude of other things. None of these seemed to have a link to her aunt's disappearance.

She tried **Googling:** blue aura. Still not much help. There was a lot of information about the psychic meaning of a blue aura. People with a blue aura apparently had the ability to convey their thoughts and ideas well, and their heads and hearts were well balanced when making difficult decisions. They prized truthfulness and clarity in all their relationships. "That makes sense about Aunt Laura," Susan said to the plastic frog sitting on the napkin holder in the center of the table. "She's a bookkeeper. Those would be great traits for her to have. Maybe that psychic is on to something."

Susan closed the computer and looked again at her list. I feel alone and don't know where to turn. I'm pleased that Joe Boulder will be at the shop when I open and I hope that he will be able to make some sense out of the information I have. Oops, it's time to get ready for work, hope my day will get better.

As Susan arrived at the bookstore, she noticed that Boulder was leaning against her shop window. "Hi Mr. Boulder," she called, digging out her keys from her bag. "You're an early bird."

"Call me Joe and, yeah I've brought the worms!" he said, as he lifted up a white box from the pastry shop in town. "I didn't know what you'd like, so I bought a lot of good stuff."

"Well, come on in, Joe. I'll put the coffee on."

"Ack! Who's that? Who's that?" Nicky screeched as the two entered the bookstore. Susan shut off the alarm, uncovered the birdcage and then put her purse on the counter.

"Come on in back," she said. "We can talk there."

Once the two had settled down and had coffee and pastry in front of them, Boulder looked at Susan. "So?" he said. "What's all this you were trying to tell me about yesterday, something about a Big Blue?"

Susan got her purse, pulled out the note she had received and handed it to Boulder. He slipped the note out of the envelope and studied it for a few minutes. The envelope's postmark was smeared, and he noticed that the writing on the envelope and the note was printed by hand with a ball point pen. He put the note down and looked at Susan.

"This is quite a warning you got," he said. "What do you make of it?"

"That's just it. I don't know what to make of it."

"Who knows you're searching for your aunt?"

"Oh, just about anyone knows," said Susan. "Bud Thorne, Ryan Brewster, Jonathan Fox, my mother, Chelsea, and anyone they've talked to. And I haven't really been secretive. Anyone in the shop could have heard me talking about it. And then there was the psychic."

"The psychic?" Boulder asked.

"There was this woman who came in to the store and when she saw Bud Thorne's article on the counter, she told me that my aunt was dead and that she wasn't alone. A few minutes later, she saw a blue aura around the picture of my aunt."

"How does this woman know all this?"

"She said she knows because she's a psychic."

"Well, it could be true. Sometimes psychics can shed some small light on a situation, but in most cases their information is found to be false, so I wouldn't get too worked up about this. Do you have her contact information?"

Susan handed him Wanda's card.

"Do you mind if I keep the letter and the card?" Boulder asked.

"Okay, but first let me make a copy of them." After Susan made copies, she handed the papers back to Boulder.

"I know a little about Big Blue," he said. "One of Fox's stablehands told me a story about a horse named Big Blue. He was owned by Charlie Ayers, who bet the horse and his entire stables then lost it all in a huge poker game with a stable owner, Jack Walsh. I actually played poker once with Jack, and he was a real horse's . . . well, you know what I mean."

"A horse," Susan repeated. "What would a horse that is owned by Jack Walsh have to do with my aunt?"

"Don't know," said Boulder. "Do you think your uncle would be able to tell us?"

"Maybe, it couldn't hurt to ask."

"Why don't you call him now and see if we can go talk with him together."

"Okay Joe, but first I want to know where you've been and . . . have you come up with anything?"

"Give me another cup of java, if you don't mind, and I'll tell you about my visit with your mother and Laura's friend, Annie Somers."

Susan poured two fresh cups of coffee then looked at her watch. It was eight o'clock. "Joe, I have a little time to talk. Chelsea gets here at nine so . . . what'd my mother have to say? Where'd you meet her?"

"I flew down to Florida and met her at a restaurant, Crabby Bill's. You know the place?"

"No, but go on."

"She certainly holds a grudge against her sister. Wasn't a bit happy talking about her. She preferred to put her emphasis on Ted Watson. How much do you know about him?"

"Not much. I have the picture that I showed you with him and my aunt. Mother has told me some things—all of them negative."

"Well I didn't get anything from her except that she thinks poorly of Ted. Pardon me but I found her to be bitter about this whole thing."

"That's my mother. She holds grudges like no one else I know."

"Sorry about that, Susan. Anyway, yesterday I flew to DC and visited Laura's friend, Annie Somers. Your mother suggested she would know more about the relationship. You know her?"

"No, but I imagine Jonathan knows her."

"She told me she grew up with Laura; they had a lot in common. Annie went on to tell me about Laura's bad marriage to Ted–that's about all. I have to digest all of this back in my office–maybe I can come up with something else to look in to. Oh, by the way . . . Annie had a spell of some sort after we finished talking and ended up going to the hospital. She is very stressed over all of this; maybe we should tell Fox. He can decide if he wants to call and give her some support." Boulder yawned.

"I guess your trip was more tiring than informative?"

"Yeah. Hey, I've got to go. I'll write up some notes about my trip if you want."

"That's okay, Joe. You know what you're doing. I think we should call Fox and talk to him. You do what you have to do this morning then come back about noon and we'll call him."

CHAPTER 33

I will go with thee to thy uncles.

Fox had been diagnosed in the early spring. His internist said he had Type 1 Diabetes. Fox knew what that meant, since his father had had diabetes. He had often watched his dad self-inject insulin when he was a child back on the farm. Now, after all these years, he couldn't believe he too had to take insulin.

***

Fox's cell phone rang. He saw Susan's name on the caller ID.
"Hello there, Susan, what's up?"
"Well Jonathan, I'm here in my shop with Joe Boulder, the private investigator I hired. Remember?"
"Yeah."
"Well, we've got to meet with you sometime, today preferably."
"Oh, what's going on? I'm home right now. Can you come over about one?" Jonathan's voice had a gruffness to it.
"Yes Jon, we can leave here shortly."

The front door of the bookstore opened and Chelsea came in carrying a Styrofoam food container from Sal's next door.

"Chels, this is Joe Boulder, the PI I hired. Joe, meet my assistant. We're on our way to see my uncle. Take care of things will you?"

"Like sure Mrs. J. Sure." As they went out the door, Chelsea scratched Nicky's head and said, "I wonder what that's all about."

Jonathan Fox ushered Susan and Boulder into his office upon their arrival. "You made good time getting here from Manasquan."

"Not much traffic," Boulder replied as the two men shook hands.

Jonathan motioned to the sofa under the side window. "Please sit down."

Looking straight at Susan, he asked, "So what's this about? What's so urgent you had to see me today?"

Boulder took the lead and told Fox about the note and the psychic. Fox immediately leaned forward in his chair, his eyes widened and he raised his brow. "Okay, okay. Big Blue is dead!" Fox said.

Susan and Boulder exchanged glances.

"My stablehand told me he died rather suddenly of tetanus that developed after a nasty cut to his foot. It was in the spring sometime."

"What did they do with the horse's carcass?" Boulder asked looking over at Susan and seeing a look of caution on her face.

Fox folded his arms across his chest and swiveled side to side in the chair. "Well, you know Jack Walsh. He always puts on the pomp," Fox sneered and continued, "He invested in a piece of land with Tom and Ellen Havens, big horse people too, over in Cream Ridge. They have a 14-acre pet cemetery over there and one portion, off Yellowbrook Road, is burial grounds for large animals . . . pets, I should say. Anyway, my stablehand, Jake, told me that Walsh buried Big Blue there and then erected a huge memorial statue of Big Blue as well. I never went over to look at it since I'm not in cahoots with Walsh, that's for sure. You know, Jack has his Shore Thing Stables over that way too."

The more Fox spoke about Walsh, the more agitated he became. He clenched his hands into a fist and shook his head before he said, "Tell me again what that letter said. Hand it to me so I can read it."

Jonathan reached out for the letter; his hand shook as he grabbed hold. Blinking his eyes to clear them, he read: **She didn't leave . . . Check out Big Blue . . . .** The color rose again in his face. He stood up and grabbed his keys from the desktop. "I've got some time this afternoon, let's drive over there and pay Tom and Ellen a visit. The name of the place is

Our Pet's Haven," Jonathan said, handing the paper back to Boulder.

After a 45-minute drive, the trio arrived in the parking lot in front of the office. There was a large marquis decorated with cut stone, with the name **Our Pet's Haven** across the top. A driveway wove through a large expanse of park-like grass. Small, flush headstones dotted the area on each side. The atmosphere was serene. As Susan got out of the car, she saw a gazebo at the distant end of the road and many smaller paths off the main road that led to other memorials.

In a hushed tone she said, "This is quite a park. I can see why someone would want to bury their pet here; it's beautiful!"

Boulder and Fox walked ahead of Susan into the office and held the door for her. Inside, they were greeted by a man who introduced himself, "Hello, I'm Tom Havens. Sorry for your loss."

Boulder glanced at Susan then said," We're here to . . ."

Fox interrupted. "We don't have a loss. We want to know where Jack Walsh's memorial is located . . . you know . . . the one he erected for his horse, Big Blue."

"Oh yes, it's a beautiful one. You see, here at Our Pet's Haven we try to give our utmost attention to . . ."

Jonathan held up his hand. He was having difficulty controlling his emotions. A twitch appeared in his cheek and he absently rubbed at it. He slammed his hand on Haven's desk. "I just want you to tell me where Jack Walsh's horse, Big Blue, is located. I don't need the whole spiel."

"Okay, okay," Havens said, putting up a hand to ward off Fox. "Here's a map of the grounds. The area for large animals is on the far right side right next to a pine-covered, forested area. Take the main road, then, make a right then go past the gazebo. There are two rows of pampas grass that lead to Big Blue's grave."

Jonathan began to sweat; drops of moisture dripped onto his jacket. "Come on you two. Boulder, here are the keys, you drive." he said.

Susan lagged behind as the men headed for the front door. "Thanks, Mr. Havens. My uncle's a little upset. I'll take care of him," she said, nodding toward Fox.

They got back into the Bronco and turned right, onto the lengthy driveway. Boulder drove slowly past the main cemetery grounds following the twists and turns in the road. He saw a sign - EQUINE RESTING PLACE.

CHAPTER 34

No one ever drowned in sweat.

Boulder pulled Fox's vehicle over to the side of the paved road near a large, blue-marble monument. Jonathan jumped out and sprinted to the foot of the memorial. Susan caught up with him and Boulder, after reaching for his jacket in the back seat, followed.

"Look at the date," Fox shouted, not addressing anyone in particular. "Big Blue died just days before Laura disappeared."

"It could be a coincidence," Boulder said putting his hand out to restrain Fox.

"Maybe," Fox mumbled. Perspiration beaded on his upper lip. He turned aside and ran back to his Bronco. After opening the hatch, he grabbed a shovel out of the back and returned to the grave site. Susan and Boulder had no chance to interrupt his actions or ask what he was doing. Fox dug up some of the ground in front of the marble monument with such force that he lost his balance for a moment. He tossed the first shovelful of dirt to the side. Digging again, Fox stumbled, pitched forward and landed face down on the small pile of dirt.

Susan ran over to him and checked for a pulse but she was unable to get a verbal response when she called his name. After calling several times, she yelled to Boulder, "Call 911." Susan reached in Fox's pockets to see if he had any medicine or some other indication that he may have a medical problem. She found a used diabetic test strip in his jacket pocket. "I think Jonathan might be diabetic. Here's a used strip and he has a strange smell about him. Tell the EMTs what I've found."

Five minutes later, Susan and Boulder heard sirens. A state trooper's car, followed by the Allentown First Aid Squad, entered the road on the side of the grave where Fox had fallen. Within two minutes, State Police vehicles joined the group.

The first aid squad immediately checked Fox. His blood pressure was low, his pulse was weak and rapid, and his breathing had become labored.

"His breath really smells like acetone," one of the EMTs stated. "He's probably a diabetic and too busy to take his insulin. Hey Ed, look at this. His glucose is 900." The EMTs worked quickly; they started an intravenous line and phoned in their findings to an emergency room doctor. As they loaded Jonathan into the rig, he opened his eyes but mumbled incoherently. In minutes the EMTs transported their patient to CentraState Medical Center in nearby Freehold.

The State Trooper, whose badge read Captain Thomas J. Lewis, arrived on the scene. Susan and Boulder walked over to him and introduced themselves. Trooper Lewis asked immediately, "What's going on here?" Neither Susan nor Boulder answered him, since the owner of the cemetery, Tom Havens, approached them at the same time.

"I called Jack Walsh as soon as you left my office," he said as he stepped down from his golf cart to stand with the three of them.

Jack Walsh arrived minutes later. Havens looked at Susan and said," I didn't like the looks of Fox when you were in my office. The guy was behaving oddly. I thought Walsh should know that someone was interested in Big Blue's grave." He turned and directed his next words to Trooper Lewis. "As I said, I called Walsh and told him that someone was interested in Big Blue's grave."

The trooper nodded and directed his attention to Susan and Boulder. "So why are you here? Who had this shovel?"

"My uncle, Jonathan Fox, thinks my aunt is buried here."

"That's a bunch of bull," Walsh blurted out ignoring the trooper. "Why would your aunt be buried here?"

The trooper turned away from Walsh and continued questioning Susan. "Why does your uncle think that?"

Susan told him about the letter she had received and the psychic who was in the bookstore. The trooper wrote something in his black notebook and was interrupted again by Walsh.

"I'll prove she's not here."

"How will you do that?" the trooper asked, straightening his hat.

"Heck, that's easy. I'll get a backhoe here in twenty minutes. We'll dig up the grave and you'll see. There's nothing here except my beautiful Big Blue."

The trooper snapped his notebook shut and looked at Walsh. "So, you're going to dig up the grave?"

"Well, yes. That's what I said. Havens has already called his workers."

"Since this may be a crime scene, it has to be staked out and a forensic team called in. We can't risk any evidence being damaged by a back hoe."

"Evidence? What evidence? I just told you there isn't anything here. What crime are you talking about?"

"Well, if there's a body . . . ."

"There isn't," Walsh yelled. He pulled his cap off his head and slammed it to the ground.

"If there is a body," the trooper repeated, "then there is, at the least, foul play and possibly a murder."

"A murder? Whose murder?" Walsh insisted.

"The murder of my aunt," said Susan, her voice breaking.

CHAPTER 35

Who questions much shall learn.

Susan stepped away from the men. What if my aunt's body is here in the grave? Who put her here? Why did someone kill her? Does Jonathan know anything? As the thoughts ran through her head, she heard Trooper Lewis talking to dispatch at police headquarters on his radio.

"Steve, we might have a human body here . . . yeah . . . here at Our Pet's Haven Cemetery." His voice had a touch of laughter in it. "We need to notify the Monmouth County Sheriff Department. They'll send Officers and the K-9 unit. It may be just what we need."

Jack Walsh paced back and forth. "I had no idea about any of this," he yelled. He took out his cell and called his stables. "Rudy, get over here to Big Blue's grave. There's trouble here and I need help. Get a damn backhoe over here. . . and quick . . . sure the cemetery has one but I want another one." He ended the call and turned to Trooper Lewis. "My crew will be here with a backhoe soon."

Havens stamped his foot and shook his head. "This is unbelievable. The deer and raccoons graze here almost day and night but I've never seen a human body here before." He looked over at Susan. "Are you okay?"

"I'm okay. I'd like to get over to the hospital. Jonathan doesn't have any children and maybe there are some questions I can answer, or papers, or something I can do there. I'm no good here." Susan turned and started to walk slowly in search of Boulder who had walked over to look at Big Blue's marble statue.

Trooper Lewis walked up to her, placed his hand on her arm and said, "If we find a body, there won't be much left of it, if it's been in there for a few months." He sniffed the air and continued, "All these pine trees and flowers cover up any strong odor if there is a body."

Susan shuddered and Boulder took her elbow. "That was quite a scene there with Walsh."

"Yeah, I know. Did you hear him say anything that will help us, Joe?"

"Not really. Here're the keys to Fox's Bronco. You'll need them to get to the hospital. I want to hang here and see for myself what's going on. I'll hitch a ride home from one of these guys. Drive carefully and I'll talk to you later today. Hope Fox comes out of it okay."

Twenty minutes later a pick-up truck entered the cemetery from Mill Road which ran parallel with the property. At the same time, several police officers and the K-9 unit arrived. Two men got out of the truck and released the backhoe from the trailer. One of the men approached Walsh. "Hey there Jack, what's up?"

Walsh shook his head, his face reddened and he inhaled slowly. "Well, seems like these people think there might be a body in with my horse. The only way to prove them wrong is to dig a little and that's why you're here. Be the hell careful though. I put a lot of money in the memorial and I don't want it damaged."

"Okay Boss, where do I start?"

The officer with the German Shepherd cadaver dog stepped in front of Walsh. "Just a minute . . . let my dog do his job first. It might save us a lot of trouble." He took the dog over to the front of the memorial and let him sniff the ground. The dog moved to the right side and sniffed for a few seconds more. Almost immediately, when the dog reached the side of the plot, he sat down.

"Bring the backhoe over here and start digging," the Officer-in-Charge said, "Be sure to remove just the top soil; you'll have to hand-shovel the rest." His voice was loud in the silence of the cemetery.

Walsh, standing a little apart from the police, swiped his hand over his eyes and perspiration ran down the sides of his face. "I can't believe this," he sputtered. He turned and spit on the ground behind him.

After several scrapes of the bucket, Walsh's stablehand loosened about two feet of dirt on the right side of the grave. Walsh, Havens and Boulder, along with the investigation team, peered at the opened earth. The backhoe operator deposited another load of dirt on the side toward a grassy area and the men saw a light-colored piece of cloth and a mushroom-colored long bone on top of the pile. Another man from Walsh's truck grabbed the shovel that Fox had used and moved several more clumps of soil. Each had small light-colored fragments which appeared to be bones. A boot had surfaced, along with a moldy-looking strap.

"There are bones here all right," another officer called out above the sound of the backhoe. "Turn that machine off. Now!"

"Whoa . . . hold it," Havens yelled. "Let's see what we've got." Getting down on his knees he leaned over the deepest part of the hole. "Holy crap. Nobody touch a thing." Havens shouted, visibly shaken.

"Everyone, please move back," Trooper Lewis instructed. He looked up and saw that a van with the **Asbury Park Press** logo on the side had arrived as well as more members of an investigation team from Monmouth County. He handed a spool of yellow crime scene tape to a sheriff's deputy who walked up beside him.

"I'll call Dr. Dinberg and get him here too," he told Trooper Lewis. "He's the coroner in Upper Freehold. We can't let anyone touch these findings until he looks at what we've got." The deputy proceeded to unwind the spool of yellow crime scene tape to secure the area.

CHAPTER 36

If I am dead, you can find where I am lying.

Boulder leaned against a pickup truck at the end of the driveway leading to the grave site. He had a panoramic view of the investigation from the spot where he was standing. The entire area, including the entrance to the pet cemetery, was blocked off. The area looked like a scene from the television series *CSI*. There were several black-and-whites as well as a few black unmarked deputy cars which had arrived. The memorial site, now cordoned off, was limited to those in authority. One police photographer snapped pictures from every angle, and two people decked out in white suits and boots, meticulously screened each scoop of dirt.

I just hate cemeteries, Boulder thought. I know people say how beautiful, serene and historic they are, but all I know is that they are full of death. It doesn't matter that this one has only pets. I wish I had gone to the hospital with Susan but I know I have to remain here to get information.

Jack Walsh stood with his two stablehands out of ear shot. He was extremely agitated. His face had a purple flush and seemed slightly distorted, as if he were talking through his teeth. As he talked, his hands flailed with every word he uttered. His stablehands listened as he vented in frustration. His move to deter a police investigation by offering to dig up Big Blue's grave himself had backfired. He became angrier by the minute. Every five minutes he stomped to the end of the crime tape and demanded. "When is this going to end? When is Big Blue's grave . . . there's nothing here."

"Hey, we found something," a deep, graveled voice yelled from a spot where other investigators were digging. "Looks like body parts. They're badly decomposed. Do you think we've got human remains?"

"It can't be," Walsh yelled from where he was still standing.

"We've definitely found pieces of a skeleton," a female inspector responded. "There's a gold-colored ring and a few other items scattered about, too."

"How long do you think they've been here?" asked a young officer who was standing alongside the opening in the ground.

"I think . . . for at least a few months," the female inspector answered. "There's a tarp here too and bones appear to have shifted about. We'll know more when we collect all the pieces then examine them in the lab. There's nothing more conclusive than that right now." The female inspector's tone was matter of fact. "Johnny, get me some more evidence bags and I'll need some smaller brushes."

"Hey Boulder," the lead detective yelled.

"What?" Boulder did not move from the spot next to the truck.

"Did Laura Fox wear a ring?"

"How should I know? You'll have to ask Fox." After a pause, Boulder added, "Should I call Susan Jeffries?"

"Who's Susan Jeffries?"

"She's Laura Fox's niece. She hired me to investigate the disappearance of her aunt. She's the one who left to go to the hospital with Jonathan Fox."

"Give her a call if you want. We'll have to verify the ring later anyway. The investigation will be able to move along quicker the more information we get."

Boulder pulled out his cell but was interrupted.

"Get your ass off my truck," a large burly ranch hand yelled as he walked up next to Boulder.

CHAPTER 37

There are times to speak your mind.

Jack Walsh watched the activity around the monument for several minutes more then approached the lead detective.

"Hey officer, I've got to get back to work at my stables. Do you need anything from me? I've told you I'm in the dark as to what's going on here. Haven's in charge; it's his land."

"Well, you've spoken your mind. We'll be talking to you again soon. I advise you to stay in the area until we've completed our investigation."

"Yeah, I'll be at Shore Thing Stables when you want me." Walsh kicked a clod of dirt with his boot and walked back to his truck parked alongside the driveway. He shook his head. *I wonder who knows I buried Big Blue here besides a couple of my stablehands and Havens. How did that knucklehead, Fox, find out? And what's with those bones?*

Jack pulled out of the cemetery entrance and headed toward the road home. As he approached the lot where he usually parked his pick-up, he saw Sprint, one of his older staff, leading Have Faith across the grounds to her stable. Jack waved his hand out of the window indicating to Sprint that he wanted to speak with him.

"Sprint, did you pick up the load of hay over at Burnsides yet?"

"Sure did Boss. We've got enough hay to last the whole winter. That's if you don't buy another Thoroughbred," Sprint grinned. His smile showed that he could use a few teeth implants.

"Don't worry. I've got enough trouble to handle right now. Put Have Faith in her stall and come over to my office. I've got some questions for you."

Ten minutes later, Sprint pounded on Walsh's door.

"Come in," Walsh yelled. He sat at his desk twirling an empty glass around on the blotter. You want a drink? I got some Jack Daniels here." A perfect set of teeth showed when he spoke.

"Sure Boss. My day's work is done for the most part."

Walsh opened the bottom drawer on the side of his desk, grabbed the whiskey and another glass and poured Sprint a drink.

"Boss, what did ya wanna ask me?" Sprint sat down across from Walsh.

Jack leaned back in his swivel chair and stroked the stubble on his chin. "Did you hear about the ruckus over at Big Blue's grave?"

"There was some talk in the barn earlier when I stacked the hay. I picked up snatches. Seems they're looking for a woman's body over there. Ted and Rudy came in after lunch and I heard them talking, but they were hush-hush."

"Anyone else comment?"

"Not that I heard. I remember when we buried your horse. That's some cemetery; they keep it up real nice. Haven's got himself a good crew." Sprint stopped and looked at Walsh who appeared to be daydreaming; his eyes were closed and his brow was furrowed.

Walsh was listening to Sprint but thinking about Fox. *That Fox grinds my gears. He thinks he's such a big shot with all his Thoroughbreds. He sure learned a lesson when Have Faith took the Belmont in June. He knows I keep my word when it comes to saying I'll win. Even in those pitiful Saturday night poker games, I've shown him what I stand for.*

"Hey Boss, you need me anymore?"

Walsh shook his head. "Nah, you can go. Just let me know if you hear anything. There'll probably be some police coming here. You can count on it."

Sprint left the office and returned to the barn. A stablehand was hunkered on a footstool on the side of a stall with his cell phone cupped to his ear; he didn't hear Sprint enter.

"That's what I said," he exclaimed into the phone. "They found a body over at the pet cemetery where we buried Big Blue. . . Don't ask me so many questions, you already know the answers. Just keep cool and I'll keep you informed. . . Sure, Walsh is upset; Havens called him to go over there when he saw that Fox was snooping around. You know how this might affect Jack's reputation."

Sprint tried to get the gist of the rest of the conversation but the man mumbled too much. Sprint's hearing was giving him trouble. He slipped out the barn door and went over to his bunk in the back of the stable.

Walsh sat in his office a while longer. What a mess at Big Blue's grave, he thought. How the heck did someone manage to bury a body there? It has to be someone who knows I had that memorial built for Big Blue. I hate that Fox. He ticks me off. Maybe he was over there making sure his wife is still right where *he* put her.

Walsh refilled his glass with more whiskey. He finished the drink and made his way to his house to talk with his wife, Marie. His pace was out of tempo and he stumbled up the walkway. Marie opened the door and smelled the alcohol on his breath. She helped him to a chair and brewed some strong coffee. His tone of voice was harsh and he slurred his words. "I-I don't like this one bit."

"You need to settle down, Jack. You're not in the barn talking to your stablehands. You've had too much to drink and now you're too upset to explain anything to me."

After drinking several mugs of black coffee, he sobered up and told Marie everything about the events of the afternoon. She listened to him. There's nothing I can do, she thought. But at least Jack got it off his chest and calmed down.

Boulder was watching as Walsh left the cemetery. He's really on the edge of exploding, he thought. I'm getting out of here too; not much more I'm gonna learn today.

A newspaper reporter stood on the edge of the driveway. His boss had called him and requested that he follow a story on a break-in at a 7-11 in Asbury Park. Boulder overheard his conversation and when the reporter ended the call, Boulder hailed him. "Say, mind if I hitch a ride back as far as Colts Neck? I parked my car at Fox's main house this morning and need to pick it up."

"No problem. It'll cost you a bit; we reporters aren't paid enough to go out of our way," he said with a laugh.

"Name your fee, I got a few bucks."

Boulder settled in the passenger's seat of the Honda Civic and started talking. "Sure is a shame. The horse's grave looks like it was rototilled. I imagine that Jack Walsh is snorting bullets on his way back to his stables."

"You're right ya know. I've seen him over at the racetrack on the days I covered the races. He sure gets fired up. Matter of fact, he demands a lot from his hands and sticks near them to make sure they follow his orders."

"Have you interviewed him after a race. . . say one that he's lost?" Boulder asked.

"Ha. You're kidding me. Walsh lose? Well, I guess he doesn't win every race but . . . ." The reporter saw Boulder's cheek twitch. Must have a tic, he thought.

Boulder yawned widely and stretched although, due to his bulk in the small car, it prevented him from easing the stiffness in his shoulders. "Say Ernie, I appreciate this lift. I've got to get in to my office and make some calls but then, maybe I'll start again in the morning. Maybe I'll just spend the evening nursing a couple of scotches and listen to the news."

Ernie grinned and nodded his head.

Thirty minutes later, the men arrived at Fox's place. Boulder shook Ernie's hand and thanked him again. "See ya 'round."

Boulder glanced at the front door of the house and remembered that Fox had locked it when they headed to the cemetery. He didn't bother going onto the porch but opened his own car door, climbed in and turned the key in the ignition. Yeah, I'll call it a day. First, I should call Susan and see how she made out, he thought. When he punched in her cell number, he got the message that his call was being transferred to voicemail. Boulder turned his car and headed to Route 35 and within minutes he pulled in to the parking lot at TGI Friday's restaurant. Steak night, he thought. I deserve it.

CHAPTER 38

Envy makes one resentful of something enjoyed by another.

Jonathan responded quickly to the intravenous insulin in the emergency room. The doctor determined that he needed to remain overnight, since his blood pressure was low. After a length of time bickering with anyone who would listen, Jonathan agreed to stay the night.

Susan arrived and promised she would sit with him for a while. Their conversation centered on her family and his.

"It was envy, Susan," Jonathan began. "Your mother found fault with whatever Laura said. Laura was as pretty as a picture. She took pride in keeping herself in good shape and she kept busy by volunteering time to various charities. Virginia thought it was Laura's responsibility to raise a family instead. It was your mother's way or no way at all. Laura no longer kept in touch with her."

"I wondered why they never got along but I know they had several arguments," Susan said.

"Well, Laura was determined to do what she wanted and didn't like Virginia's meddling. By the way Susan, before I forget, would you go to my office?"

"What do you need?"

"There's a broken picture of Laura lying on the floor in the corner. I threw it when I was angry and never bothered to clean it up. It's been there this whole time. I'd like to have it here at the hospital. Also, try to retrieve the files I have in the computer concerning Jack Walsh. There are some in the old file cabinet too. Bring anything you can find here to me as soon as you can."

"How do I get into your office?"

"The keys are on the same ring as my Bronco's. That's how you got here, right? I'll call Jake back at the stables to meet you."

When Susan arrived, she noticed lights on in the house. She entered through the front door and went up the stairs. She saw a grey-bearded man sitting in the swivel chair at Jonathan's desk.

"Oh hello Mrs. Jeffries, I'm Jake, Mr. Fox's right-hand man. He stood up and offered a calloused hand to Susan. "Mr. Fox sounded pretty good when he called me. Boy, he really left this office in a mess. After Laura disappeared, I don't think he cared much about anything. I told him I would clean up a bit."

"Jonathan wants the picture of Laura that he threw across the room that night, Jake. May I see it?"

"It's right here. I straightened the frame, but the glass was broken."

Susan took the picture and looked closely at the woman who smiled back at her. She looks so much like my mother, she thought. Her heart quickened. Well, I guess I shouldn't be surprised since they're sisters.

"Ms. Jeffries, a . . . do you need anything else? If not I'll get back to the stables. If you need my help, let me know. Close the front door when you leave. It will lock itself."

"Thanks Jake. I'm picking up a few personal things for my uncle, then I'm returning to the hospital."

Susan listened to Jake's heavy footsteps descending the stairs. She looked out the office window above the sofa and saw his long, clumsy strides take him to the stables. How convenient that Jonathan can observe his workers from his office, she thought.

After Susan retrieved the files that Fox had requested, she went over to the stables to tell Jake she was leaving. "Thanks for your help, Jake. I'm going back to the hospital now. Here's my cell number if anything comes up."

Susan didn't notice anyone around while thanking Jake, but over in the shadows Pete watched as Susan turned and walked back toward her car. Susan you're as beautiful as ever. I've got to make plans to see you, he thought.

CHAPTER 39

*The evil that men do lives after them;
the good is oft interred with their bones.*

Susan's cell phone rang as she drove into the hospital parking lot. As soon as she answered it, Boulder said, "I hate to tell you this, but they found body parts in Big Blue's grave."

"Oh no, I had a bad feeling about that. How did they find them?"

"A cadaver dog sniffed the ground and the police started digging in that spot. They found a piece of clothing and skeletal remains and now the forensic team and coroner are there. It shouldn't take long to identify who it is. By the way, how's Fox doing?"

Susan clutched the phone tightly in her hand and said, "The doctors are keeping him overnight. He's still weak. I guess I'll stay with him a while longer. Joe, there are so many questions floating around in my mind. Whose body parts? Why? We need more information."

"Susan, I hate to tell you this, but there were reporters arriving on the scene, and I'm sure this will be broadcast on the news shortly. You'd better get to Jonathan and tell him something in case he watches the news and draws some of his own conclusions."

"You're right. Thanks Joe. Please keep me updated. I'll talk with you later." Susan rode the elevator, lost in thought. She walked down the third floor hallway and entered Fox's room. He lay on the bed with his eyes closed; a little color had returned to his face. He opened his eyes and Susan handed him the picture. He smiled as he looked at it and touched Laura's face with his fingers.

"Jonathan, I have some information from Boulder. The police found body parts in Big Blue's grave. There are reporters at the cemetery now and it'll be on the news soon."

Fox interrupted her and said sadly, "Susan, I'm not surprised that they found her. I know in my heart that's she's gone and I'm glad that it's finally over. When she didn't show up for the Belmont and wasn't with Annie, I knew that she was dead. She would never have stayed away from me or the horses for that long."

"I'm so sorry, Jonathan. We have to wait for positive identification and then we'll know for certain."

Tears welled up in Jonathan's eyes as he looked at Laura's face in the picture. He spoke quietly and said, "Maybe since the police couldn't find her in June, they'll find out now who murdered her and why." He closed his eyes and turned his head away.

***

During the next two days, the investigation team ran tests on items found at Our Pet's Haven. The article of clothing was a shirt with an embroidered logo F&H. There was a gold-colored ring and a silver necklace with the letter L attached and a leather boot with remnants of dried blood.

The local Channel 5 News broadcasted the story of the unusual finding of a woman's body buried in a horse's grave. Although positive identification was not released to the media, word leaked out that Jonathan Fox, prominent owner of Fox & Hound Stables, might finally have the answer to his wife Laura's whereabouts.

CHAPTER 40

The end of a relationship does not end living.

Susan stood next to Jonathan's hospital bed the following morning. "I don't know how you feel, but I think we should tell my mother and Annie Somers about the news reports. They may have seen it on the television already."

"I suppose you're right," he said, his voice trailing off.

"I'll call my mother and ask Joe Boulder to call Annie since he spoke to her recently."

"No, I'll call Annie. She was my wife's best friend. I'll do it even though it'll be difficult. I have a feeling she won't be surprised but she'll be terribly depressed."

Susan arched her eyebrows, which she had a habit of doing when she had a recollection. "Joe told me that Annie was in the hospital with a relapse of her heart problem. You might want to speak to her husband instead. He can use his best judgment when to tell her," Susan said.

Jonathan pushed his hands under him to sit up straighter in bed. "I can't believe this is happening. Laura's gone." He pounded his fist on the bed rail.

Susan pulled back from the side of the bed. She looked at his cardiac monitor and said, "Jonathan, please calm down."

Fox yelled, "I don't care about my blood pressure or diabetes but I do care about Laura and can't stop thinking about her. When she didn't attend the Belmont, I knew something was wrong. She would never have left on her own without contacting me. But who would have murdered her and why on earth for?"

The nurse on duty came into the room and asked if everything was all right. Jonathan assured her he was okay. Susan checked her watch; it was 12 noon. She smiled and squeezed his hand to indicate she was leaving. "Jonathan, I'll be back tomorrow. I've got to get over to the bookstore. Find out when you'll be discharged and call me. I imagine there might be a few news people and photographers wanting information about Aunt Laura."

"I think you're right," he said.

Susan grabbed the door handle and turned around to ask, "Is there anything you need?"

"Time, I need time to think about Laura."

Susan left and went out to the nurse's station to speak to the head nurse. "I'm Susan Jeffries, niece of the patient in room 317. May I speak with you?"

"Certainly."

"My uncle received some tragic news about his wife's death and the circumstances surrounding it. I'm sure the media will show up to ask him questions."

The head nurse tilted her head appearing puzzled. She stared at Susan for a few seconds. Susan continued talking. "My aunt was murdered and I want to restrict visitation. Please don't let reporters in to interview him."

"Oh my, how terrible! Yes, I certainly will accommodate you."

"Thank you."

Susan walked down to the end of the hall and sat down in an overstuffed chair. She turned toward the large glass window and looked below to the parking lot. She saw TV trucks and people standing around. They're just waiting for their chance to get a story, she thought.

Susan dialed her mother on her Droid.

"Mother, it's Susan."

"I was ready to step out the door to play Mahjong with my card-playing friends: Marie, Maddie, Barbara, Teresa and Ida . . . why'd you call me?"

Susan tapped her fingers on the arm of the chair impatiently, with her eyes closed, waiting for her mother to finish her litany. "I have some news far more important than your card game. Aunt Laura's been found."

"Oh, where was she found?"

"Mother, she's been murdered."

At first, there was silence on the other end of the phone. "What? Laura's been murdered? Oh my! That's absolutely terrible. When did this happen? Who did this? What did . . . ?"

Susan interrupted her barrage of questions with a quick answer. "I'll let you know all the details as soon as I can. I wanted to call you before you saw it on TV."

Virginia's voice cracked as she tried to talk, then Susan heard her mother sobbing. It was one of the few times Susan had heard her mother express any emotion.

"I'm sorry, Mother, but I have to go now. I'll call you later." She left the hospital, jumped into Jonathan's Bronco and drove to her bookstore.

***

"Hello, Kirkland Somers? It's Jonathan Fox. I want to speak to you about my wife, Laura. Is Annie there with you?"

"No, she's in the hospital. I can tell her you called when I go over."

"Please don't. I have terrible news to tell you and. . . ."

"I know what you're going to say," Kirkland interrupted, "and I appreciate your calling us at such an arduous time. Annie always hoped for the best but she suspected the worst after Laura had been gone for months."

Catching his breath and trying to hold back tears, Jonathan said, "Kirkland, she was murdered."

"What? I didn't think you'd tell me that. When did it happen? I better figure out a way to tell Annie right away."

"The police are gathering more evidence right now and will tell me more as soon as they can. My niece, Susan, told me they found a body in a pet cemetery. Some of the things they found are Laura's I'm sure. It might speak loudly that whoever did it is connected to the stables. Just a guess. . . ."

"Please keep me posted on any new developments, Jon. May we offer our deepest condolences? Let me know when you make the arrangements for her service. If Annie's well enough, we'll both be there. I hope they get the person who did this to her. Take care, Jonathan."

CHAPTER 41

A person' true character is revealed when he's drunk.

At a small bar on the south side of Miami, Franky Alvarez sat hunched over his glass of Bacardi Gold. Neat. He enjoyed the taste of rum and usually only had a couple, but today he was on his third glass without a thought of stopping any time soon. Last night had been just as bad. What was I thinking, he mused as he straddled the stool.

When he saw the newsflash come over the TV at the bar, his mind was rattled for a moment. Once that body in Big Blue's grave's positively identified, the cops, or Fox, might put two and two together, he thought as he took a large swallow of rum. He continued drinking heavily into the evening. What a fool I was to get involved with bribery. I just didn't have a choice. My sister needs the money I send. She means the world to me and she deserves some happiness. Without money that jerk she's married to would divorce her in a heartbeat and she would have nothing. I couldn't allow that. I had to do it.

With his mind blurred by drink, Franky remembered the telephone call he'd made the night before. Drink does make you stupid. Why the heck would I try to blackmail a murderer? This whole thing was an accident but it was still murder and I'm an accessory, like it or not. Franky's mind sloshed in his skull.

He broke out in a cold sweat. I have to get out of town by tomorrow, but where will I go? I can't sponge off my friends much longer. I can't find a job and I'm broke. After this visit by Walsh's ape, I'm afraid for my life. I just want enough money to get to another country. What a terrible mistake I've made.

Franky staggered out of the bar. He headed in the direction of his friend's house. Weaving along, he stayed close to the stores in an outside strip mall, often leaning on them to help him keep his balance.

Franky never saw the man behind him. He didn't have time to think. The man held his head and the razor sharp knife slit his throat. It was over in a flash. Franky lay in a pool of blood as the killer slipped away in the darkness.

CHAPTER 42

Sip some wines but with others, drink the whole bottle.

Susan finished at the bookstore and headed home. She pulled into her driveway and slowly got out of the Bronco. Her mind was still in turmoil as she searched in her purse for the keys to open her door. Dropping her purse and Jonathan's keys onto the table in the foyer, she went into the kitchen and opened the refrigerator. She reached for the bottle of Chardonnay and poured the cold, crisp wine into a glass then walked into the living room and sank into the soft pillows on her couch.

"What an awful day," she said to the empty room. "I can't believe all that's happened." She took several sips of wine and then steeled herself before turning on the TV. There it was . . . **BREAKING NEWS: HUMAN REMAINS FOUND AT OUR PET'S HAVEN CEMETERY.**

The commentator reported that the remains of an unidentified woman had been found in the same grave as the horse, Big Blue, a Thoroughbred which was owned by Jack Walsh, a prominent stable owner. He then speculated on the fact that Laura Fox, wife of Jonathan Fox, another well-known horse owner, went missing about the same time that Big

Blue was buried. Walsh, the stallion's owner, refused to comment to the press. Jonathan Fox, who was at the scene, had been taken to CentraState Medical Center before the body was uncovered.

Susan shut off the TV, finished her wine and poured a little more into her glass. I can still hear Mother's sobbing, she thought. This must be hard for her. And poor Uncle Jon, he has such pain in his eyes when he looks at Laura's picture. She took a sip of wine and thought about her aunt. How I wish I could have known her better. I've got to give Tony a call, she thought. He can tell me what to do next to help find the person who did this.

Susan dialed Tony's cell phone and spoke softly after the beep. "Tony, have you seen the news? Are you available? Get back to me; I need you."

Susan finished the wine and pulled herself together. My day is done, she thought. I'll head over to the hospital in the morning to check out Jonathan and get him settled back at his home. I'm exhausted and I'm going to bed.

The following morning, Susan woke to the sun streaming in the bedroom window. She smiled for a moment enjoying the beautiful October morning and then remembered the events of the day before. She bounded out of bed and went into the kitchen to brew some coffee. I need some caffeine, she thought. Next, she called the hospital to check on Jonathan and learned he would be discharged later in the morning. She turned on the TV in the kitchen. There was nothing new. The police hadn't given a final statement yet on their findings, Jack Walsh hadn't spoken with the press, and no reporters had been permitted in Fox's room.

Susan poured herself a cup of coffee, drank it quickly and put the empty cup into the dishwasher. I'll take a quick shower and get to the hospital early, she thought. I know I'll have to dodge reporters in order to get Jonathan back to his home.

An hour later, Susan arrived at the hospital. There were several news trucks in the parking lot. She parked a distance from them and kept her eyes averted as she headed to the main lobby and walked to the elevators. One burly-looking reporter hailed her and started asking questions. "No comment," she said. He tried again. "No comment." Finally the elevator door opened and she stepped inside. The reporter looked annoyed as Susan stared directly at him and repeated, "No comment."

Dr. Santos was with Jonathan, signing his release form, when Susan walked into the room. He went over medications with him and advised him that he had to follow his orders. He emphasized that the next time something happened he might not get through it as well. Susan heard the doctor say, "Diabetes is not something to play with."

Susan waited for him to finish, then asked, "What do we do about the press in the lobby and in the parking lot?"

"I recommend that you go through the emergency room. Get the car and I'll have Jonathan waiting for you. This way you can avoid the main hospital area. Hopefully, he'll be home before members of the press get wind of it."

Susan followed the doctor's suggestions and both of them were on the road without having to endure endless questions from the press.

Jake met the Bronco as soon as Susan pulled up to the house. He assisted Jonathan into the living room and settled him into his easy chair.

"You still need to get some rest, Jonathan. I heard what the doctor told you, and now, with the police investigation opening up again, you need to keep your strength up. You don't need a relapse," Susan told him in her soft voice.

"Everything is under control here too, Boss," Jake stated. "Listen to the lady and take care of yourself."

After complaining to both of them, Jonathan gave in and leaned back in the chair. "Susan, please turn on the TV. I need to know what's going on."

Susan picked up the remote, turned on the TV and both watched in shocked silence as the newscaster read the startling announcement. **"We have just learned that the body of a murdered man** found this morning, in Miami, Florida, has been positively identified as Franky Alvarez, a well-known jockey. Alvarez worked for Jonathan Fox, of the Fox and Hound Stables, until recently. This comes on the heels of finding the body of Laura Fox in the same grave as the famous Thoroughbred 'Big Blue'. Folks, what is going on in the racing world?"

Jonathan was the first to speak. "Franky? I can't believe it. He was a good man. I guess I went a little crazy the day 'Catch' lost. First Laura, and now, Franky." Fox shook his head and looked over at Susan.

"Why don't I check on Joe Boulder and see what he's doing," Susan suggested. "I told him I'd touch base with him today. I bet he knows more than those newscasters. I'll call him on the way back to my store and check with you later."

It was 4 p.m. when Fox woke at the sound of rapping on his front door. Hope it's someone with food, he thought. He went down the hall to the foyer and saw two men dressed in suits standing on the porch.

"Jonathan Fox?"

"That's right."

"I'm Rob Stallings and this is Stewart Kraft from the Medical Examiner's office."

"Come in." Fox said as he shook their hands. "What do you have to tell me? I've been in limbo for a couple of days."

"Well sir. This is still a bit preliminary since there are lab procedures being done, but we can give you a little heads up on some findings." Stallings opened a briefcase on his lap and took out several papers. "The coroner confirmed that the bones in the horse's grave at the cemetery were indeed human remains. The dental record matches that of your wife, Laura Fox. It will take six to eight more weeks before all the testing is complete. Dr. Dinberg said the cause of death appears to be blunt trauma to her skull."

Fox stood up, walked to the front window in the living room and gazed out. When he turned around, he appeared calm but stated in a hoarse voice, "I'll see that whoever did this meets his match." He wiped his hand across his eyes.

"Well as I said, Mr. Fox, we don't have many answers just yet."

Kraft motioned for Fox to reseat himself. "Another thing sir, there were some items found—a gold-colored ring and the remains of a blouse with F&H on the pocket confirmed to be your wife's also. There was also a leather boot and a boot strap found too. Her blood was found on a blue tarp under some bones."

Fox held his head in his hands and mumbled, "My sweet Laura."

Stallings shuffled the papers to get Fox's attention. "We have some more work to do and will get all of the information filed. In the meantime, the police will be talking to you. Did you get copies of the death certificate from the funeral director?"

"Yeah, I have copies here somewhere. I've decided to have Laura cremated when you're done processing or whatever it is you guys do."

"We'll keep in touch as we proceed. Sometimes it can take six to nine months depending on circumstances. This office will inform the police as we get more work done."

The men stood up and walked out to the hall. "Sorry we had to tell you this. You have our condolences."

Fox closed the door and punched his fist into the wall to his right. "Now I guess I talk to the police and see what comes next."

CHAPTER 43

Shafts of pale amber sunlight fell across the reddening October trees.

The four stablehands at the Fox and Hound Stables, Scott, Jake, Jim and Cody, stood under the old oak behind the barn as they always did on their late afternoon breaks. The air was unusually warm for October and the expanse of the tree branches gave good shade. The tree was their water cooler-a gathering place to talk and complain. Each man had heard about Laura Fox's murder on the nightly TV news or on their truck radios.

Jake opened a pack of chewing tobacco and stuffed a wad into his mouth. He had a habit of chewing when he talked about something disturbing. "Fox's gonna be a changed man without the missus. Not sure anyone is surprised after all these months; Fox may have had an inkling about things. It's a damn shame, because she was one great lady."

"You know what I heard? Susan, her niece, offered her DNA if the police needed it for identification," Scott said as he lit a Marlboro.

Jim was quick to add, "I heard that Laura had a sister, but no one seems to know much about that."

"Yeah, that's Susan Jeffries' mother. I understand they were gonna use dental records since that's quicker than DNA," Jake said.

Scott listened intently to the comments then said, "You know what? Someone broke into Fox's office. It happened a while ago. That's all I know."

Cody tapped his foot against the tree as he waited to speak, "Something else, not only was Laura murdered, but I read online that Franky Alvarez was found stabbed to death in Miami. Wonder why. He was a swell jockey and we all liked his quiet and friendly manner."

"When Franky worked a horse on the track, he'd lean forward, as far as he could so he could talk into the horse's ear," Jake said. "Ever notice that?" After a brief pause, Jake concluded, "He was one of the best."

"Yeah, he was. They haven't found much information about the reason he was murdered. It was reported that Franky had been drinking a lot," Scott said sadly. "They also knew about him losing the Belmont. News travels fast. I think that really ruined his reputation. He probably couldn't get another job as a jockey."

"Wonder what Franky planned to do in Miami once he left Jonathan's stables," replied Jim. "Maybe he wanted to return to his family in Cuba."

There was silence now underneath the old oak tree. Each man was deep in thought. Jake turned his head as he spat on the ground.

Jim cleared his throat and said, "Fact is, that two people from Fox and Hound Stables were murdered."

"Yeah," Scott said as he took a final drag on his cigarette. "Makes you wonder if there's a connection between the two. This whole thing makes me curious."

CHAPTER 44

People who are angry may not be very wise.

Later in the evening, the tall man's phone rang with a jarring tone. I wish they'd put ring tones on all the phones, he thought. As he picked up the receiver, he glanced at the caller ID for a second wondering if he should answer.

"Yeah? I told you not to call me here. We're not supposed to make contact, and you're using your own phone? Can't you get this into your thick head?"

"They found her body or what's left of it. I feel so damn bad. All this for a race? She didn't deserve it."

"Whoa . . . ya got to get it together. If we keep quiet there's no way they can pin it on either of us. You made damn good money too. What I want to know is why'd you kill Franky? Killin' Laura 'twas . . . an accident, right? You didn' mean to hit her that hard, right? Ain't that right? Then, why'd you kill Franky? And don't tell me you didn' do it!"

"Okay you moron, he had to be shut up. He was tryin' to blackmail us."

"What do you mean us?"

"You're in this up to your eyeballs and you'll be in prison for life as an accomplice. Maybe even for murder."

"It will be my word over yours. Now get off the phone and don't call me again. If my name gets into the wind, you'll be as good as dead."

The drunken man ended the call and poured another drink. We have to be quiet. No one would listen to us anyway.

The caller hung up the phone. That guy has never shown any remorse for what happened, he thought.

CHAPTER 45

Do not accuse a man for no reason, when he has done you no harm.

The day after Fox's release from the hospital, Susan sat drinking her morning coffee and thought about Jack Walsh. I'd never seen him until the day he showed up at the pet cemetery. His size and burliness really made me feel uncomfortable. I know from the way he talked that he meant business. He spat out his words like an angry cat. Susan's cell phone rang.

"Hello Jonathan. Are you up already? What happened to the doctor's order to rest?"

"Got a lot on my mind Susan. First thing, before I get nabbed by those reporters, I want to go over to see Jack Walsh. Don't try to talk me out of it either. I want you to come along sort of like my sidekick, if you don't mind."

"Well, I have to get over to my bookstore at least by noon today. What are your intentions? Did you find anything in those files I gave you at the hospital?"

"Nothing but a list of Walsh's wins at Monmouth Park Racetrack and names of his jockeys and the horses. Laura kept track of his purchases of stables in Ohio and Maryland too. There's competition buying horses and he always wants to be ten steps ahead of the rest of us. I want to find out for myself what he knows."

"Okay, Jonathan. I'll get ready. You can pick me up in an hour."

"Good. See you soon."

Fox laid down his cell and grabbed his morning coffee. *She's turned out to be a rather nice young woman. Doesn't act at all like her mother*, he thought. *She's a lot like Laura.* He put his cup down sharply on the table. "I'm getting some information out of Walsh if I have to strangle it out of him, I promise you Laura," he said aloud.

An hour later, Fox and Susan headed for Upper Freehold. He knew the road to Shore Thing Stables. His friend, Chuck Ayers had held poker games in the back of the main stable for many years before Jack Walsh won the stables and Big Blue in one of the games. Fox missed his friend. Ayers had a good sense of humor, a sharp tongue and, even though he looked like Napoleon, he never had a complex.

"Yoo hoo, Jonathan," Susan said in a quiet tone of voice.

"Oh yeah, sorry, I was just thinking about a friend who used to own this place." Fox pulled his Bronco into the lot beside the first stable and saw Walsh's truck parked on the side.

"Here we are. Let's check the barn first. Walsh boasts about how he lends his guys a hand getting the horses out in the morning. We'll see how good his talk is."

The two of them walked side by side into the barn. The hay smelled sweet and the inside floor was newly swept.

"He keeps a clean house so to speak," Susan said.

There was a small room toward the back where a light shone through the entry. Fox walked swiftly toward it and saw Walsh sitting at the desk. He had his head in his hands.

"Say there Walsh," Fox called in a loud voice.

"What are you here for? You're supposed to be in the hospital."

"So you think. Is that all you have to say? Isn't there an explanation you owe me?" Jonathan leaned both hands on the desk and bent over in front of Walsh, the spittle from his mouth landing on Walsh's face.

"Don't start with me," Walsh shouted. "I don't know anything. Why aren't you talking to the police and getting this solved?" Walsh stood up and saw Susan standing behind Fox. "What did you do? Bring her here for protection? Look man, I don't like you or her either," he continued, glancing in Susan's direction. "The only straight fact here is that I built a memorial for my horse and it's been desecrated." He moved his chair away from the desk and sat back down.

"Okay, tell me who had a hand in this . . .this monument," Fox yelled. "Surely someone helped you put Big Blue there. You had to make the arrangements. Who'd you tell that you had a fresh grave?"

"What do you mean? What are you implying?"

As the two men faced one another, Susan saw movement outside the office. A man with a long scar on his face stood at the door staring at Walsh. Susan looked directly at him. I've seen that face before, she thought.

"Hey Walsh, get out here quick. I think there's trouble with Have Faith; she's down."

CHAPTER 46

Moral indignation permits envy to be acted on in the guise of virtue.

Fox followed Walsh outside. Geez, this may be bad, he thought. I know how it feels when a horse goes down. He looked at the gathering of men. Walsh's horse, Have Faith, stood among them snorting and shuffling her right front foot on the ground.

Walsh stroked his nose to calm him.

"Whoa there, girl," he soothed. "Anybody here know what's happened? Lift up that leg and look at the shoe."

Two stablehands lifted the horse's leg and the men saw that the shoe had loosened. "We just put these shoes on her the other day. Must not have been a good fit," one of the hands said. He picked at it a moment and extracted a stone that had lodged under it. "Here's the trouble; this was imbedded in her foot," he said tossing a small stone onto the ground.

"Take her back to her stable and get her checked out. Get me the name of the guy who put it on her. I can't race my horses with slip-shod shoes." Walsh's tone of voice sharpened with each word.

"Get going . . . we can't stand around wasting time." Walsh turned to re-enter the building.

Fox stood waiting and followed him inside. "Sorry to see that, Walsh." Fox didn't say anything else until he stood in front of Walsh. "You know Jack, we're not finished here. I want some real answers. I don't care about your feelings. I'll be talking to the police later today and I'll get the real facts on what they found over at the cemetery. Then I'll be back. Don't think for one minute that you're off the hook here. You've been messing around in my business that's for sure. You brought my Laura here and dumped her body in a horse's grave." Fox's face reddened and he grabbed the front of Walsh's shirt and pulled him into his face. "And get this, you jerk, when the truth comes out you'll be dumped in prison. We're leaving." Fox shoved him backward and Walsh fell onto the desk top.

Susan and Fox were silent during the ride back to Manasquan. Susan's mind never strayed from the image of the man whose eyes she'd seen somewhere before.

Fox parked his Bronco in her driveway and she opened the passenger door.

"Bye, thanks for. . . ."

"Susan, sorry I dragged you over there. I needed someone with me to keep me from killing him." Jonathan gave her a crooked grin and continued, "I'll wait for the cops before I do that again, but I do need answers."

"Uncle Jonathan, I'm on your side. I'm all you have now and I'll help you in any way I can." She got out and turned away fighting back tears.

As the Bronco pulled away, she reached for her cell phone. "Chelsea hi, I'll be in there in a while. Everything okay? . . . Good. I have something to check on here then I'll come in and fill you in." She went inside the house and entered the dining room. She reached for the stack of family photos on the table and pulled out the one with Laura and her first husband. "I knew it, I knew it! Ted Watson. Those eyes." Susan said, as she held the photo and walked to the window. "There, there it is, that scar on his face and the tattoo on his arm."

Susan went into the kitchen, poured a cup of leftover morning coffee and placed it in the microwave. Is Ted Watson working at Walsh's stables? she thought. Had he been stalking Laura? Susan carried her coffee into the dining room and sat at the table. Her hand shook as she picked up the photo again and stared at Ted Watson. Aloud she said, "My mind just won't quit." Her cell phone rang, "Oh hi, Chels, yep I'm coming . . . . A weird-looking lady? Yes, I know who you're talking about. Try to keep her there. I'm on my way."

When Susan arrived at the bookstore, Chelsea was standing with Wanda Lubowski, the psychic who had told Susan to check on Big Blue. The two were standing by the self-help section of books and giggling.

"Well you two sure look like you're having fun. Let me in on it."

"Oh hi Susan," said Chelsea. "Wanda just told me the funniest joke and I can't stop laughing."

"Hi Wanda, what's the joke?"

"Are you ready? A frog telephones the Psychic Hotline and is told: 'You are going to meet a beautiful young girl who will want to know everything about you.' The frog says, 'That's great! Will I meet her at a party, or what?' 'No,' says the psychic. 'Next semester in her biology class'." With that, the two started laughing again.

"Cute," said Susan. "What brings you by again? I hope you haven't had any more vibes about my family."

"Oh no, Susan, nothing like that. It's just that I was in the neighborhood and want to thank you again for letting me use your phone when I had that flat tire. And I'm also curious as to how your situation is progressing. Have you figured out what's happened to your aunt?"

Susan told Wanda everything that had happened. "But the police still don't know who killed her, and there were several items found where she had been buried. We can't figure out their significance. Say . . . do you think you could help with that?"

"I'm willing to give it a try," said Wanda.

"Oh that's great. I'll call the detective in charge and see what we can arrange. I hope he's open to working with you."

"Me, too," said Wanda. "You can never tell. Sometimes the cops are agreeable to help and sometimes they think I'm just a nut."

"You know the old saying," chimed in Chelsea. "Sometimes you feel like a nut . . . ."

"Chelsea!" Susan and Wanda said in unison.

CHAPTER 47

We need to realize that our enemies are in disguise, they could be right under our eyes.

Pete Carter had the day off from Fox and Hound stables and decided to look up Susan Jefferies. He parked his truck in the lot near Sal Catalano's restaurant.

It was noon and the lunch crowd had started to file in. Sure seems like a popular place, he thought as he entered the restaurant. A young waiter, with his arms full of menus, greeted him.

"Hello sir, where'd you like to sit?"

Pete glanced around the large dining room and noticed a small, six-foot bar counter on the side. "Over there's okay. Sure looks busy in here."

"Yeah, we're always busy. Papa Sal does a good business. Say, I like your jacket. Hmm . . . Fox and Hound Stables, up there in Colts Neck. You work there?"

"Yep."

The waiter grinned and led him to the bar. "Here's a menu. Let me know when you're ready to order."

Pete removed his jacket and hung it on the back of his stool. He pored over the five-page menu anticipating the choices he had in front of him. Another guy sat down next to him. "You're new in here? Try Sal's special, it's good."

"Thanks."

Pete flagged down the waiter, ordered the special and a glass of red wine. Sitting back on the stool, he watched the door. I hope Susan comes in, he thought. She has such pretty auburn hair and green eyes. I remember the day we drank wine together on the yacht. Seems like a million years ago.

A young girl with jet-black hair opened the door and spoke to the young man holding the menus. "Hey Vinnie, like what's doin'?"

A spark lit in Pete's brain and he unconsciously rubbed the back of his head. I've heard that voice before, he thought. Wasn't that the girl who hit me over the head in the back of Susan's store? I was lucky to escape that time. He listened to more of their exchange.

"I'm doing good, Chelsea. Haven't seen you on campus lately."

"Like, I'm there every evening. Right now, I've come to get some take-out. Ms. Jeffries is in the store today for a few hours so I offered to get lunch."

"You want the usual then . . . pepperoni stromboli and . . . ."

"Like, you're right-on Vinnie, the usual."

Pete continued eating and watched the two friends standing closer to the bar bantering back and forth. Suddenly, he heard the girl speaking to him, "Like, mister, your jacket's sure nice. You work at the Fox and Hound Stables?"

Pete dropped his fork and looked at her. "You bet. I'm a stablehand for Jonathan Fox. You familiar with the stables? You ride?"

"No way, like, never even been on a horse." Chelsea looked in the direction of the kitchen as an apron-clad redhead brought her take-out order toward her. Chelsea continued, "Do you know anything about what's happened to Fox's wife? The news report this morning said they found her body. Like, my boss, Ms. Jeffries, knows Mr. Fox. Say, I've got to get back to the store. When you finish your food come on over. Susan might want to ask you some questions. Like, you see she's investigating her aunt's death."

"I might just do that, young lady. Thanks."

Chelsea sauntered to the door, waving goodbye to Vinnie.

Pete Carter finished eating, picked up the check and walked to the register. After paying the bill, he followed Chelsea's path to the door. He hiccoughed the taste of merlot into his throat. *I'm nervous as ever,* he thought. *Love makes saps of us all.* Once outdoors, he traced his own steps back to his truck. He wasn't ready to go to Susan's store yet.

After sitting for 15 minutes, he left his truck, walked toward the building and opened the front door.

"Who's there? Lunchtime," squawked Nicky.

Pete pretended to be interested in the display of mystery books in the window. I've never read one of these in my life, he thought. Not wanting to attract too much attention to himself, he walked into the tearoom addition and sat down at a lone table next to the window.

"May I get you some water? Everything is set up but we're not open for business yet."

Pete looked up. "Susan, it's nice to see you again."

Susan Jeffries jumped at the sound of his voice. "Have we met before? What did you say? Who are you?" She looked directly at him and stepped back.

Pete chuckled. "I'm Pete Carter, ma'am. I'm a stablehand over at the Fox and Hound Stables."

"You're not Carter. You're Paul, Paul Thomas. Why are you here? Get out or I'll . . . ."

"Wait Susan, please wait. Give me a chance to talk. I'm not here to cause you any trouble. I just want to explain . . . ."

"Explain what? That you're on the run?"

"No, I sent that note to you about your aunt and Big Blue a few weeks ago. I overheard a telephone conversation out at the racetrack and put two and two together. I thought you should know."

Susan saw that Pete, or rather Paul, was determined to stay. She sat down across from him at the table. Her hands trembled and she fought the tears which welled in her eyes.

"Just listen to me, Susan. Fox is a good guy and a good boss. He doesn't know who I really am or anything about my past. He hired me in his stables and that's that but . . . I've heard a lot of talk going on and I just want you to be safe. You know I want to be your friend. I never got you out of my mind; that's why I came back. I told you I would."

Susan sat forward and looked Paul straight in his eyes and said, "I thought you were gone from my life. You should have stayed away from here. You don't belong in Manasquan or in the United States. You're a menace and your disguise didn't fool me for long. Get out of my bookstore or I'll call the police." Susan stood up, walked to the back of the bookstore and slammed the door.

Paul stood up as Susan went out then bent down to scribble on a napkin that was lying on the table.

I never thought Susan would recognize me especially so soon after we met. I remember Susan's beauty. It was a jolt to his ego that she had become irritated with his presence. He hadn't planned on that kind of reaction.

Paul walked back to his truck thinking, I can't believe that Susan really saw through my disguise. I messed up big time. A good disguise was always part of my job; I was good at it. What should I do now?

CHAPTER 48

Restore normalcy with a cup of tea.

"Susan," Chelsea said in a cheery voice as she entered the kitchen in the rear of the bookstore. She saw Susan sitting at the table holding her head in her hands. Chelsea had heard Susan talking loudly with Paul in the tea room. "Hey, you're trembling. Like those are some juicy tears! Chill out. I'll make some tea. Tell me anything you want. Lean back in your chair and catch some quiet vibes."

"Thanks Chels," Susan managed to mutter in between her tears of anger. "I'd love the tea and I really do need to pull myself together."

"Yeah, whatever you want, Susan. I'll take care of the store until time to lock up."

Susan sat for a while thinking about her encounter with Paul. I thought he was gone for good. How could he have sought me out and think he could fool me with a disguise? I know he'll be back; he's not finished with me yet. There have been so many upsetting incidences lately and now this. I'll close early, go home and call Tony. He'll know what to do.

Chelsea went back into the tea room and cleared the table of the rumpled napkin and glass of water. As she reached for the napkin, she noticed writing on it. She read the words and held her breath. I hate to hand it to her now, she thought. She's too upset. Chelsea put the napkin in her pocket and finished straightening up.

"Chelsea, can you count the money and put it into the leather pouch?" Susan asked.

"Sure Mrs. J. You turn out the lights and I'll meet you out front."

After they left the building, Chelsea followed Susan home thinking, I've got to be sure she's safe. I'll give her the napkin tomorrow.

An hour later, Chelsea called Susan from her cell. "Yo. What's up? Feeling better? Did you make something to eat? Can I come over to give you some help?"

"Oh Chels, I'm so glad you called. I'd love to have your company. Want some mac 'n cheese? It tastes better if you can share it with someone. Come over as soon as you can."

"Like, I'm already here. I followed you home. Open up after three knocks."

Susan welcomed Chelsea as though she hadn't seen her for a long time.

"Glad to see that you got your face back. I worry big time about you."

After some small talk while eating, Chelsea couldn't stand the note burning in her pocket. "I . . . a . . . like found this on the table in the tea room."

She slid the note slowly across the table. "Sorry I didn't speak up sooner but you were so upset."

"Don't worry about it Chels, you were just using good judgment," Susan interrupted. She opened the napkin and read: **I'll prove you wrong.**

"Did you read this, Chels?"

"Yeah, couldn't help it. Who wrote it?"

"That jerk, Paul Thomas. He changed his name to Pete Carter and disguised himself. Chels, promise to keep this conversation to yourself. Keep a look out for him. You'll recognize him I'm sure. I called Tony and left him a message but he hasn't returned my call. Hope he calls soon. In the meantime, I need to make some plans. Aunt Laura's memorial service is in two days and I need to talk to Jonathan.

"Okay Mrs. J. I'll be mum. Like it's time for me to split," said Chelsea. "Call me if you need me Susan; otherwise see ya tomorrow."

CHAPTER 49

Everything a man does is in question when there is suspicion about his motives.

Saturday morning Susan was determined to use her day off to look into her suspicion that the man she saw at Walsh's stable was Ted Watson. Susan's usual routine was to shop and clean her house. I haven't spent much time here this week though, she thought. I'll let go of routine today. She grabbed a yogurt, swallowed a mouthful of orange juice and picked up her jeans jacket. October mornings are chilly on the East coast. Susan programmed her GPS for Shore Thing Stables in Cream Ridge and set out on her mission.

Forty minutes later, she thanked the GPS voice, "You did a good job gal. Keep on, keeping on," she said laughingly.

The main gate, which she and Jonathan had driven through the day they visited Walsh together, stood open at 9 a.m. She didn't see anyone outside in the yards. She parked her car in the nearest lot and casually walked to the barn. Now what should I say if someone comes up to me, she thought. Something like, I'm here for riding lessons? Susan chuckled at her own suggestion and readjusted the purse strap on her shoulder.

In the next few seconds, she heard a clanging noise coming from inside the barn. She stopped abruptly as the door opened; a stablehand stepped onto the gravel. He was carrying four large tin cans that were banging together. The racket was deafening and echoed across the lot. He looked up at Susan and called out, "Mornin' ma'am. Nice day."

"Good morning sir. Yes, it's nice out this morning." He looks mellow, Susan thought.

"Kin I help you?"

"I. . . I'm looking for a man . . . ."

"I'll bet you are," he replied grinning. "There's Walsh here, he's the Boss. I'm Rudy. We've got Sprint and then there's Ted."

"A . . . that's a lot of men." Susan smiled and flipped her hair. "It's quiet here. They must have Saturdays off."

"Nope. They're about the place. What can I do for you?"

"Well . . . I'm looking for Ted. He was married to my aunt years ago . . ." Susan began, but as she spoke, Jack Walsh walked through the door.

Looking at Susan, he charged, "So, you're back. Did you bring the big Fox with you?"

Susan's stomach felt like rocks were tumbling inside. "No. Matter of fact, I'd like to speak to you," she said, speaking in a low and sexy tone.

Walsh looked at Rudy. "Get those cans over to Burnside. He needs them today, not tomorrow."

Susan hesitated then asked, "Ted Watson. Is he here? I thought I recognized him the day Jonathan and I were here. I have a photo and he's in it with my aunt. You know, he was married to her at one point." Susan opened her purse and pulled out the picture.

"Well, I don't know anything about that," Walsh said. "I hired him from some stables in Ohio. He's a hard worker."

"He has to be to do this kind of work," Susan agreed. "I understand he wanted to own prize horses years ago."

"Why are you asking me about Watson? What's your real purpose? Did Fox put you up to it?"

"Why would he do that?" Susan batted her eyelids and smiled.

"Because he'd like nothing better than to see me fail." Walsh was annoyed. He licked his lips and pressed them together. His hands moved constantly as he spoke. "You've no business snooping around here. Tell Fox not to make you do his dirty work." Walsh turned and stomped back toward the barn.

"Well, tell Ted that his ex-wife's niece was here to say hello," Susan yelled as she stood on her toes, craning her neck to see around him into the barn.

Susan glanced around to see if anyone had been listening to them talk but saw no one. She breathed in the stable air and decided she should leave.

When she approached her car door, she heard a loud hissing sound and saw that her front tire was rapidly deflating. Darn, now what should I do, she thought. Susan reached in her purse for her cell. I'll have to call AAA to come out here to fix it for me. I don't see anyone here who could help me. Gee, I wish I were brave enough to ask Walsh to help but I'm afraid he'll really toss me off his property and probably call the police on me for trespassing, she thought. She punched in the numbers to AAA and while she waited for an answer she detected movement and the sound of boots scraping in the dirt behind her. A stablehand approached her. "Hello miss, you okay? Need some help?"

Susan flipped her cell shut without waiting for an answer on the other end and looked up. "Hi. I guess I do. I have a flat tire. A . . .say, you're Ted Watson aren't you? I have a picture of you with my Aunt Laura."

"Don't know about any picture ma'am. I can get this fixed for you though. Open the trunk."

Susan unlocked the trunk and tried to talk with the stablehand again. "You work for Mr. Walsh here?"

"Yep, been here a long time. Don't see many pretty ladies around though. Why're you here so early on a Saturday? There ain't no riding lessons 'til afternoons."

Susan looked closely at Watson. A long time huh, she thought. As Ted knelt down to fix the tire, Susan saw the scar on his chin. Now what do I ask him? "Say, how long has it been since you saw my aunt, Laura Fox? You know she's been killed right?"

"No I don't. I work here at these stables and keep to my business. Maybe you should ask Walsh about whatever you're here for. I'm just fixin' your tire."

Within the next ten minutes the tire was swapped for the spare and Watson turned to walk back toward the barn. "No charge, lady. Have a nice day." He strode away leaving Susan standing next to her car with a lump in her throat and no information.

Susan started the engine and backed out of the parking space. She said softly to herself, "Boulder's got to come over and talk to Ted to see when he got here and why. I wonder why he didn't own up to being my aunt's ex?"

Susan drove through the gate.

CHAPTER 50

One may be lonely if one is different.

It was Sunday and Chelsea felt lonely. Living with her mom was okay most of the time but there were days like today when she needed to get out and talk with other people. The kind of people who hung out at Maggie's in Lakewood.

Chelsea liked Maggie's. It had a friendly atmosphere, good food and it was really three bars in one. There was the Tiki Bar, the Underground and the Uptown.

Chelsea's favorite was the Underground, sports bar by day and club by night. Today she decided to head there for a really juicy burger, a tall, cool brew and maybe some good gossip.

The jumbo screens scattered around the room flashed the action of baseball, football, soccer, and hockey. White text scrolled across the bottom of each screen so the patrons could see the scores and tell what was going on without having to relinquish bar talk or bar music. Today the music was louder than usual. Mannie, the head barman, took her order and plunked a tall brew down in front of her. Taking a long swig, Chelsea casually observed the others at the bar.

They were a colorful mix: forty-somethings just off the golf course, T-shirted studs just off their construction jobs and the occasional senior reliving a past life.

A man nudged Chelsea's elbow as he sat down next to her, smelling of fresh air, hay, and manure.

"Hey there," he said, flagging the barman, "I didn't think I'd know anyone here. How's it going?"

"Um, like do I know you?" Chelsea asked, thinking that this was just some pickup line and getting ready to give the guy the cold tattooed shoulder.

"Sure you do! I met you in Manasquan, and you even invited me to your store. Aren't you the chick who works for the Sandcastle Bookstore?"

I know why he looks familiar, she thought. He's the dude that made Susan so upset. Susan didn't say much about him, but anyone who gets under Susan's skin is no friend of mine. "Oh yeah," she said as she looked at him. "But I don't know that I should even look at you, never mind talk to you. You made my boss really upset that day."

"I guess I did. I didn't mean to. Actually, I've known her quite a while and I like her a lot."

"Well you got a funny way of showing it." Chelsea took a bite of the cheese burger that had been placed in front of her.

"My name's Pete, Pete Carter. What's yours?"

Chelsea ignored him and took another gulp of her brew.

"Hey! I'm talking to you." He reached out and touched her arm again.

Chelsea yanked her arm away and looked at him. Actually, he's kind of good looking, in an older man kind of way, she thought. "I already told you," she said, "I don't talk to people who upset my boss."

"What if I could tell you something about me that would change your mind?"

"Huh?" Chelsea put down the burger and picked up her beer. I could always dump it on him if he gets fresh, she thought.

"I met Susan right after her husband was killed."

"Murdered," Chelsea corrected him.

"Yes, murdered. I had some business dealings with his murderer, but I was not involved with his death."

"Then, what . . . ?"

"Yeah, I know it sounds kind of crazy. But I met Susan and fell in love with her then. She saw me as the enemy, but I wasn't. I left the states to let her cool off and came back a few months ago to see if I could convince her to become my friend."

"That's nuts," Chelsea said, taking another burger bite.

"I guess it seems that way. But I saw her just before I left back then. I went to her shop, but someone hit me over the head and called the police. I managed to escape them and get back to Venezuela. By the way, Pete Carter isn't my real name."

"I know. Susan told me."

Chelsea was beginning to remember that night in the shop: Susan had been arguing with a guy in the front part of the shop. Chelsea had grabbed her baseball bat and hit this guy over the head.

"OMG!" Chelsea said.

"What?"

"I remember that day. It was me who hit you on the head."

Pete grabbed her arm. "Just do me a favor. Listen to my story."

Mannie refilled their drinks. The bar was getting more crowded. This is a safe place, Chelsea thought, and maybe the information this guy gives me will help Susan. "Let her rip, Pete, or whatever your name is. This better be good."

"Well first, my real name is Paul Thomas. I live in Venezuela and own several businesses there. I knew Susan's husband even before she did. He and I dated the same girl and he took her away from me. I was friends with the girl's father and unfortunately I got involved with him in some drug trafficking and money laundering deals. I didn't think about if it was right or wrong. It was money for me and for her father.

"Susan's husband found out about one of our deals. My partner had Mark killed before he could turn us in, and I couldn't stop it. I felt so bad about his death that I made it my business to see if I could help his widow. But that backfired. She saw me only as the bad guy. And it's true, I'm not guilt free as far as those deals were concerned, but I didn't want anything to happen to Mark. That's what I was doing in the shop the night you clubbed me over the head. I wanted Susan to know the real truth, and also how I felt about her. But once I escaped from the police, I knew I just had to leave the country."

"But now you're back," said Chelsea. "What do you think's going to happen?"

"What I think is that I'm going to see if I can talk with Susan and get her to see my side of the story. I want her to see me for who I really am. And if I'm lucky . . ."

"Yeah?" asked Chelsea.

"If I'm lucky, the most beautiful, most faithful, and kindest woman in the world will hear my story and not hate me."

As Chelsea listened to Paul she thought, I'm beginning to believe this cockamamie story and actually starting to like this guy. "You'll have to have a lot of luck for that to happen," she told him.

"Yeah," he said, "and a friend to help me." He looked at her with raised eyebrows.

"Dude," she said, "so now you want me to be that friend? You must be kidding."

"No, I'm not kidding. I'm dead serious. Um, strike that. I mean really serious. Would you help me? I only want to talk to her. That's all. Honest."

Chelsea pushed her empty plate away and signaled to Mannie for the check. "I'll think about it," she said. "That's all I'll promise. Just to think about it."

Paul smiled warmly.

He has the kind of smile that worms its way inside me and wriggles right down to my heart, Chelsea thought. Surely thinking about it can't hurt. She returned his smile and stood up. "I've got to go."

"Wait," Paul said. "When can we talk again? How soon do you think you'll be finished thinking?"

"Don't know," she said. "I'll see you around." She gave him a little wave and walked out the door.

That wasn't the answer I wanted to hear, Paul thought. But I know where she works. At least she agreed to think about it. He paid his tab and sauntered out of the bar with a new lightness in his step.

CHAPTER 51

To weep is to make less the depth of grief.

When Susan arrived home from work on Monday, she picked up her cell and punched in Jonathan's number.

"Jonathan, do you have time to talk a little about Aunt Laura's memorial service. . . . Great, I ordered food from Sal's café next door . . . Yes. I've ordered enough for 100 people. All the pastries will be coming from there as well. Are you sure that will be enough? . . . Okay, I'm just checking. . . . Really? Kirkland says Annie will be able to come? That would have made Laura so pleased. I'm looking forward to meeting both her and her husband."

Susan listened as Jonathan continued to talk about the phone call he had received from Kirkland then said, "I'm glad you talked with him. I'll let you go now. Call me if you need anything else, otherwise I'll see you at the service tomorrow."

***

The morning of the service was perfect; the early October air was crisp and invigorating. Fall leaves dotted the lawn outside Susan's kitchen window. Susan sipped her coffee thinking about the day ahead. She knew her mother was flying in early to Atlantic City but would only be spending the day. I guess mother is still jealous of Laura and doesn't want to meet anyone up here, she thought. I wonder if Ted Watson will be at the funeral and I wonder if mother will recognize him. This should be interesting.

After finishing her coffee, Susan headed upstairs to dress. She looked at the clock. Wow, nine o'clock already, she thought. I'll have to hurry. She swiped her lips with gloss, put on a light-weight jacket and headed to her car.

Tony had called earlier and agreed to meet her at the funeral home and then go to the repast at the Fox and Hound. Boulder also called and told Susan that he planned on going to the repast and hoped to talk with Kirkland and Annie again; he had enjoyed his visit in Maryland and was still anxious about Annie's health.

Susan was curious to meet Annie Somers. She wanted to know so much more about her and her friendship with Laura. She imagined they had some good times together when they were younger.

Susan arrived at Muller's Funeral Home with fifteen minutes to spare and quickly went to the front to sit next to Jonathan. She gave him an affectionate hug and kiss then looked around the room. Her mother was sitting in the back row with her lips pursed and a sour expression on her face. Virginia didn't smile or nod when she saw her daughter. Well really, Susan thought.

Tony walked up to Susan and gave her a hug and smile that made her heart melt. She introduced him to Jonathan and the two men chatted for a moment. Susan was not fooled by Tony's casual demeanor; she knew he was assessing everyone in the room.

Several stablehands from various horse farms in the area stood in the far corner and Susan noticed Ted Watson among them. Boulder was standing with them speaking with Jake who had a sad look in his eyes.

A tall, attractive man walked into the room with a small fragile woman holding on to his arm. Everyone watched as Kirkland Somers brought his wife, Annie, up to Jonathan and seated her next to him. "Jonathan, I'm so sorry for your loss."

"Thank you, Kirkland." Jonathan looked at Annie with tears in his eyes. Annie glanced at the smiling picture of Laura on the table next to them and began to weep. "I'm so sorry, Jonathan. I wish there was something I could have done. I miss her so much. I know you do too."

"I loved her, Annie, and to think that the night before she disappeared we argued. It's eating me up inside."

"Jonathan, Laura would have forgiven you. She loved you too much to let an argument come between you. Don't let guilt about that night haunt you. Laura wouldn't have wanted that."

"Thanks, Annie. Now tell me, how are you feeling? How was your trip up to New Jersey? I hope it wasn't too much for you."

"Well, I'm doing a little better. The doctors don't understand why I'm not improving as quickly as they think I should be. I keep relapsing and having to go back to the hospital. They're trying to get to the bottom of it."

Annie turned when she felt a hand on her shoulder. It was Boulder. "Hello Annie, how are you doing?"

"Much better, Mr. Boulder. Nice to see you," she replied.

The Funeral Director stepped up to the podium and asked everyone to return to their seats so the service could begin. As the hymn, Amazing Grace, began to play, Susan's eyes welled with tears. The Pastor's words were a heartfelt testimony to Laura's sweet and generous personality. When the service ended, the Funeral Director invited everyone to go back to the Fox and Hound Stables for the repast.

CHAPTER 52

Confrontation can clear the air.

The repast was held on the patio alongside the grand Fox house. The yard was kept impeccably. In the distance, several Thoroughbreds grazed at their leisure. Small round tables and chairs were situated both inside and outside on the porch and patio. Susan greeted Sal who was busily overseeing the tables as well as the refreshments. "This really looks great, Sal. You've done a lot of work and everything is in perfect order. Jonathan told me he's pleased with the wonderful spread."

Family and friends were arriving, many seating themselves or gathering at the bar. Tony seated Susan and Annie at one of the small tables and brought them each a glass of wine. "Everyone looks comfortable. Is there anything I can get you? I'll send the waiter over with some appetizers. The food looks good."

"That would be nice, Tony," Susan replied. The waiter brought finger sandwiches and fruits to the table.

Tony wandered over to talk with Boulder; Susan slowly sipped her wine and watched the two men. She noticed that Boulder kept eyeing Annie while they talked. *He seems concerned for her,*

Susan thought. Glancing at Annie, she could understand why. Annie appeared pale and fragile. This trip must be a tremendous strain on her heart, Susan thought.

Jonathan's friends milled around, getting reacquainted and comforting one another. Susan noticed Walsh walking towards Jonathan. They engaged in a brief conversation. Walsh turned abruptly and walked away; neither man put out his hand.

Boulder sat next to Annie. "It's nice to see you again, Annie. Your drive from home must have been long and tiring."

"Oh hello again, Mr. Boulder. Everyone has been taking good care of me. I'm quite settled."

Susan greeted Boulder then excused herself and walked to the bar. She wanted to talk with Kirkland but she didn't see him. Probably inside the house, she thought. While Susan waited to be served her wine, Virginia walked up behind her. "Mother," Susan said. "How are you holding up?" Susan was shocked to see tears in her mother's eyes.

"Susan, I can't believe Laura's really dead. And murder! It just doesn't seem possible in this family. What had she gotten into?"

"Mother, we don't know yet, but Boulder is working on it. We'll get answers and I think very soon. Why don't you visit with Annie, she would appreciate that. This has taken such a toll on her mentally as well as physically."

"I'll do that Susan; maybe it's time to mend a few fences. First, I'll get another glass of wine."

Susan thanked the bartender, picked up her wine and scanned the crowd for Kirkland. She walked around the patio but didn't find him among those seated. Odd, she thought, I wonder where he went. Oh well, now's my chance to go to the barn and check the new foal Jonathan has been talking about. I haven't had a chance to see him, yet.

Susan wandered over to the stables and saw Kirkland standing in the doorway. When he looked up, he said, "Susan I'm surprised to see you over here. Is everything okay with Annie? You probably need a breather from all those people."

"Yes Kirkland I do, so I came over to see the new foal. But since you're here too, I'd like to talk with you about Annie. She's so sweet and we had such a nice talk. She told me that the doctors still can't find the reason for her relapses. She seems so frail and I can't believe the doctors gave her the go-ahead to make this trip."

"Susan, no one can stop that woman when she has her mind made up. Even the doctors told me it would be better for her to come here instead of fretting back home. However, she's getting weaker. Let's head back. It's time for her medicine, and I want to make sure she takes it."

As they left the stables, Kirkland grabbed hold of Susan's elbow and guided her toward the patio. They headed directly to Annie's table. She appeared more relaxed as she sat talking with Boulder and Virginia.

Virginia stood up as they returned, motioned to Susan and the two walked over to the edge of the patio. "I've got to have a cigarette," Virginia whispered. "I'm going over to the stables; do you want to come?"

"Mother, I hate the smell of cigarettes; besides, I just came from there. Here, let me hold your wine for you."

"No you don't. I want to take it with me and drink it in peace."

Virginia excused herself from the group and walked hurriedly across the yard toward the stables. She stood outside the main doorway, lit the cigarette and took several small puffs. After a few minutes, she crushed it in the dirt and poked her head in the doorway. She saw a familiar looking man standing by one of the stalls. That's got to be Ted Watson with that awful tattoo on his arm, she thought. He has that same face but he looks a little older. Virginia moved inside and approached him. "Is that you Ted? Ted Watson?"

"Yeah, it's me. Who wants to know?"

"So, this is how you elevated yourself in life-mucking horses? As I remember, you promised my sister Laura you would be the proud owner of a first-rate stable someday. How things have changed."

"You don't know anything about me. Besides, I don't work at these stables. So, shut up, you bitchy old lady."

"Who are you calling a bitchy old lady, Mr. Watson? First, I'm four years older than you and that doesn't make me an old lady without your being an old man. Second, you're the very reason Laura and I stopped talking to each other after she married you. Everyone knows you're a cheat with a bad temper and have a jealous streak in you. That's why Laura had stalking charges against you."

Though Virginia never got along with Laura, she disliked Ted. Now she was willing to defend her dead sister. Virginia continued to grill him. "You worked for my father and mother on their farm and they were good to you but you stole from them. Why are you such a low life?"

Ted Watson reached for his jacket which was hanging over the side of one of the stalls. "You don't understand anything. I loved Laura. She meant everything to me but she never trusted me after I took the money from your folks."

"You mean stole. You loved yourself more than you did Laura."

"I know I had faults back then but I still loved her."

Virginia stared at him. "Annie Somers told me you even tried to hit on her," she yelled.

Virginia's voice became louder and floated across the yard. Susan and several guests stopped talking when they heard the angry voices. Susan left the table and walked quickly across the yard and into the stables. "Mother, what are you doing in here? Who are you yelling at? This isn't the time or place to be arguing." Susan shook her head in disgust and noticed Ted standing there.

Virginia took her half-filled glass and tossed the wine in Ted's face. As he wiped his face, Susan and Virginia walked outside. "I was so surprised to see him standing there," said Virginia, "I had to give him a piece of my mind."

Virginia shook slightly and seemed unsteady on her feet after the ordeal. She said to Susan, "I'm getting out of here right now."

"Mother, you can't leave now. I drove you here, remember?"

"Give me the keys to your car and I'll drive myself back to your house."

Susan tightened her lips and blurted out, "You'll have to find someone to take you home, I'm staying. You've made a spectacle of yourself. Some of the other people heard you yelling too. I'm tired of trying to accommodate you. I'm going back to the guests. Goodbye."

CHAPTER 53

The medication can be worse than the illness.

It was a long day for Annie and she sat appearing more exhausted when Susan returned to the patio.

"Where's you're . . . umm . . . mother?" she asked softly.

Susan looked at Annie and thought, she seems a little confused. "Oh, mother's going back home angry as a hornet. She had a fight with a man in the barn." Susan reached for her glass and finished the remaining wine in one gulp.

"Susan, I'll go over to the barn and see what went wrong," said Kirkland. "But first Annie, it's time for your medicine. Actually we're a little late." All three looked up at him as he took two white capsules from a bottle in his pocket and handed them to her."

Annie smiled. "Thank you dear, you never forget." She took the medicine, picked up a glass of water from the table and drank it. Boulder looked up and saw a speculative look flicker in Kirkland's eyes.

Boulder and Kirkland exchanged a few words about the new foal. I'll have to get over to the barn to see him, seems like he's a hit, Boulder thought. "See you around Kirkland," he said and headed to the bar.

Ten minutes later, Boulder stood bantering with some of the stablehands at the bar when he heard Susan call out for help. He ran back to the table and saw Annie slumped forward. "Call 9-1-1" he said. Susan already had her phone in hand. "The ambulance is on its way," Susan shouted.

Boulder carried Annie inside to the living room couch and laid her down. Jonathan, Susan and Kirkland followed him. Boulder looked down into the pale, grey face. Annie's eyes were closed, her breathing was shallow, and when Boulder felt for her pulse her heart rate had definitely slowed. Boulder stood aside and let Kirkland kneel next to her. What's going on with Annie, Boulder thought. This is the second time I've seen her collapse soon after taking her medication. He smoothed the front of his jacket and straightened his tie. Odd, he thought.

The paramedics arrived, checked Annie's vital signs and lifted her into the ambulance. Kirkland climbed into the back and, as the vehicle pulled away en route to CentraState Medical Center, the siren sounded.

Boulder turned to Susan and Jonathan. "I've got something to look into. I'm sorry this has happened, especially on your sad day. I really have to take off, Susan. I'll keep in touch.

As he walked to his car, Boulder thought about Dr. Charles Kramer, his friend, who headed up the laboratory at CentraState. A while back, he had researched some background information for the doctor, and since then Dr. Kramer had sent him quite a few clients. The two acquaintances occasionally met at Monmouth Park Racetrack or at one of the Friday night poker games they both enjoyed.

Boulder tapped in the doctor's number on his cell. "Chuck, it's Joe Boulder. . . Nah, there isn't anything ailing me, but I have something interesting for you to check into. I think something serious is going on with a friend of mine and I'd like it if you could find out what's wrong. The woman, Annie Somers, is being transported to CentraState hospital as we speak. Annie collapsed a short time ago here at a repast at the Fox and Hound Stables. This is the second time I've been with her in the last few weeks and each time she collapsed after her husband gave her medicine. It's weird. And today I noticed a very strange look in his eyes as she took it. Do you think you can find out anything for me?"

"Joe it's a little hard for me to go to the emergency room to take a look at her unless they call me but I know they'll be drawing blood and doing an EKG. I can look at those findings. The lab tech will post the results in the computer, and if there is something way out of whack in her blood they'll want me to look at it anyway."

"Doc, Annie has a bad heart and has had surgery recently down in Maryland."

"That's good to know Joe. First thing they'll do is look at her electrolytes and enzymes. I'll be able to see what's up. The EKG may show something too."

"Thanks Doc, I really appreciate it. Call me back on my cell when you find out anything."

CHAPTER 54

A willow sways restlessly in a storm.

Susan was restless. She paced back and forth between the bar and the stack of tables being taken down. There was no word yet on Annie's condition. She looked toward the far side of the patio and saw her mother holding a glass of wine in her hand while trying to light a cigarette. Oh Lord, she thought. Susan crossed the patio to Virginia. "I thought you were going home."

"I'm waiting for you. Besides, y-you have the k-keys."

"Mother, sit down here before you fall. You've had enough to drink." She reached out to take the glass.

"No, no, no you don't." Virginia held the glass by the stem and gulped the remaining wine.

"Mother, please sit here and don't move until I come back."

Virginia leaned her elbows on the table and rested her head between her hands. "Okay, okay."

Susan stepped in front of her mother to block her from being seen by Jonathan's lingering guests. She saw Jonathan standing on the other side of the patio. He looked comforted by his friends' attention. It was a good idea having the repast at the stables where so many people could connect with their memories of Laura, she thought. As she turned to check on her mother, Tony approached her and grabbed her arm. Susan looked up and smiled. "Where have you been? I've missed you." She slipped her hand into his.

Tony's eyes caressed Susan before he responded. "I've been at the stables; the foal is simply beautiful. While I was there, Kirkland and Watson came in. They didn't see me at first, so I continued watching the foal for a while. I recognized Watson from the picture you had on your dining room table. He hasn't changed much."

"Yes, so I've noticed."

Tony squeezed her hand and said, "Sorry Hon, but I have to leave now. I got a call from the Captain at the station. Don't know when I'll see you next, but you know I'll be back as soon as I can." Tony pulled Susan behind the large oak tree which bordered the patio and gave her a long kiss. "Take care of things. Don't get yourself in trouble while snooping around."

CHAPTER 55

Information is not the same as knowledge.

Paul watched the ambulance leave Fox's home. He headed to his room at the stables and dug out his laptop computer. He kept it hidden in a duffel bag under his cot. After logging in, he pulled up some of Boulder's files that one of his contacts had sent him. He saw the notations Boulder had made regarding his visit to Annie Somers. He read that she collapsed shortly after taking meds given to her by her husband.

Paul logged off. He replaced the computer, left the stables and approached the backyard of the house. The caterers were cleaning up the remaining tables and many of the remaining guests were standing in small groups saying their goodbyes. Paul strolled over to Jake. "Hey man, anything extra you want me to do?"

"Did you get Red Fox's stall mucked? He sure can kick up the straw in there."

"I did it while everyone was eating. By the way, we had a few people come in to see 'Laura's Boy'."

"Yep, sure is a dandy foal," Jake said.

"What happened to that woman? I heard some talk...."

"She collapsed. The Boss was really upset as if it wasn't enough with his wife and all."

"Does Fox know her well?"

"He and the missus were close to her; she was the missus' best friend from when they were kids."

"So, are they staying here then?"

"Don't really know. I think Fox told me they would drive home tonight but now we'll have to wait and see. His car's still in the driveway. Everyone gave in their keys so the cars could be moved if need be. Mebbe you kin pull up Somer's car closer to the house so the caterers can leave. I'll git the keys for you."

"Sure enough, I can do that," said Paul.

Jake handed the keys to Paul and went back to the patio to help with loading the tables. He turned and yelled, "Hey Pete, it's the red Audi."

I'm glad my disguise still works with these guys at the stables, thought Paul. That's sure a nice ride, Paul thought when he approached the car. He opened the door, started the engine and drove to the side of the house out of sight of the backyard activities. Here's my chance to do some investigating. He looked under the seats, on the dash and in the arm rest. He found nothing but change and candy wrappers. Then, he tried the glove box. When he opened it, he saw a plastic-covered manual, a small leather envelope with registration and some insurance papers. On the bottom of the compartment, he noticed a large grey file envelope. It matched the interior of the car and he almost missed it. He removed the band and opened the envelope.

"Wow," Paul said aloud. Inside the envelope were at least one hundred betting slips from the Charlestown Race Track. The slips were in varying amounts but all of them were huge sums. The dates indicated they were from the past few weeks. Someone has a gambling problem, Paul thought. He took some pictures of them with his cell and then put them back.

Paul went around to the back of the car and opened the trunk. He noticed some dark stains in the wheel well. Could be nothing, he thought, but I'll take a photo anyway. He started to close the trunk when he spotted a lone white capsule in the fold of the loosened carpet. He took it and casually dropped it into his pocket. He checked to make sure he had locked the car doors and went back to the patio.

"Here's the keys, Jake. The car's on the side of the house. See you back at the stables."

Paul walked back to the barn and thought how glad he was that he had been in the right place at the right time. He had seen Kirkland and Ted Watson talking at the side of the barn earlier in the afternoon. They sure looked chummy but not overly happy, Paul thought. He also remembered seeing notes about both men in the files from Jonathan's office, indicating that they had met several years ago at the Virginia Derby in Colonial Downs in New Kent, Virginia. Funny, that was noted in the files, he thought. At least my trip to Jonathan's office proved informative. They seem to know each other well.

Something isn't right though; I feel the hairs going up on the back of my neck. I still have connections. I'll see if my friends can dig anything up on this Kirkland guy. My gut tells me there's something screwy going on and for Susan's sake I'm going to find out what it is. Anything I find out could put me in good with Susan.

CHAPTER 56

Numbing pain at night with drink lasts only until morning.

Jake limped through the Fox and Hound stable yard. Arthritis in his knee added to the constant pain of a war wound which had made one leg shorter than the other. He pushed open the door to his room, entered and closed it behind him. It was a small room—no bigger than a prison cell and very confining. He shoved the captain's chair he had rescued from Fox's dumpster to the rickety table that served as his desk and sat down. He pulled a small leather trunk from under the table and unbuckled the worn leather straps that kept the lid closed. He opened the trunk, revealing several notebooks, various medals and combat ribbons.

Jake rubbed one hand over his stubbly beard and massaged his aching leg with the other. He rummaged through the notebooks and pulled out a brown covered spiral notebook that was water stained and dog eared. Placing the notebook on the table, he shoved the trunk back with his foot.

"Fine kettle of fish," he muttered to himself. He opened the notebook and stared at the first page of scrawled writing. "My whole life is here in this book. Not much to speak of. Nobody to tell it to. No one who cares."

Getting up, Jake reached up to the wooden shelf nailed precariously to the wall and took down a pint bottle of Old Smuggler Scotch Whiskey and a water tumbler. He poured a two-finger measure of the golden liquid into the glass and downed it in one swallow. The heat of the drink burned his gullet on the way down and began to work its calming magic. After a few more swallows, Jake replaced bottle and glass on the shelf and plopped back down in the chair. Once again he picked up his notebook and started to read. His own story unfolded as he scanned the handwritten lines. Halfway through the book he found the words he was looking for.

I met Jonathan Fox in 1988 at the Monmouth Park Racetrack in Oceanport, New Jersey. I knew horses, and Jonathan wanted to open a stable. So we went into business together. Jonathan had the money and I had the horse sense. Before that I was a drifter, but once Jonathan bought the property and started creating his stables, I knew I had a home as long as I wanted. I owe him my life.

A tear oozed from the corner of Jake's eye and he closed the book. I owe him my life and now I've betrayed him, he thought. A knock at the door startled him and he shoved the book under the table.

"Who's there?"

"It's Joe Boulder, Jake. Can I come in?"

"It's not a good time Joe, but I'll be right there."

Jake opened the door and Boulder pushed his way in. "Listen, Jake, I'm trying to make sense of Laura's death and I thought you could help me."

"Me? What can I do?" asked Jake.

"You can help me sort out the facts here, and maybe together we can figure out what happened. What do you know about the day Laura disappeared? Did you see her that day?"

Jake hesitated. "N-no, I don't think so. I don't remember." His eyes shifted from side to side.

Boulder could tell that Jake was hiding something. How can I get him to open up, he thought. He spied the bottle of Scotch on the shelf and stood up. "Jake how about a snort between friends?" He took the bottle down, grabbed Jake's glass and a coffee cup that was also on the shelf and poured a good measure into each. "Let's drink to the future, Jake."

"We're friends, right Joe?" Jake asked after a few seconds. "Have a seat; I need to talk to someone."

"That's right buddy. What's going on?"

"I'm mixed up in some awful stuff and I don't know where to turn. I think I'm in big trouble."

"That sounds pretty serious," Boulder said. "Do you want to talk about it?"

"I don't want to, but I think I better. It's kind of a long story."

"I got the time."

"Well, here goes. I was in a real fix. I'd been gambling pretty heavy and I was into it big time. I'd been skimming some of the take from the races for a while. I mean, I meant to pay it back—all of it! Jonathan was my friend and I would never betray him. But between the booze and the money I owed, I was really in over my head. And then I heard that Mrs. Fox had discovered cash missing, and I panicked. The only way I could figure to pay it all back was to win big.

"The Belmont was coming up and everyone figured Fox's horse would win. So everyone would be betting on him. Walsh's horse would be the long shot. So if I bet heavy on Walsh's horse, and then could get Fox's horse to lose, my worries would be over. I figured Franky would go along with it and I'd share the take after I paid Fox back. But Franky didn't want any part of it. He said he wouldn't do it not even for me."

"But Fox's horse did lose," said Boulder

"Yeah, but it must have been legit."

"Well I think you need to tell Jon about the money you stole."

Jake was silent for a few minutes. Then he sighed. "I know you're right but I sure am ashamed."

"Well, just stay here, Jake, and I'll go get Jonathan. When we've talked this all out we'll figure out what the next steps are."

"Okay, Joe. I'll wait for you here."

Boulder left Jake's room and hurried to the house where he found Jonathan. After a brief rundown of what he had found out, Boulder brought Jonathan back to Jake's room, which was . . . empty.

"Gone," Boulder yelled. "He said he'd wait right here. He told me the whole story. He seemed ready to talk it all out. I never thought he'd run for it."

"Well, man," said Jonathan, "we better find him."

CHAPTER 57

One sip of this will soothe the tired spirit.

Jake was intoxicated. Scotch was his favorite drink and he had consumed too much in a short period of time. He tucked the pint bottle in the pocket of his vest. Gotta get out of here and take a walk, he thought. I don't want to talk to no one.

Behind the stables was an overgrown fire road which led to an old abandoned barn. Jake walked there occasionally to enjoy the clean, clear air of the forest. The unevenness of the road caused him to stumble but he continued to walk as fast as he could. When he came to the site of several large trees, he turned into the woods and walked to a familiar pine. There was a special spot at the base of the tree where he could sit on the cool earth and do some serious thinking. No one would ever find him since it was several yards from the road.

Boulder's steaming mad by now; he'll probably call the cops, Jake thought. Wonder what Fox thinks about all of this. Now he knows I let him down big time. I'm so damned ashamed. I could never control my gambling habit and the episode with Franky really made a mess of my life. How can I live it down? Jake pulled out the pint and emptied it in two swallows. He leaned against the rough bark on the pine tree, slid to the ground and fell asleep.

When he awoke, it was dark. "I feel like I'm gonna heave and I have a rotten headache. It's been a long time since I've felt this bad. Gotta git back to the stables; mebbe the crew is gone and nobody'll see me."

Jake tramped back along the road sidestepping the deep ruts. When he reached the stables, he saw no one. Thought there'd be a cop car parked here, he mused. A chill went down his spine.

Jake opened the back door and stepped inside. Suddenly, he heard a sound at the main door. Gotta split, he thought as he hurried back out the door, which he left ajar. As he turned, he stepped on a coil of rope and stumbled. He felt a sharp pain in his knee but continued, limping along the dirt road.

The moon shone through the trees and once again Jake found his favorite place. He needed to catch his breath. His head reeled and his heart pounded. He thought about the noise he had heard inside the barn. Who was that? I shoulda stayed to find out. I musta made some noise when I tripped over the rope. Geez, I didn't even shut the door, he thought.

Jake felt no peace as he sat under the tree. He looked up and saw the glow of the harvest moon. Fox, I'm sorry about your Laura. I shoulda told you about taking the money. I wanna pay you back but I can't face you or anyone else right now. As he continued looking at the dark sky, he began to feel the tranquility of the dark, quiet woods. He slumped to the ground and closed his eyes without another thought.

CHAPTER 58

Pressure is relieved with courage and grace.

The next morning Jake felt more confident and knew he had the courage to speak with Jonathan. He went to his small room at the stable. Not a pretty sight, he thought. It needs a good cleanin'. First things, first. I really need coffee and a hard roll. Then I'll be able to get on with my chores.

It was late morning when Jake saw Fox standing on his patio. I better talk to him now before I lose my nerve, he thought.

"Hey Jon, you're lookin' better today. Been takin' your meds like the doc said?"

"Yeah, I'm taking them. I just need to remember to take them on time. You're not looking so good, Jake."

"I got some problems. Do you have time to listen?"

"Yep, let's sit right here on the patio."

Jake sat down on the small, delicately designed, wrought iron chair directly across from Jonathan. Hmm, very uncomfortable, he thought.

"How about some coffee?"

"Okay Boss, only if it's old and black."

The coffee was bitter but the 'kick' helped him tell everything to Jonathan. Jake was uneasy and shifted on the chair as he spoke.

Jonathan observed Jake's movements and listened intently to everything he said. After Jake finished, Fox said, "I looked for you last night, Jake, but your room was empty. I heard a noise coming from the back door and thought it might be you, but I couldn't find you."

"I needed air and time to pull myself together." Jake held his head in his hands and shook it back and forth.

"I figured something was wrong, Jake. I've had a feeling for a long time. You've been a good friend and a loyal worker since we started the stables together. I'm glad we talked. Don't worry about our relationship. This won't change anything between us. We'll work something out but now get back to work."

CHAPTER 59

Some jigsaw puzzles are almost impossible to solve.

Paul hung up the phone. What a long day, he thought. He had just finished speaking with an old Miami buddy, Danny Callahan, who had worked with him years ago. He promised Paul he would look into Kirkland's finances and also Franky Alvarez' murder. Now, how do I get the capsule into Susan's hands so she can have Boulder or 'the boyfriend' check it out? he thought.

Paul lay down on his bed and allowed the events of the day to run through his mind like a jigsaw puzzle. I must be missing something he thought. Things should be falling into place now that Laura's body has been found. He drifted off to sleep with Susan's smiling face foremost in his mind.

Waking early the next morning, Paul dressed and headed out to Manasquan. He decided to eat breakfast at Sal's and then drop the capsule off at the bookstore. He could give it to Chelsea and ask her to give it to Susan. He preferred not seeing Susan just yet.

Sal strode around his café talking with customers and shaking hands with many of them. The early morning crowd enjoyed being greeted.

Paul sipped his coffee and listened to the chatter at the next table. Franky's death was one of the topics of conversation. One of the men talked about the Belmont and stated how he had bet a bundle on Catchmeifyoucan. He expressed surprise that Alvarez and 'Catch' lost.

Paul started thinking, blackmail? I wonder if that might have something to do with Franky's death. Maybe that's something to look into. Anything can happen in this day of technology. He finished his coffee and breakfast special, paid his bill and left. Deep in thought, he walked into the Sandcastle Bookstore and smiled as Nicky said, "Hello, Nicky wanna grape."

"Hello to you too Nicky. Sorry I don't have a grape today; next time," he promised. Paul walked over to Chelsea and handed her a sealed envelope. "Chelsea, please give this to Susan as soon as she comes in today. It's very important."

"Sure, I'll give it to her. She'll be in soon."

"Thanks Chelsea, see ya 'round."

CHAPTER 60

A bad dream is something going on in your head that is uncontrollable.

The memorial service and repast were over and Susan was alone in her kitchen. Her mother, an unexpected overnight guest, had retired with a cup of chamomile tea. Susan took a bottle of Kendall-Jackson Chardonnay out of the refrigerator and opened it with her favorite antique wine bottle opener. She gave the cork an appreciative sniff, although she wasn't sure what she was supposed to smell. She took a Brotherhood Winery wine glass out of the cupboard and tilted the bottle, soothed by light gurgling as the wine filled the glass. She took another sniff and then a sip. "Oh, this is good," she said aloud, as she grabbed the glass and the bottle and went into the living room.

It was an intense day, Susan thought. She settled herself on her couch, took a deep breath and sighed, "I'm glad it's over; I really don't like funerals." The last funeral Susan had attended had been her husband Mark's. She had tried desperately to forget finding his body lying on the floor of their home. After the death, she had experienced months of devastating nightmares that had invaded her sleep and left her frightened and depressed. Susan sipped more wine. She had not killed Mark but she had been involved in the sleuthing necessary to discover his killer. It was almost two years ago, and yet she felt like it was yesterday. Before he was killed, Mark had started to show more attention to her but she still didn't know what had caused his black moods and what had changed them back again.

While she was growing up, her mother hadn't seemed to care about her. There had never been any mother-and-daughter shopping trips, manicures, tea parties or girly gossip, but her dad had made up for that. He was there for her whenever she was in a school play or a swimming meet. She had been devastated when he passed away. Susan's mother had withdrawn from her even more and never tried to comfort or console her. Susan had not expected her to behave any differently. She had steeled herself and, ignoring her feelings of abandonment, made sure she was the best in everything she did. Then she had married Mark and had thought her life would be like a beautiful fairy tale.

Susan poured a little more wine in her glass. "I could have been a better wife," she said, tears trickling down her cheeks. "Mark was struggling, and I didn't help him at all." Her tears flowed more freely now and an empty feeling permeated her being. "I've failed everyone I know," she sobbed. Minutes ticked by as Susan's tears dripped off her chin. She grabbed a Kleenex from the box near her chair and dabbed at her face. She jumped as she heard a noise behind her. Virginia stood in the doorway, wearing Susan's nightgown and robe, with a concerned look on her face. "Mother, what do you want?"

"Susan, I came down to get a drink of water and I heard you crying. Why are you so upset?"

"Oh, Mother, I'm so miserable. The funeral made me think about Mark and how he died. I feel so helpless. I miss Dad so much. I miss Mark. I even miss you." Her tears flowed again and words failed her.

Virginia sat down on the couch next to Susan and put her arm around her daughter's shoulders. "I miss you, too."

"What did you say, Mother?"

"I've missed you, dear."

"Mother I can't believe you. You've never been like a real mother to me. You never even call me. I feel like an orphan."

There was a short period of silence and then Virginia said, "You're right. I haven't been a good mother. I know there are some people who are natural nurturers and then others, like me, who don't know how to love. My mother didn't know how to be a good mother either," she continued. "You never knew your grandmother, but she loved Laura so much more than me. I remember one time I was supposed to give a piano recital and I got all dressed up in my best dress. Then my mother made me share the spotlight with Laura. I have a picture of the two of us standing by the piano and Laura holding *my* flowers. It was like that throughout my whole childhood. I learned to harden myself to any warmth; I learned not to expect any love; I learned not to be hurt by anything.

"Somehow your father was able to see through that hard shell. He was the only one who could pierce my cold heart. I remember when I became pregnant with you, I developed pre-eclampsia. You were born two months early and then I went through a hard time; my doctors diagnosed postpartum depression. I guess I blamed you, at least unconsciously. I've had a lot of time to think since then and talked to quite a few shrinks."

"You've been to see therapists, Mother? I never knew."

"I didn't tell anyone. I thought it was something I had to work out myself. But Laura's disappearance and her murder have made me do some serious thinking about myself, and about you. That's one of the reasons I wanted to come home with you tonight. I'm hoping we can close some of the distance that's been between us."

"Oh, Mother. I can't even react to that now. There's so much going on and so much weight on my shoulders. I want to help Jonathan find out what happened to Aunt Laura, I'm trying to open my tearoom and make a go of that, and I need to train new staff at the store. I think I might be in love, but I'm not sure. There's someone who was involved in Mark's murder who's now come back into my life. I'm tired, I'm sad, and I just don't know what to do." Susan's tears began again as Virginia hugged her daughter closer and wiped the tears from her face.

"You know what they say, darling," Virginia said. "Today is the first day of the rest of our lives. Maybe it's time we helped each other."

"I don't know whether to believe you mother. You think we could?" Susan asked.

"Let's try and see," her mother replied. "You can start by calling me, Mom. And pass me that bottle of wine," she grinned.

CHAPTER 61

There are some questions to which nobody has the answers.

Day is done, thought Jonathan as he sat on the low porch behind his house. He zipped up his jacket as the coolness of the evening set in around him. His friends had lifted his spirits at the repast. They had helped him begin to find closure in the death of his wife, yet he knew there were still questions to be brought to the surface and answers that only time would provide. Fox looked out toward his stables and saw a faint light shining through one of the windows. I'm really blessed with good horsemen here, he thought. At least I don't have to worry about them.

Fox dropped his head in his hands for a moment and thought about Laura. What was she trying to tell me right before the Belmont? He had asked himself the same question over and over and couldn't lock onto an answer. She said we were missing money, he mused. How much? She never told me. I was so damned impatient with her that night. Fox stood up and paced. I can't believe that any of my men would try to put something over on me. I guess Laura knew what she knew and I kept a closed mind as to what was going on. Why am I agonizing over this now; she's gone and . . . gone the sun, he thought as he went into the house and slammed the door.

CHAPTER 62

Coffee is the favorite drink of the civilized world.

Susan awoke as the aroma of freshly brewed coffee drifted up from the kitchen. She dressed and pulled her hair into a soft chignon and went downstairs. "Good morning Mom, you're up kind of early."

"What do you mean, early? It's almost eight o'clock. Didn't you set your alarm?"

"That's why I'm dressed but . . . why are you up so early? Say, the coffee is yum," she said taking a small sip.

"I couldn't sleep, I've been thinking about poor Annie. She sure didn't look good at the repast."

"I know what you mean. I wonder how she's doing too," said Susan. "Maybe we can go over to the hospital to see her today."

"Well, if she's as bad as she looked yesterday, I suppose they'll only allow immediate family in to visit," Virginia replied, pouring another cup of coffee.

"I'll call the hospital to see how she's doing and see if she has a phone in her room." Susan picked up the phone, dialed the number and spoke with the receptionist. After a minute, the call was put through to Annie's room.

Kirkland answered on the first ring.

"Hello, Kirkland, this is Susan Jeffries. Mother and I are wondering how Annie's doing and if it's okay to visit her today."

"Thanks for calling, Susan. I was going to stop by to pick up my car at Jonathan's later this morning and tell him what was going on so then he could let you know. Annie's not much better. They're transferring her to Deborah Hospital in Browns Mills later this morning. Annie's doctors want the cardiologists to see her. They may have a better grasp of the situation, since Deborah is primarily a heart and lung facility. If you give me your number, I'll let you know how things progress. I wanted her transferred to DC, but her primary doctor feels this is in her best interest."

"Okay Kirkland, please remember to give her our best when she wakes up and do let us know how she's doing." After an exchange of cell numbers, Susan hung up the phone and conveyed the information she received to her mother. Virginia was leaning so close to the phone trying to listen in that she almost fell off the end of the counter.

"Mother, be careful! I wouldn't want to have to take you to the hospital too," Susan exclaimed as she put her hand on her mother's shoulder to steady her. Then, mumbling under her breath she said, "It must be terrible to see the one you love in such bad condition and not know what's causing it."

"Well, I'm sure that's true, but honestly I don't see much empathy coming from Kirkland. He was always a kind of cold fish if you ask me," retorted Virginia.

"How can you say that? He's taking good care of her and he's with her every minute, Mother. You always see everyone in the negative. You're just so cynical."

"No I'm not. And, if I am, I have good reason to be. Most of the time . . . hmm I'd say 98% of the time . . . I'm right."

"There's no use arguing with you, but why do you feel that way about Kirkland?" Her mother had piqued her curiosity.

"Well, it's just that he's so cold. He doesn't show he cares, but only that he's a caregiver. Do you know what I mean? It seems one time he wants to care for her because he loves her and the next time he does something only because he's expected to. It's a fine difference but it's huge. You should know. I felt the same way about you and Mark."

Susan's mother definitely hit a nerve with her comparison. Susan did not want to talk about Mark with her. She and her mother had never seen eye to eye on Mark or their marriage and there was no reason to start fighting over it again. "Mother you are not 100% right, and I am not talking to you about Mark. Not now and not ever. You had your chance when I needed you; now it's over and so is this conversation." Funny how old baggage never really leaves you, Susan thought. Virginia had instilled a little bit of doubt in Susan's mind as far as Kirkland was concerned, though.

Susan walked out of the kitchen and grabbed her car keys out of the amber glass bowl on the hall table. She was glad that she had showered and dressed before coming down; now she could just go to her bookstore without further incident. Wow, guess I'm handling things better, she thought to herself. "See you later Mom," she yelled as she walked out the door.

Susan thought about what her mother had said as she drove toward Main Street. She decided to call Boulder and get his take on Kirkland since he had interviewed him and Annie in D.C. She also wanted to know how he was doing in his investigating. She hadn't talked with him except for a few minutes at the repast. Frankly, I'm not sure about paying him since he hasn't found out anything useful, she thought. Oops, I'm beginning to sound like Mom. She actually laughed at the thought as she activated her phone in the car and instructed it to call Boulder. Busy . . . guess I'll call him again when I get to the book store.

Chelsea was already at the store when Susan arrived. She seemed anxious as Susan walked through the door. "Is there something wrong, Chels?" Susan asked.

"Not wrong, but that guy Paul was here and he gave me this envelope for you and said it's very important. I dialed your cell but couldn't get you. I just wanted you to have it right away."

Susan looked at her cell. "Darn, with that so-called discussion with mom I forgot to charge the phone."

Susan took the envelope from Chelsea and walked toward the back of the store. "Is everything else okay?" she asked while she walked. She used a letter opener to slit the seal carefully to avoid ripping it. Once she opened it, a large white capsule rolled onto the table. Also inside the envelope was a small, folded piece of paper on which a note was scribbled in pencil.

I know you're mad at me, but I'm trying to help. Found this in Kirkland's car. It's not a prescribed drug. Maybe your PI or your boyfriend can find out what it is. I'm following up on a different lead. I'll let you know how it goes. Be careful! I don't want you to be dead body number three. Paul.

Susan looked at the capsule and read the note again. As she handed it to Chelsea, she decided to call Boulder rather than Tony. *I know Tony will try to protect me but I want to look into this alone. I don't need to lean on him or worry him unnecessarily. Gee, could Mom be right?* she thought. *Ugh, I'll never hear the end of it.*

Susan dialed Boulder's office and the call went through. Well, at least he isn't on the phone anymore, Susan thought. On the third ring, the phone was picked up. "Joe, it's Susan. I need you right away. I have something for you to see. It's a capsule that I just received. Joe? Joe?" The line had gone dead. Susan looked at her cell. That's odd, she thought as she dialed Boulder's office again. This time the phone rang until the answering service came on. She didn't leave a message but looked at her contact list and called Boulder's cell. This time the call went through immediately.

"Joe, where are you?"

"Hi Susan, I'm with a client. What's up?"

"Joe, something strange just happened. Someone sent me a capsule and a note. I'd like you to check it out. It was found in Kirkland's car. I called your office and the phone was picked up on the third ring. I thought it was you so I blurted out the information that I had then suddenly I heard a click. I don't know who it was, but now someone knows about my having the capsule. Can we meet somewhere? I'd like to get it to you right away."

"Sorry Susan, I can't make it today. There's another case I'm on and I have to be in court to testify. I don't know how long that will be since court appearances aren't necessarily timely."

Susan was silent. I know that Boulder has other cases but I think he should make a better attempt when I call him, she thought.

"Susan, Susan, you still there?"

"Yeah, I was just thinking."

"Well, why don't you put the capsule in a safe place and I'll stop by first thing in the morning. We can have breakfast at Sal's. Meanwhile, I've made some inquiries and have some additional information for you."

"Okay, I guess that sounds like a plan. That will give me time to get some work done in the tearoom today." Susan hung up the phone and stared at it. "Now what," she said aloud. She looked at her watch and thought, Millie should be here soon. She's dropping her car off at the dealer's for a few days and she needs a ride home.

Chelsea poked her head into the back room. "What's up, Mrs. J.?"

"I'm not sure Chels. Joe warned me to be careful. With all that's been happening I'm imagining the worst."

"Like, don't let your imagination run away with you. My mom always used to tell me, 'don't trouble trouble until trouble troubles you'."

"That's just the point, my dear. Trouble has been troubling me for quite some time now. Whenever I think I can relax something else goes wrong."

"By the way, what are you going to do with the capsule? Shouldn't you give Tony or the cops a call?"

"No, I think I'll put it in the safe. I don't want to call them until I know more. I'm giving it to Boulder in the morning. Besides, it's been so long now, how would twenty-four more hours hurt?"

The door chimes rang and Millie toddled in, complaining under her breath. "What's ruffled your feathers, Millie? Was it the dealership or the drive to bookstore?"

"It's my dang bunions."

CHAPTER 63

You can disagree with a person and still remain friends.

Susan worked into the evening at the bookstore making it a long day. The tearoom needed to be set up as more equipment began arriving daily. The flooring was completed and the tiles looked beautiful. Four tables with two ladder-back chairs each needed to be set in place without looking crowded. Millie had stayed with her to help. At times, Millie had different opinions about the arrangements and Susan restrained herself from reacting to her constant chatter.

The room looked cozy and comfortable. The counter would be delivered and installed within the next two days. It was 9 p.m. and the two women were tired and ready to leave.

"We'll stop now and head home," Susan said. "The tables and chairs look great and the wall art picks up the colors perfectly. The room looks quiet and friendly. I'm satisfied . . . for now anyway. Let's vamoose Millie."

After closing the store and heading out of the parking lot, Susan talked about the changes and also about hiring some college girls to serve the customers. Millie didn't respond; she looked too tired to speak.

While driving down Main Street, Susan checked the rearview mirror and noticed headlights from a vehicle driving close behind. She turned onto the next street to try losing the vehicle. The high beams blinded her view in the mirror. I've got to get Millie home, she thought. I can't tell her about this truck; she's fallen asleep. No sense getting her upset too.

A few minutes later, Susan reached over and shook Millie. "Wake up, Millie. You're home."

"Wh-what?" Millie said in a startled voice.

"Thanks so much for helping me this evening. I couldn't have done all the work by myself. Hope I haven't worn you out."

"You didn't wear me out but I really missed my afternoon nap today. It rejuvenates me and I get more energetic if I rest a while. Now I'll put my fluffy slippers on and settle in my comfy chair to watch a movie. I do this every evening. Good night, Susan."

The driver of the pickup watched as Susan backed out of Millie's driveway.

A few minutes later, Susan approached her street and the headlights she had seen earlier reappeared. "Someone's following me. Who could it be?" she whispered and pressed the garage door opener. She drove in and closed the door. "I'm home," she said. "There are no lights on in the house, Mother must have gone to bed for the night."

CHAPTER 64

There are those who think they know and those who don't know to think.

The man in the truck watched as Susan drove into the garage. He picked up his cell and punched in some numbers. "Yeah, it's me. I followed her home. The house is dark . . . . Don't know if she's alone. I know her mother was staying with her but I don't know if she left yet . . . . No, I'm not going in there. What if I get caught? Hell, I don't even know what I'm looking for. . . . This is your mess. Frankly, I'm getting tired of the quicksand. Every turn we make, you get me in deeper and deeper. This was supposed to get us out of the hole with the loan sharks. Now, what a mess. I'm going to a bar and get drunk. You do what you have to . . . I'm done."

As Susan lay in bed, she heard the tires of a vehicle squealing as it took off. Boy, someone must be either in a hurry or really ticked off, she thought as she drifted off.

Four hours later, Susan sat straight up in bed. The security alarm was blasting; it woke her up from a deep sleep. Her mother, obviously up for the same reason, stood at her bedroom door wielding a tennis racket she had taken off the wall in the den.

"A little early for tennis, isn't it?" Susan

couldn't resist taunting her.

"Someone's trying to break in and you're in bed making jokes?" her mother shot back. "I thought you lived in a crime-free neighborhood." Her mother began waving the racket back and forth.

The phone rang and Susan reached over to the table beside her bed and picked up the receiver. "I don't know. I'll have to look. . . . Yes, I'm fine. . . . The code? Oh, it's Maverick. Let me shut off the alarm. . . . Okay, I'll keep the line open, while I'm checking it out. . . . No, don't notify them yet. It may just be an animal or something. She turned toward her mother and whispered, "Mother did you leave a window open?"

"I don't think so. Why would I do that?"

Susan turned on the light switch in the bedroom, went into the hall and stepped cautiously down the stairs. Her mother followed her from behind. Susan punched in the alarm numbers at the front door and the house became silent. The alarm was still blinking though at the patio door off the den. Susan and her shadow went over and turned it off. Then the duo checked the remaining windows and doors. Everything seemed secure. Susan kept the alarm company dispatcher informed as they made their way through the entire house. "No, there's no reason to send someone over; nothing was disturbed. Thanks for your help."

"You should still have the police come over

and check out why the alarm sounded," Virginia said as she clung to the racket, yawning widely.

"Check it out? It could have been something simple that jarred the alarm. I won't bother the police over something so trivial. Now, would you please put that racket down before you knock me out with it? What time is it?"

"It's 4:00 a.m., if your clock is right. Do you want a cup of tea?"

"That sounds good, Mom, now that I'm wide awake. Besides, I want to tell you about my day. You were asleep when I got in so . . . ." The phone rang again.

"Now who's calling?" Susan said, a hint of annoyance sounding in her voice.

"Hello." Susan answered rather coolly then said, "Oh, hi, Tony," when she heard his voice.

Virginia noticed that Susan's voice went into an instant defrost tone.

"Oh, I'm fine . . . no, nothing's wrong. It was just a malfunction . . . . No, it's really okay. . . . Yes, Mom's still here . . . . Love you too. Talk to you in the morning. Ahh . . . later this morning." Susan put the phone slowly into the cradle and smiled. It feels nice having somebody care about me, she thought.

"Tony had the alarm installed and he's one of the contacts when it goes off," Susan said as she saw her mother's quizzical look. Susan took the cup of tea her mother offered, sat down at the table and began telling her about the note, the capsule and her day with Millie at the bookstore. Susan finished with a final exhale. "Mother, you haven't said a thing."

"You didn't give me a chance. You never came up for air."

"Well, what are you thinking?" Susan couldn't believe she was actually asking her mother for her opinion.

"First, let's go back a bit. Fill me in on Paul and that whole scenario. How come he's in the picture? Wait a minute! Don't tell me he's the same Paul who kidnapped you? Have you ever told Tony about him?"

Susan gave a short synopsis of Mark's murder and how Paul was involved and the outcome. She even told Virginia that Paul had contacted her recently and wanted to make up for the past. Again, she did not pause to answer questions.

"So, what you're telling me is that he's trying to make things right by helping you with the investigation? Do you trust him? Could he be making things up to gain your confidence?"

"No, I don't trust him because I believe he has ulterior motives. But I don't think he would lie to me about what he found, either. There would be no reason to."

"So, let me see the capsule. Is it like the ones Kirkland's been giving to Annie?"

"I don't have it here. It's in the store safe. I'm giving it to Boulder this morning, and besides, I didn't really see the medication she took at the repast."

Virginia leaned close to Susan's face. "Oh, I did. It was a white capsule. I remember because it was huge! It was the size of a horse pill. Matter of fact he gave her two."

"Then it's probably the same. But I don't know what the medication is. Paul might have questioned it because it didn't have any markings which probably led him to believe it's something that's not made pharmaceutically. It could be nothing, but I want Boulder to check it out."

"Do you think Paul might have tried to break in tonight to get the capsule back?"

"Why would he do that, Mom? Besides, it may be a legitimate medication," Susan said as she got up and poured more hot water in her cup.

"I'll bet the house it isn't," muttered Susan's mother under her breath.

Kirkland was hiding in the dark pantry at the far end of the kitchen. He mumbled to himself, "Boy that was close. I didn't see any sign on the lawn saying the house was alarmed. I should have taken off but I have to find out what this busybody and her daughter know. He listened intently, trying to understand the conversation in the kitchen. Who the heck is this guy Paul? I've never heard of him before. Why was he messing in my car and in my business?

So the capsule is in the store, he thought. I have to get it back. I can't believe I got so careless. Annie will soon be dead. I got her to take two more capsules this afternoon; she was so confused she didn't even know who I was. He chuckled to himself. I don't think this hospital will help her any more than the one in DC. They'll just put natural causes on the death certificate. I won't sign for an autopsy either. There'll be a cremation and that will end it. My worries will be over and I'll get my life back in order. Too bad, but I have no other choice, he thought. Whew, there are too many spices in here. Kirkland felt hot and was having difficulty breathing.

Kirkland heard the two women place their cups in the sink and go upstairs. He tiptoed through the kitchen. Great, he thought. They never put the alarm back on. He opened the patio door, stepped out then jogged to his parked car. Almost on the home stretch, he thought as he calmly drove away.

Susan heard something and went to the bedroom window. As she looked down the street she saw a car pull away and turn down the next block. She decided to stay up and go for her early morning run on the beach before opening her bookstore. She grabbed fresh clothes, left a note for her mother and headed out.

CHAPTER 65

If all the details fit perfectly, there's probably something wrong.

Back from her morning run an hour later, Susan went over to Sal's and ordered coffee. When the front door opened, it was Boulder. He joined her at the table and they talked a bit about all of the recent events.

"So where's this mystery capsule?" he asked Susan while blowing on the hot coffee.

"I've got it in the safe in my back room."

"Well, let's go over and take a look at it." Boulder gulped the remaining coffee and left a tip on the table.

Once she was back in her bookstore, Susan opened the safe, drew out the envelope and handed it to him.

Boulder took the capsule out of the envelope, examined it then replaced it in the envelope and put it in his pocket. "I'll turn this over to the police."

"Joe, I'm worried about whoever picked up the phone yesterday. I blabbed about the capsule and they hung up."

"I'll check into that, Susan. Don't worry. I have a cleaning person who comes in during the day, and my guess is that she picked up the phone and then just hung up again. But I'll double check. And another thing, my friend, Dr. Kramer will be in his lab today and I'll give him a call. He can look at the results of Annie's blood work from the ER and let us know if anything's out of whack. I'll let you know what he finds out as soon as I can."

"Thanks Joe, I really appreciate it."

"Listen Susan, I don't have any firm evidence but I want you to be careful around Kirkland Somers. There are some things that don't add up and I want to check them out. In the meantime, just watch your step."

Susan watched Boulder walk through the shop and out the door, waving to Chelsea and giving Millie a wink. Boy, Susan thought, that conversation didn't make me feel better. Mom said she didn't like Kirkland and now Joe's telling me to be more careful around him. Maybe I'd better pay attention to them.

Ten minutes later, the front door opened again and Susan heard Chelsea talking with someone whose voice sounded familiar. Looking toward the front of the store, Susan saw Kirkland standing near the cookbook display. He spied Susan and called out, "Hey there. Nice shop you've got here."

Walking toward him Susan said, "Thanks Kirkland. We've been working really hard. What brings you to the neighborhood?"

"Well, Annie's doing a little better so I thought

I'd stop by to let you know. Thanks for your concern."

"I like your wife, Kirkland. I'm glad to hear she's feeling better. Do you think she would like a book to read? I'd be glad to send one along with you—no charge."

"That's nice of you Susan, but I don't think she's up to much reading yet. I'm intrigued by your shop. Do you get much business?"

"I do okay," she answered him reluctantly.

"That's good, that's good. I know you've had it pretty rough lately, what with your uncle's problems and all. By the way, have you seen that PI guy? What's his name?"

"You mean Joe Boulder?"

"Yeah, that's the guy. Has he come up with anything yet?"

"As a matter of fact, I saw him a little while ago. And yes, he's working on some interesting leads, but I can't talk about them."

"Oh, sure, sure, glad to hear things are going well," Kirkland said. "Well, gotta go, he said looking at his watch. "I think Annie will be awake now and I want to help her with her breakfast. I'll let you know how she's doing."

"You do that. I hope she's better soon."

Kirkland turned and walked out the door without a backward glance.

"You know, Chels, there's something I don't

like about that guy."

"If you want my opinion, Mrs. J., like I think he's a phony. I wouldn't trust him."

"Neither would I, Chels. Neither would I."

CHAPTER 66

Life is like a Twinkie, we all want ours to be a piece of cake.

Boulder headed straight to his office after talking with Susan. He checked his e-mails and then sat at his desk to enjoy a TWINKIE and reheated coffee. *I'm so glad these cakes are making a comeback, sure would miss 'em.* He checked the bottom drawer of his desk. *Gee, I've only got two more packages,* he thought. He finished swallowing his first bite when his cell rang.

"Hey Joe, good morning."

"Hey, yourself Doc, what's up? Got anything for me?"

"Yep, but first, I see they transferred your friend Annie Somers over to Deborah. They've got an extensive cardio rehab over there, you know . . . if she needs it."

"Doc, come on, let me in on what you've got."

"Well, it looks like your gal has had too much bicarb. She was admitted in metabolic alkalosis."

"Whatever that means." Boulder stuffed the remaining bite of the snack cake in his mouth.

"It means Joe that somehow, little by little, she's been taking large doses of, well . . . you know it as baking soda. It looks like she's accumulated enough in her plasma to put her in alkalosis. I mean, enough for her to be confused, have muscle weakness and even heart arrhythmias. If someone was helping her with her meds, they might have been slipping in sodium bicarbonate too many times a day. Between you and me this looks intentional. Her sodium level in the blood, drawn on admission, was nearly 300."

"I see. I thought she acted very tired and weak but she had just arrived from Maryland so nobody seemed that concerned. Susan Jeffries told me she seemed a little confused. Do you think she'll do okay now?"

"Oh, yeah, they treated her with intravenous right away to balance her plasma but her EKG must have shown changes for them to send her out to Deborah. Do you know the name of her doctor in Maryland? I'm going to recommend that the doctor here arrange to have her records from Maryland sent up here. It may be interesting to see past sodium levels when she collapsed."

"Good idea," said Boulder as he scrolled through his cell looking for Susan's number.

"Yeah Joe, I hope this helps you."

"I think it will. Thanks for the information. I owe you another one. I'll let you go; I know you're busy."

Boulder ended the call, sat in his chair and muttered, "This is another avenue all right." After a few seconds, he looked at his watch. I've got to get over to the courthouse, he thought. It's already eleven o'clock and I'll be tied up until who knows what time. I'll call Susan tomorrow, first thing, and tell her what I found out.

CHAPTER 67

I am restless and discontent.

Virginia dusted Susan's knick-knacks and swept the kitchen floor. I'm getting more restless with each day, she thought. Susan isn't spending much time with me with her demanding schedule at the bookstore. There's nothing I want to do today but go home to my friends in Florida.

Somehow, I can't get interested in the bookstore, she thought. It keeps Susan busy, but I thought we would be spending more time together. When she comes home tonight, I'll talk to her about leaving. I've stayed here long enough and experienced more excitement than I've had in years.

***

Business was slow in the late afternoon at the store and Susan decided to close earlier than usual. It was becoming darker now and only a few cars passed the bookstore during the last hour. Even Nicky was quieter than usual. He didn't ask for a snack.

"What's the matter Nicky? Feeling tired? Got the blahs?" Susan asked.

"Blah, blah, blah," Nicky imitated and put his beak over his left wing to get some shut-eye.

It's been really quiet this week, Susan thought. Maybe I'll find some soft background music for my customers to enjoy while they shop. I think I'd like that myself.

While driving home, Susan thought, maybe I'll take Mom out to dinner tonight. She might like the Broadway Grille. I've neglected her and concentrated only on my work these past few days. At least she's spent some time at the bookstore and met Chelsea and Millie. Mom got annoyed with Nicky. He would talk back to her and she wasn't amused. Susan laughed at the thought.

Upon arriving home, Susan smelled the aroma of food as she left her car. She was surprised to see that her mom had cooked dinner and set the table.

"Hi Mom, it sure smells good in here. What a nice surprise! Such a treat-to stay home tonight. I'm exhausted. It's been so hectic these past few days."

"Sit down and relax," Virginia answered. "I'll pour some wine for the two of us. Tonight's my treat for you and you haven't tasted my cooking in years. You've been working so hard lately. It's no wonder you're tired."

As Susan sipped her wine, she noticed that her mother had packed her bags and placed them near the door.

"Oh Mother, you have your bags packed. Why are you planning to leave?"

"How long did you think I was going to stay? I want to go back home and be with my friends. Besides, you're always so busy and on the go. I can't keep up with you and your busy schedule."

"Mother, we've just gotten to know each other. I don't want you to leave just yet. Stay for a few weeks longer. I could drive you down to Florida and stay with you while my bookstore is closed during the Christmas holidays. It would be fun, don't you think so?"

"No. I don't intend staying here any longer. You know the saying: 'Fish and relatives smell after three days.' Well, there's a lot of truth in those words and I'm not going to let that happen. I called the airport in Atlantic City and made arrangements to catch the 10:38 flight tomorrow morning. It'll be simpler that way. Maybe you'll take me there?"

"Oh Mom, of course I will, but only if you promise to call me often. I'll do the same. We've got to keep in touch and continue to make up lost time. In the meantime, maybe you'll consider cutting down on your smoking habit."

"Yeah, I hear you," said Virginia with tears in her eyes. Instead of turning away, she reached for Susan for a long assuring hug.

The evening was filled with lots of conversation and Susan learned that her mother had a good sense of humor.

"I'm glad I came here, Susan. I met some nice people including your Tony. Most importantly, I mended fences which were broken by years of misunderstanding. Also, I've been selfish in the past and I plan to correct that. We'll keep in touch, that's for sure."

Virginia got up and refilled the glasses with wine. "Honey this is the best time we've had together in a long time."

CHAPTER 68

Fair Dinkum.

The door swung open with the jingling of the bell. Susan had arrived earlier than usual so she could get some things done before she had to take her mother to the airport.

"Hey Mrs. J, You'll never guess what!"

Susan smiled at her assistant, who exuded early morning energy. "Well I guess you better tell me then."

"I've been given a chance at a wicked cool assignment. But I don't think you'll like it." Chelsea said as she plunked her back pack down behind the counter. "It's great for me, but it will mean I can't work here for a while."

"What on earth are you talking about?"

"My professor has a brother in Sydney who has a marketing consultancy business. He's looking for an American intern for a semester to work in a tea shop there. The shop is just opening and I think I could learn so much to help you." Chelsea stopped for a breath.

"Chelsea Keating, you've got to be kidding." Susan said. "I'm in the middle of trying to find out what really happened to my aunt and I'm trying to wiggle my way through all of the remaining red tape connected with opening the Tea Cup Room. I can't do all of this without you on board. I've grown to depend on you like I do my right arm."

"I know, I know, Mrs. J. But I've got it all figured out. You said you were thinking of hiring someone to help manage the tearoom. I don't have to leave for a couple of weeks, and I can help you get all the new people in place and even do some of the training myself. I know it can work, and I really want to go. It'll count as my grade for the next semester in Marketing and get me in good with the Prof, too. What do you think?"

"I think you're nuts, Chelsea, but that's nothing new. And why to Australia? Don't they have marketing internships here? Do you have to go? And what about your mom? What does she say?"

"Like my mom's cool with it," Chelsea said. "She just said to be sure it was okay with you. So . . . is it?"

"Well, what about expenses? It must cost a lot to fly to Australia. Are they paying for it? You can't afford that—not on what I pay you, you can't."

Chelsea laughed and Nicky echoed her chortle with a flap of his wings. "Mom and I have that figured out, too. They aren't paying for it, but she took out a life insurance policy on me when I was a baby, and we're going to borrow on that. It will pay for my flights over and back. And my uncle is giving me a loan to pay my expenses while I'm there. Like

I'll be living with a family, which will be way cool anyway but I'll need to have money for stuff like souvenirs. It's all planned and I just need you to say it's okay with you."

"Seems like you've done an awful lot without telling me," Susan muttered.

"I didn't hear you, Mrs. J. What'd you say?"

"Oh nothing," Susan answered. "I'm just trying to get my head around this news you dumped on me. It's a lot to take in. I must be nuts to say this, but if you give me more information on the internship, where it is, when it is and all the details, I'll think about it."

"You're the bomb, Mrs. J. I knew you'd go along with it."

"Hey, wait a minute, Chels. I only said I'd think about it. You need to get me the info and I'll see what I can do. In the meantime, I need to hire a manager for the tearoom and an additional clerk. Take a look through those resumes we received. Go on Craigslist and find some good candidates. Also, why don't you check with your school and see if there are any interns that want to work for me."

"Like I'm on it," Chelsea said as she grabbed her iPad and turned it on. "I'll have all the info you want in a little while. I'm good."

"Yes you are, you traitor. I know you're good. So you better make it good for me."

"I got the message, Mrs. J. It'll be fine, you'll see."

Chelsea tapped away on her iPad while Susan waited on a few customers. During the transactions, Susan smiled and made small talk, but her mind was busy thinking about what Chelsea had asked.

CHAPTER 69

Each person is unique and unrepeatable.

Later that afternoon after she had gone home, Chelsea went into her bedroom which was decorated like a Lady Gaga tour bus. Posters of her favorite rockers and bikers decorated the walls and silver rings hung on black painted tree twigs, stuck in sand-filled pots on her dresser. Books and stuffed animals shared the black-painted vintage desk top with her HP Notebook. She had painted the desk a shiny black and then distressed it with a tire chain. She loved this retreat, so different from the rest of the apartment, which was kind of ordinary in a 'mother chose these' sort of way.

I've got to find someone, or maybe two someones to fill my spot at the bookstore while I'm in Australia. And I better be quick about it. The new employee has to be someone who's dependable, available and smart. But not too smart, Chelsea thought. I don't want to lose my bookstore job to a substitute.

Chelsea kicked off her Doc Martens, plopped on the bed and leaned back on her pillows to think. Her thinking turned into napping until there was a light rat-ta-tat on the bedroom door.

"Chelsea dear, it's time to eat."

"Huh?" grunted Chelsea. "Oh, okay, Mom. I'll be right there."

As she walked into the eat-in kitchen, Chelsea detected the mouth-watering aroma of her mom's homemade spaghetti sauce. "Yum," she said. "What's the occasion?"

"Just felt like making my sauce. Would you get the salad out of the fridge?"

"Sure."

"What have you been up to all afternoon? I didn't hear a peep out of you."

"Well, Mom, I was trying to figure out who could take my place at Susan's while I'm in Australia, and I couldn't come up with anyone. In fact, I kinda fell asleep."

"I think you're burning your candles at too many ends," her mother chuckled. "What about that girl you were telling me about in your accounting class? You know; the one who is so smart that everyone wants to be in her study group?"

"Oh, you mean Randy," said Chelsea. "Randy Carr. I'm not that close with her, but I did hear her saying she was looking for a job. She'd be great at the register; she knows her way around numbers, that's for sure. And like maybe she can help Susan with the bookkeeping, too. I'll see her in class tomorrow and ask her."

***

The next day Chelsea burst through the door of their apartment and grabbed her mother, giving her a whirl around the living room.

"Hey, hold on there," her mother laughed. "What's up?"

"You had such a good idea, Mom. I talked with Randy today and like she is so interested in the job. Turns out she likes books, too, and she's going to come to the store tomorrow to meet Susan and see what's involved. I think Susan's going to like love her—but not as much as she loves me."

Chelsea's mom laughed and hugged her daughter. "Good going, honey."

"Thanks. That's one more thing I can cross off my list. I can't wait to see how she and Susan get along. There's just one thing . . . ."

"What's that, dear?"

"I hope her handicap doesn't get in the way."

"Handicap? What do you mean?"

"Well," Chelsea hesitated. "Um, she's like, a little person."

***

Chelsea rushed through the door of the bookstore at 8:45 the following morning calling, "Hey, Mrs. J. Have I got news for you!"

Nicky chimed in with "I got, I got, I got!"

Susan turned from straightening the shelf with new books and looked at her enthusiastic assistant. "What's the news, Sunshine?"

"Well, you know, like, you told me to see if I could find someone who could help out while I'm in Australia?"

"Go on."

"That's it! I found her. Her name's Randy Carr and she's like a genius, and she'll be coming in today to meet you, and I know you'll like her and . . ."

Susan laughed. "Hold on, hold on. Slow it up a bit, will you?"

"Okay, Randy's coming in today. I know her from my accounting class and she's like a brain. She's looking for a part-time job and loves books. Oh look, here she comes."

Susan was speechless, a state that was not at all typical for her. The door opened, and through it walked a beautiful young woman with short blonde curly hair, fashionable leopard-framed eyeglasses and a brown leather Bulga hobo bag slung over her shoulder. She was short in stature, about four feet tall, wearing two inch heels and a smile that lit up her whole face.

"Hey Randy," Chelsea whooped, running over and sharing a fist bump with the newcomer. "Glad you made it. This is my boss, Susan, er. . . Mrs. Jeffries."

Susan laughed and held out her hand. "Susan will do just fine. Welcome, Randy, it's so nice to meet you. I've heard a lot about you from Chelsea."

"But I'll bet there's one thing she didn't tell you," laughed Randy. "You had the strangest look on your face as I came through the door. I'll bet you didn't know I wore glasses." Randy laughed again as Susan looked even more confused.

"No Randy," said Chelsea, "I didn't tell her that you were nearsighted." The girls looked at each other and burst into giggles. "Actually, I did forget to mention that you were a little vertically challenged."

"Mrs. Jeffries, I mean Susan, please don't let my height disturb you. It doesn't affect my brain power, and with a step stool or short ladder I'll be able to do anything you need."

"Well, I must say I was a bit surprised. But I've watched that show on TV, *Little People, Big World*, and wished I knew the Roloff's. There doesn't seem to be anything they can't tackle. And I'm sure that if Chelsea says you'd be a great help here, I don't have to worry about anything."

"She's great, Mrs. J." said Chelsea.

"Okay then. Let's have Millie watch the store while we go in the back room, have a cup of tea, and talk details."

"Oh Millie, I need you to watch the store for a while."

"Certainly Susan, I have plenty of books to stack."

Millie turned toward Chelsea and raised her eyebrows questioningly as if to ask why Chelsea was in on the interview. She's an employee just like me, Millie thought.

A half hour later, Susan, Chelsea and Randy walked out of the back room laughing. Susan spoke up first. "Millie, Randy will be your new co-worker. I'm delighted to have her on board in my store. She'll be quite an asset."

Millie extended her hand to welcome Randy and said, "I'll be very pleased to work with you. Now let's all have that second cup of tea."

***

Susan finished straightening up the worktable after everyone had gone home. She liked Randy Carr and had hired her to start the following day. She was happy that Chelsea had found someone to fill in for her so soon.

Susan turned the sign on the door to 'closed' and walked back to the counter to grab her purse and the money bag for the bank. She wished Boulder would call her with information from the doctor at the hospital. Susan stood at the counter and let her mind wander to Annie. I know something's going on with her. She was so weak and just couldn't get her words out at the repast. Sure is strange. Susan grabbed her purse and car keys as her cell phone rang. She noticed Paul's name on her caller ID and let it go to her voicemail.

CHAPTER 70

Never burn your bridges. You don't know when friendship might be needed in the future.

Paul looked at the notes he had scribbled while talking to a contact. Well Susan, he thought, I've got some information for you. But now I need to get it to you.

He paced around his small room and thought about his villa in Venezuela. It's time to get out of town again. I'm not getting anywhere with Susan but maybe after I give her this information her attitude might change.

Paul had punched in Susan's cell number and heard the voicemail prompt. "Susan, don't hang up; just listen. I have some very interesting information for you. I heard back from my contact in Washington, DC. Kirkland Somers is in with the mob for millions with his gambling debts. After the Belmont Stakes, he paid off some of them. What he needs now is for his wife to die, and soon, so he can get his hands on her estate.

"Also, on the day of Laura's repast, I saw Kirkland talking with someone out by the barn. Listen Susan, I've decided to head back to Venezuela. You know how I feel about you. Maybe next time we meet, your feelings for me will have changed. Remember, I helped you find your aunt's body and I gave you the capsule. Give all this information to the PI or the boyfriend. Don't go off by yourself. I don't want anything to happen to you. Goodbye for now my dear." Paul hung up the phone.

Well, Paul thought, I came here hoping to become Susan's friend, or better still, more than a friend and I've told her all I know. Now it's time for me to pack up and head out. I could use a drink before I leave town and there's no better place than Favorites.

Heading down to the OTB, Paul was mentally listing what he needed to escape. Paul had another disguise in mind, with appropriate passport and other necessary forms of identification. He had all the clothing and make-up. But I'm the master of disguise, he thought. Tony will be livid that I got away again.

Paul walked into Favorites and spotted Cody at the bar, beer in hand, chatting with the bartender. Probably has the hots for the cute chick behind the bar. Oh yeah, he thought. He's smitten.

Cody looked up as Paul sat down next to him and said, "Hey guy, what's up? I just hit one that paid $28.80 to win. Had $10.00 on it."

Paul ordered a beer, put a $20.00 bill on the bar and turned to Cody, "Good hit man, anything else?"

"Not yet," said Cody, "But I'm watching one of Walsh's horses in the next race at Charlestown. If the odds stay high, I'm putting a hefty wager on him."

Paul started to handicap the horse then looked back at Cody. "He really has a good shot in this race Cody, looks like he's ready. I really like the jockey too."

After finishing his beer and ordering another, Paul went to the betting windows and made his wager. When he returned to the bar, he said to Cody, "Hey pal, I want to thank you for the past four months. It's time for me to head out of New Jersey and back to Venezuela for a while. Thanks for getting me the job. And if I can impose just one more time, don't tell anyone that we met here tonight. Next time I'm back in the states we can catch a race at Monmouth."

"No problem man, now let's watch this race. They're putting the horses in the gate now and Marine's Glory is still 23 to 1."

The two men watched intensely and cheered their horse on. It looked like the favorite was going to win, and the crowd went wild. From the back of the pack, flying like the wind, their horse pulled ahead by a 'head-bob' at the wire.

A few minutes later the two cashed in their winnings. Paul placed his hand on Cody's shoulder and shook it briefly. "This is goodbye, my friend. I've learned a lot from you, probably more than I ever needed to know about the behind-the-stables-scene but I'll not forget you. Sorry to cut our friendship short again," Paul said.

"Hey man. You've had a lot on your back these past few months, I could tell. I'll be here when you come back. Matter of fact I'll be doing real well." Cody grinned, shook Paul's hand and walked back to the bar.

As Paul walked toward the door, he gave the winning horse on the TV screen a salute.

***

As soon as Susan arrived home she listened to Paul's message on her cell. What'll I do now? she thought. I have to tell Boulder and Jonathan what I know, but it's all too much for me tonight. I'll deal with this tomorrow.

CHAPTER 71

We can always choose to look at things differently.

The next morning Chelsea was at the register while Susan went to the back room to make the phone call to Boulder. "Joe, I'm so glad I caught you," she said after he picked up." I got a call from Paul Thomas late yesterday and he found out some interesting facts about Kirkland."

"Yeah? What did he find out?"

"Well, first of all, Kirkland owes the mob millions to cover his gambling debts. Paul thinks that Kirkland might have been hoping for his wife's death so he could get his hands on her money."

"That sheds a different light on things, doesn't it?" Boulder asked. "I really like Annie, but from the very first I got a funny vibe from Kirkland."

"I'm worried about Annie too. Kirkland keeps giving her the meds, and she's collapsed after taking them. Do you think Kirkland is tampering with the doses?"

"Could be. I know Deputy Brown in the Sheriff's department in Upper Freehold. I think they have jurisdiction over there by Deborah. I'll give him a call and ask him to check into what's going on. Maybe he can station a police officer outside Annie's hospital room and at the same time run a check on Kirkland."

"Oh, I'd feel so much better if you would do that." Susan said.

"I'll make that call now and then I've got to get back to court. Why don't I call you and let you know what Brown finds out?"

"I've got an even better idea. Why don't you meet me at Jonathan's this afternoon. Then you can tell both of us at the same time. Jonathan wanted us to keep him posted."

"Good idea, Susan. I can meet you there after 3:00 this afternoon."

"Okay. See you then."

Susan's next call was to Jonathan. "Jonathan? You sound kind of funny. Are you all right?"

"Hi Susan . . . Yes I'm fine. Think I'm coming down with a cold or something. What can I do for you?"

"I've found out some information about Kirkland, and Boulder's looking into it. We'd like to come over there around 3:00 today, if that's okay."

"Sure that would be fine. This is the quiet season for the horses. I decided not to take them to Florida to run on the warmer tracks. There's been too much going on and frankly I've lost my desire to race," Jonathan said despairingly.

I hope Jonathan can come to grips with everything, Susan thought as the call ended.

"Hey Mrs. J," Chelsea called from the other room. "Randy wants to know if we have any special napkins on order for the tea room, like ones with books. I wasn't sure. Could you come out here?"

Susan went up to the front of the store and was looking through the orders when her phone tone indicated an incoming text from Boulder.

You were right about Annie.

Susan stared at the message.

"Mrs. J. What's up?"

"Chelsea, that's from Boulder. I was right. Kirkland may be giving Annie something harmful. I don't know what to do first. Let me see if I can get hold of him." Susan punched in his number but the call went right to voice mail.

"So like what are you going to do?" Chelsea asked.

"I've got to tell Jonathan. I think he might be interested in what's happening to Annie. I'm going over to the Fox and Hound stables to see him with Boulder at 3 p.m. I don't want to tell him anything over the phone." Susan put her cell in her pocket. "Oh darn, I forgot to call Tony." Susan punched in his number and held her breath. She relaxed when she heard his confident reply.

"Lt. Russo. Oh, hi Susan, how are things going?"

"Oh they're going. Do you have a few minutes? There's a lot I need to tell you."

After Susan updated Tony, there was a long silence on his end.

"Tony? Are you still there?"

"Susan, I'm trying not to reach through the phone and wring your neck. I've told you, you have to be careful," Tony yelled. "Now, I find out that you've known about Paul being in town and that you've talked to him? He kidnapped you and he's a wanted felon. Don't you remember that? What were you thinking and why did you wait until now to tell me? I'm putting out an all-points bulletin on him. He's got to be to be caught. I've got to go now."

"I don't think I've ever heard Tony so angry. Good thing he's over in Brick. Maybe he'll calm down before we see each other," Susan said to Chelsea who was looking oddly at her. "I'm not sure whether I want Tony to catch Paul or not. Now how confusing is that?"

Susan looked at her watch, it was 2:15 p.m. "Hey, Chels, I've got to take care of this. Do you think you could close the shop for me at five o'clock? I'll be over at Fox and Hound if you need me."

"You go, Mrs. J. Like I've got it covered."

As Susan drove out of the parking lot, she thought about Tony. She hadn't told him originally because she knew he'd get angry. "Oh, I so don't want to lose him," she whispered.

CHAPTER 72

Truth may be where the evidence leads you, but you may not want to go there.

Kirkland Somers pulled into the parking lot at Deborah Heart and Lung Hospital in Browns Mills tired and nervous. I tried to gain Susan's confidence in order to get my hands on the one piece of evidence I couldn't afford to lose–the capsule, he thought. I have to finish Annie off and tie up any loose ends. There's a few more capsules in the bottle that will do it. The police won't have a clue. If Annie dies everything else will be circumstantial. A capsule doesn't make a murder. Besides, I could say I was just trying to help. I didn't necessarily know it would hurt her. It's not a poison. Yeah, I think I can pull this off.

Kirkland stepped off the elevator on Annie's floor. He looked down the hall and saw a plain clothes cop standing at Annie's door. He could spot one a mile away.

"Damn, I'm too late. Now I have to get out and fast. I bet they have an APB out on me.

Kirkland got back into the elevator, pushed the DOWN button and exited at the lobby. He unobtrusively dropped the pill bottle into the trash receptacle. He knew he couldn't risk taking his own car so he asked the receptionist if there was a cab company she could recommend, there in the middle of what he called the sticks. She called for a pick up. "It'll be here in about ten minutes."

The cab was an old white station wagon but it would suit his needs. He gave the driver the address and started to plot his next move. Only one loose end to tie up, he thought.

As they pulled out of the lot, the driver turned and said, "You sure you want to go that far in a cab? I only take cash you know."

Kirkland replied gruffly, "Yes I do and I got the cash. Just drive and mind your own business."

Kirkland looked idly out the cab window and noticed a large plane heading toward the clouds. An idea flashed into his mind. Of course, he thought, I've heard Walsh talk about his private plane. His Piper Cherokee is parked at his stables and it will be my quickest way out.

Kirkland had the cab driver drop him off at the west entrance to the Shore Thing Stables. He wanted to make sure that Watson was alone. Standing at the side of the gate, he texted him.

Are u alone? Need 2 talk.

Yeah. Meet u at barn 3, texted Watson.

CHAPTER 73

It's is when you are an adult that you experience suspicion.

Susan and Boulder pulled into the driveway of Fox and Hound stables at the same time. How weird is this, thought Susan.

They greeted each other and Susan grabbed Boulder's arm. "Hey, Joe, I was right after all, Kirkland really is giving Annie something isn't he?"

"Yeah, I probably shouldn't have told you in a text," Boulder said, scratching his ear. "Sorry. But I wanted you to know right away and I wasn't able to actually talk with you at that moment. Dr. Kramer was right when he said Annie was getting too much medication. The police lab took the capsule I gave them and found sodium bicarbonate in it. Kirkland was literally trying to kill her. Her heart couldn't have taken much more. The Colts Neck police contacted the doctor taking care of Annie and then arranged for protection for her. They really acted quickly."

"Wow, that's huge," Susan said. "I don't know if I'm relieved or angry."

"Me, too. I'll be glad when they pick up Kirkland."

Susan knocked on her uncle's open door.

Jonathan came to the door looking tired and depressed. Susan asked him to sit down, so that she and Boulder could explain everything that they had found out. As Fox listened to their stories, he grew incensed. Susan fixed him a tumbler of bourbon and water.

"Drink this Jonathan," she said. "This will calm you down. I have a plan and I think Ted Watson may be the loose end. Why don't we head over to Walsh's stables and see if he can tell us anything. As soon as we start questioning him about Laura I think he'll give us Kirkland."

Boulder chimed in, "I agree with her, Fox. Watson is the type of guy who would turn in his grandmother for a deal. Why don't the three of us confront him? It looks as if you're going to owe Walsh an apology. It doesn't seem like he had anything to do with your wife's death. Let's get this over with. The cops are looking for Kirkland now and if we get anything from Watson we can call them from Walsh's."

Boulder drove the three of them over to Walsh's in Jonathan's Bronco. Walsh came out of the house with a now-what-expression on his face.

Fox put out his hand and said, "Jack, I owe you an apology and here it is. I'm sorry. I know you had nothing to do with my Laura's murder. Now, I know who did it and why. I was so angry that I assumed it was you."

Walsh took the out-stretched hand. "I accept, Fox; it takes a big man to admit he's wrong. I'm sorry about your wife; she was a good horse-woman and a good human being. Now, what's going on, why are you here and how did you find out who did it?"

Susan, Jonathan and Boulder all began talking at once. Finally, Boulder's voice rose above the rest and he said, "We need to find Ted Watson. Where is he, Walsh?"

"Over in barn three checking on Have Faith."

"Let's head over there and I'll fill you in on the way."

CHAPTER 74

Wrath and anger are hateful.

Watson pressed the send button on his cell just as the group walked in.

Fox strode over to Watson and grabbed his shirt with both hands. As adrenalin and anger rushed through his body, he picked Watson up and threw him against the wall. "Want to talk about the day my wife died, Watson?"

Winded and taken by surprise, Watson didn't have a chance to respond. "You couldn't have her so you made sure I couldn't have her," shouted Fox.

"I. . .it wasn't like that; it was an accident. I didn't do it. It wasn't me," he whined.

Wow, that was quick, Susan thought. Suddenly, she was gripped from behind and felt the cold, hard steel of a gun pressed against her neck.

Kirkland's hard, calculating voice startled all of them. "If it weren't for you and your aunt, I'd be home free right now. And you," he pointed at Watson, "get the hell over here. You're coming with me. The rest of you, head toward the tack room or I swear I'll shoot her right here, right now. And Jack, you know that plane you're always bragging about? Well, now it's my way out. I'm taking this dame with me and, as long as she follows orders, I won't hurt her and I'll leave her when we board."

Kirkland started slowly backing up still gripping Susan. She felt like she was being held in a vice. Now, how can I get out of this, she worried. I don't believe for one minute that he'll let me go. This guy'll kill me without the slightest hesitation, just for the fun of it. She remembered a move she learned in a self-defense class. Using the maneuver, she suddenly felt his grip loosen and she elbowed him in the groin. Not as hard as I wanted, she thought. Kirkland buckled over in pain and let her go.

As she stepped away, he raised the gun and aimed it directly at her.

A shot rang out from Walsh's gun. It was Kirkland who lay on the ground with a bullet in his head.

Boulder punched in 911 as Fox checked the body on the ground.

"Nice shot," Fox said to Walsh. "You saved my niece's life. I'll never forget that."

CHAPTER 75

Sometimes silence is better than talking too much.

The State Police and ambulance came within minutes of each other. Kirkland's body was examined and taken away. Ted Watson couldn't stop talking. "It was all Kirkland. He's a big time gambler. The Belmont was a perfect plan. He bribed Franky and demanded he throw the race; the poor sap would do anything for his little sister. Then Franky tried to blackmail us, so Kirkland went to Miami and got rid of him. He flew home a few hours later. When he showed up at the hospital, no one knew he was gone. Kirkland got some of his debts paid but still had to pay Annie back. He poisoned her so he could collect her money. Killing Laura with a muck rake at the stables was an accident. She was just in the wrong place. She should have been at the track with you Fox."

Ted looked over at Walsh and Jonathan. "I told you it wasn't me. Walsh you know me, I'm a hard worker, ain't that right Boss?"

Jack Walsh turned away.

After everyone's statements had been taken, and Walsh's revolver had been bagged as the murder weapon, the police advised Walsh not to leave town. "I have no intention of leaving town. I shot Kirkland to save Susan, and there's plenty of witnesses. Call me anytime."

After the police took Watson away, Susan called Tony.

"Detective Russo."

"Tony" said Susan, "It's over. They have Aunt Laura's killer. And he's dead. You won't believe what I almost got myself into this time. But thanks to Walsh I'm okay."

"Susan, where are you and what's going on?"

"Tony, I'm at Walsh's stables. I'll tell you the whole story later. Why don't you meet me at my house in about an hour. Boulder and I are taking Jonathan back to his house. My car is parked there. Once I make sure he's okay, I'll head for home. It's been a whale of a day."

"I'm anxious to hear your whole fish story. Maybe my news will make you feel better. I want you to know that I put an APB out on Paul but haven't heard from anyone yet that he's been caught. And I want to know what you almost got yourself into. Meet you back at your place."

***

Boulder drove Susan and Fox back to the Fox and Hound Stables.

"I know that Annie has been told about Kirkland," Boulder said. "But I'm heading over to Deborah to see her. I'm really worried about her."

"Okay Joe, I am too. Thanks for everything and keep me posted on Annie's condition. Let me know if there's anything I can do for her."

"Will do Susan. Good-bye Fox, see you around."

Susan chatted a moment with Jonathan then said her good-byes. She knew Tony would be waiting for her when she arrived home and she wanted to tell him the entire story. She hoped he had calmed down by now.

Boulder thought about Annie as he headed to the hospital. *What is it about her that makes me feel like a teenager in love for the first time? Since my divorce years ago, I've dated many women and had some serious relationships too but I've never felt like this before.*

He arrived at the hospital and stood in the doorway to Annie's room. Her eyes were closed and he noted that her cheeks had some color to them. He quietly walked to the side of the bed and touched her hand. Annie opened her eyes and looked up at him. "Hi Joe, I can't believe it. I can't believe Kirkland killed Laura and tried to kill me. I should have known something was wrong. I knew he gambled but not to the extent that he lost everything and owed the mob."

Joe sat on the edge of the bed as Annie sat up. He put his arms around her and held her close.

"My poor Laura," Annie said. "I miss her so much." The tears welled up in her beautiful blue eyes.

"Annie, gambling is a disease; Kirkland couldn't stop. Killing Laura was an accident and once you take a life, it's easier the next time. Killing Franky was a necessity, to his way of thinking. Kirkland couldn't take the chance that he would talk. Then trying to kill you, that became necessary also; he needed your money. It's not your fault in any way. He was a consummate actor."

Annie wiped her eyes and looked at Joe. "Thanks Joe, for everything. Gambling certainly changed him from the man I knew and loved into a complete stranger. I still feel I should have known something was wrong, but he had me fooled completely."

Still holding her in his arms, Joe asked, "When are they letting you go home?"

"The doctor came in after the police left and he's going to release me tomorrow. I need to head back to DC to make arrangements for Kirkland's funeral. It will be private under the circumstances." Annie sighed deeply and fought back her tears.

"Let me know if you need a ride to the airport; I'll be happy to take you."

"Thanks Joe. I'm trying to decide what to do about Kirkland's car. I have my own at our house and I prefer driving mine when I'm in DC. My car seems to know where to go when I'm there," Annie said with a smile. "I may fly home and keep it garaged somewhere here for a while."

"Say no more Annie. You can keep it in my garage until you decide what to do with it."

"Thanks again Joe. Then I'll need to take you up on that offer of a ride to the airport. Let me have your number and I'll text you later with my flight information."

Boulder gave Annie a quick hug and said his goodbyes. "I'll be back to see you in the morning before you're discharged. We'll make some plans then."

Heading to his car he thought about Annie. I'd like to be part of her life. Once she can make service arrangements, I'll drive down and be there for her every step of the way.

***

Jonathan watched as Susan left the driveway then turned toward his stables. He walked across the yard kicking up leaves in front of him. The sounds of whinnying pleased his ears as he got closer. I can't believe how peaceful the stables can be, he thought.

He opened the main barn door and stepped inside. None of his stablehands greeted him. "Hmm, they're a hard-working crew," he mumbled.

Blinking back tears that washed in his eyes, he walked through the barn to Another Foxy Lady's stall. The horse held her head high and kicked the wall as he approached. "Looking for a carrot, my Lady?" Fox asked. He reached over the gate and rubbed her nose. "You have a fine little foal; Laura would be proud."

Overwhelming peace engulfed his mind and body. It's all over, Fox, he thought. You've got to get on with life. He propped his elbows on the top of the gate and held his head with his hands, staring again at Laura's horse, "Your little 'Laura's Boy', will be a winner someday-I'll wager my money on him."

Fox heard someone approaching. He looked over his shoulder and saw Cody.

"Hi Boss," Cody said.

"Just the guy I want to talk to. Remember the day I asked you if you'd like to learn how to buy yourself a Thoroughbred? Well, I'm in the market for one. Still interested?"

"Sure thing, Boss. How soon?"

"Tomorrow, Cody. I'm ready to move ahead. I know my wife is at peace now and I've got to get back to my routine."

Fox clapped Cody on his shoulder and the two walked out of the stables into the cool autumn air.

CHAPTER 76

Wrapped in a hand sewn quilt made by grandma, you feel her love.

Tony's car was parked in front of the house when Susan arrived. She walked in and was pleasantly surprised. Soft music was playing in the background and Tony was opening a bottle of wine. He looked at her and said, "I heard what happened from the guys at work. Are you okay?"

"I can't believe Kirkland killed Aunt Laura and Franky and was trying to kill Annie too-all for money. If it hadn't been for Walsh, I would have been his third victim."

Tony finished pouring them each a glass of wine. After taking her in his arms and passionately kissing her, he led her over to the couch. They both sipped their wine, deep in thought, as they watched the boats sailing on the ocean. Everything was so peaceful and calm.

"Susan, I realize that I could have lost you so easily today. I'm still angry with you for not telling me about Paul. I hope we get the no-good felon. You know how I feel about you. I want you around forever. You've been through a lot these past few weeks and I have a surprise for you. You need a few days off. Chelsea and Millie can mind the store.

There's this neat bed-and-breakfast in Cape May. I've booked it for this weekend. A nice long weekend."

"Thanks Hon, that's just what I need after today. For a moment, I thought I wouldn't be seeing anyone ever again. Kirkland's voice was so cold and unemotional that I was sure he was going to kill me. Well, it's over. All of us can finally get on with our lives."

Tony refilled their glasses, and gently kissed her again.

CHAPTER 77

Is this the end or a new beginning?

The next day in her bookstore, Susan sipped the oolong tea she was becoming partial to and thought about her weekend with Tony in Cape May. "I feel so relaxed," she said to Nicky as he perched on top of the small refrigerator. "I wanna grape," he squawked.

Susan continued to reflect on the past few months . . . my Aunt Laura was a victim of a vicious crime but all that's happened helped introduce me to Aunt Laura's husband, Jonathan, and we've become close. Initially, Mom was so uncooperative. I just don't understand where she's coming from sometimes. But Annie's attempted murder influenced Mom to share her past with me and we've become closer too. That's good. Now Mom's gone back to Florida and I hope our communication will be better than it's been.

Susan shifted her weight to a more comfortable position and continued ruminating. Chelsea has been my right arm throughout this whole ordeal, opening and closing the shop for me. She's been instrumental in helping train my new staff for the bookstore and the tea shop. But now, I'll have to learn how to get along for a while without her. I hope she's successful in Australia or as the Aussies call it, OZ.

The bell on the front door interrupted her reverie and she smiled as Chelsea breezed through the door and plunked her bag on the counter. "What's up, Mrs. J," she called, pouring herself a cup of tea and joining Susan at one of the tables closest to the window.

"Oh, I'm just thinking about everything that's happened to us and kind of wishing you didn't have to leave," Susan replied. "It just won't be the same without you, and Nicky will be devastated."

"It won't be so long. I'll be back before you know it."

"Let's hope so. Do you have everything ready?"

"Like, I sure do. My backpack is packed, and I think Millie and Randy are ready to work here on their own. Wish I could be a fly on the wall to see how they do without me."

"I'll be sure to let you know, Chels. And if they mess up, I'll blame you."

"That's right, blame me. I won't be here to complain about it. This is my last day here. Is there anything special you want me to focus on?"

The chimes rang again and a familiar figure waved at the two of them.

"Wanda," both Susan and Chelsea said at the same time.

"Hiya, gals," Wanda said. "I was in the neighborhood and wanted to see how you were doing."

"What? You couldn't foresee?" Chelsea poked her in the arm.

"We're fine, Wanda," said Susan. "This is Chelsea's last day before leaving for Australia and an interesting internship."

"Good for you, Chelsea. Would you like me to do a reading to see how it will go for you?"

"No thanks, Wanda. Like I'm better winging it and not knowing in advance. But thanks for the offer."

"Chelsea, where's Randy today?" Susan asked.

"Like she'll be here in a little while–oops, pardon the pun! She had to go to the bank and open a new account."

The door opened again and Millie came in, pulling a package of sunflower seeds out of her bag and giving Nicky a few.

"Looks like the gang's almost all here," Susan said. She introduced Millie to Wanda and stood up. "I've got to get some work done, but why don't you two get to know each other. I think you might have some things in common."

"I'm a psychic," Wanda said to Millie. "What do you do?"

"You mean aside from mixing things up? I'm here helping in the shop while Chelsea's in Australia. What exactly is a psychic?"

"Oh, my dear, that's a very long story. Let's have a cup of tea and I'll try to tell you the short version."

From the back room, Susan looked out at her bookstore world. "You've come a long way, baby," she said to herself. "All the mysteries are solved, my shop is running well and the Tea Cup Room will be a big hit."

CHAPTER 78

When your journey ends abruptly and you don't know what to do, bite your lip and turn back home.

Paul Thomas sat in the first class section of the plane that was taking him back to Venezuela. He sipped the champagne the steward had given him and stretched his legs. He raised the glass in a silent toast: "Susan, I'm leaving again but my song hasn't changed. I still love you and I always will. I'll be back."

EPILOGUE

It is well to read everything of something, and something of everything.

Fliers had been posted all over town: tucked under windshield wipers, tacked on supermarket bulletin boards, wrapped around lampposts, and handed out on campus by Chelsea and her friends.

Already by 6:30, people started drifting in: some chewing gum, some sipping water, some finishing up the last few bites of a slice of pizza.

By 6:45, Susan put in a quick call to a nearby funeral director, pleading to lend some extra folding chairs.

By 7:00 p.m., Susan's little shop was getting uncomfortably crowded. Thank goodness I enlarged the store recently, she thought. Susan closed the front doors against the autumn chill, as latecomers grabbed one of the folded wooden chairs and made themselves as comfortable as possible.

At 7:15, Susan flicked the lights on and off a few times and stepped up to the microphone. "Thank you for coming this evening. I hope you enjoy tonight's reading by this particular Jersey shore author."

Lillian introduced herself as one of the local Eight Women Writers and gave a brief biography of each writer. She stressed that this was a work in progress and there would be time at the conclusion of the reading for comments, questions and answers.

Angelo

And trouble deaf heaven with my bootless cries,
And look upon myself, and curse my fate.
Shakespeare's Sonnet XXIX

Another morning. It was always the same. As the old man awoke, images of his past drifted uninvited to the surface of his mind. Depression plastered his back to the mattress in much the same way as gravity pins the back of a thrill-seeker to the metal cage of a spinning carnival game.

***

Angelo was a teenager again. Hormones were raging. He was the only son of a widow who had all she could do coping with her grief and somehow managing to put food on the table and a roof over the heads of her three children. Angelo's friends were still into playing stick ball in the street and iron tag in his Brooklyn neighborhood. They hung on the back of buses for free transportation or just for the fun of it. They borrowed their sisters' roller skates to attach to milk crates, building crude but effective go-carts..

Angelo was the first in his crowd to begin seeing girls as something other than giggling females who took pleasure in ratting on boys. They were always raising their hands for the teacher to call on them, making the boys look dumb in comparison. "I know, I know. Call on me!" they'd chorus.

Angelo started becoming aware that girls always smelled fresh and clean, very unlike himself and his buddies. He liked the way girls tossed their shiny curls and was mesmerized by the bounce in their walk. He wished he could talk to someone about these new and strange urgings of his body, but who would that be?

One hot summer evening, Angelo got so engrossed in the view through his window that he did not notice that his curtains were wide open. His neighbor happened to look across the courtyard and saw Angelo ogling her. Startled, she quickly reached up for the window shade, which instead eluded her grasp and sprung to the top of its roller. She stood on her toes to reach higher and, in her haste, lost her balance and fell out the casement window.

Angelo looked down in horror, instinctively sensing that the image of her limp, lifeless body sprawled on the concrete would haunt him forever. It didn't help any when he heard, months later, that the girl's parents split up after the sudden death of their only child. It affected Angelo even more when he heard that, a few years later, the girl's father took his own life. Angelo, of course, could confide in no one.

***

    The old man roused himself from his reverie. Nature called with an urgency that was not to be ignored. Angelo rolled his bulk to the side of the bed, slipped his feet into his slippers, and padded gratefully to the bathroom. He knew he would be okay now. For some reason, once he got up and going, he was pretty much okay for the rest of the day.
    After showering and toweling off, Angelo reached for his shaving brush, per his usual routine. As he was about to lather up, he hesitated for a moment. He glanced at the calendar. Uh oh, October 1st, he thought He replaced the brush in its holder. Angelo would not be doing any more shaving until after the holidays.

    This lumbering, slightly stooped gentleman scrambled daily to seek ways to atone for the sins of his checkered past. These days, if a kind word or a soft touch could mitigate the sting of criticism directed at someone nearby, Angelo jumped to the task. If standing on a picket line for a cause he believed passionately in might make one person reconsider, his time that day was well spent.

Soon it would be December. Local children's charities were well acquainted with Angelo's availability for children's parties. They looked forward to seeing Santa in his red suit handing out gifts. Having children pull his beard or poke him in the stomach was becoming a bit tiresome to Angelo after all these years, but he could not find it in himself to say no.

Angelo glanced at his calendar. "Christmas will be here soon," he commented to himself. "I think I'll check with the pastor of that church down the street. I'd like to do something a little special this year." Angelo looked up the number and dialed it.

"Grace Lutheran," a deep voice answered. "This is Pastor Grant. How can I help you?"

"Well, Pastor," Angelo said, "My name is Angelo. I don't belong to your church but I'd like to do something nice for someone at Christmas."

"That's a fine thought, Angelo, and of course you don't have to be a church member to do that. What did you have in mind?"

"Well, I have some extra cash, and I know there are people who might go hungry, or need some presents for their kids this season. I thought about looking for likely people in the grocery store, but with all the problems with stalking lately that might not be a good idea. Is there someone you know that could use some help? I'd like to remain anonymous, of course."

"What a great idea. We have a food pantry here, and each week we serve almost a hundred people that way. We take donations of food, of course, but also money. Do you think that would be something you'd like to donate to? And of course we can always use extra hands to help with that."

"Sounds good, Pastor, but I kinda wanted to do something a little more personal. Is there a family or two that could use the help directly? Maybe there's someone in your congregation who's having a hard time?"

"There is one family I can think of. The father has just been laid off and the mother is a waitress at a local diner. They have two little girls and are looking at a very sparse Christmas."

"They sound perfect," said Angelo. "Can I buy them some food and toys and maybe give them some money?"

"Your offer will make them believe in Santa Claus," Pastor Grant chuckled.

"You don't know the half of it," Angelo retorted. "Now to the nitty gritty. How do we get this done?"

The two men agreed on a time when Angelo would bring the gifts to the church, and the pastor promised to get them to the family before Christmas without revealing the source of the gifts.

After an exchange of mutual thanks, the two ended the conversation. Angelo walked to the mirror hanging in his hallway, and laid his finger aside of his nose. "On Dasher, on Dancer," he said. "It's time to go shopping."

To be continued.

***

The ceiling fans clicked softly, rhythmically in the crowded bookstore. Somewhere in the back room, an ice maker dumped a load of ice into a waiting tray. Someone cleared his throat. Someone else shifted in his seat. The lights flickered then brightened. A middle-aged gentleman started clapping. Others joined in. Soon there was thunderous applause, reverberating against the walls and spilling out into the cool night air. There was a question and answer period.

"I'm curious," a young woman said, asking the first question. "As an English teacher, I have a particular liking for Shakespeare's works myself, but

Catchmeifyoucan

it seems odd to see one of his pieces quoted in a contemporary novel. Would you explain your thought processes for doing so?"

"I'm happy to do so," the author answered. "You may or may not know that there's an unwritten rule that writers should, when writing for the 'man on the street,' write at a fifth-grade level. Eight Women Writers prides itself on breaking some of the so-called established 'rules' of writing. This is one of them. I have a fondness for some of Shakespeare's works too, in particular his Sonnet XXIX. So I decided to show our readers that human nature is the same today as it always was. I like to think that Angelo is a modern-day version of the person Shakespeare had in mind when he composed this particular sonnet."

The questions and comments finally eased up and people started leaving, some first congratulating the author and then thanking Susan for the evening's entertainment.

On behalf of myself and my co-authors, I, too, want to thank you so much Susan," Lillian said enthusiastically, as she shook Susan's hand.

"Now get that book finished," Susan said, "I want to see it on my shelves."

This is the second book written by Amea Lake, the pseudonym, of Eight Women Writers from Jackson, New Jersey;

Adelaide Sooy Weidknecht
Mary Ann Tobin Kerns
Elaine Warinsky Turansky
Alva Rickel Hall

Lillian Sortland Tesoriero
Anita Langbein Paerg
Karin Porter Holldorf
Eva Saks LaBrozzi.

Also by Amea Lake:
The Sandcastle Mysteries:
Death and Deception at the Jersey Shore.

Since our story takes place at the Jersey Shore, Eight Women Writers acknowledge the strength and courage of those who were affected by Superstorm Sandy in October 2012.